I0534492

the plight of exa

Jason Kay

the plight of exa by Jason Kay

Please follow me on twitter @JasonKaySays

For...

My entire fam-bam

Gina

The CC5

My TKD folk past-and-present

The 456-crew past-and-present

PROLOGUE

ONE MONTH AGO, Ashley Ryker's eager eyes dissected the lavish board room as her heels love-tapped the glistening tile beneath her. The elevator chimed behind her and the pewter doors glided to a close. The board of directors glued their eyes to the Aussie beauty as she raked a drifting blonde hair behind her ear and strided all the closer to them—finding her seat at the end of the long ashwood table.

Dr. James Bankhart, the CEO of Omicron, eyed Ashley from the opposite side of the table. Ashley could see his meticulous beard and ogling eyes between his Italian shoes that were carelessly propped on the lengthy table.

"Dr. Ryker, you're looking perfect as always."

"I know, Jim."

"Ok. I'll get right to the point as to why you're here. Omicron has been bleeding money these past eleven months. We think you can help us with that."

"Why me?" she asked.

"Because you're a scientist – *and a chaser*. You're exactly what we need."

Ashley kept her cool wit despite her deeply hidden secret being so boldly thrown in her face. "How'd you come to such a conclusion?"

Bankhart ignored the question. "As you probably know, the man to your left is Dawson Wrangle."

Ashley swiveled her head to her left and took note of the ugly and aged man with long gray hair and an odd yellow-gray skin tone. His sunken eyelids were tired. His fingertips were as blue as the tip of his bulbous nose and his thick lips. He looked like death.

"Pleasure, Mr. Wrangle," Ashley fibbed.

"Just, 'Dawson,' ma'am."

"Just, 'Ashley,' Dawson,"

"Dawson's the *Ahi* maven," Bankhart said before shoving his face into his scotch and soda. "The king of the fire-throwers in the flesh."

"Is that right?" Ashley granted the old man her full attention.

"Please, don't act like you don't know, Ashley," Bankhart implored. "It insults our intelligence."

"*Former*, Ahi maven." Dawson corrected. "I'm here because I'm a few short years from the grave. I'm sick of my post as the Ahi maven and I'm ready for retirement."

"Ashley, we have the reconstruction formula," Bankhart interrupted.

"And I have ten million dollars in bearer bonds," Dawson slapped the black Samsonite on the table in front of him.

"And I have what?" Ashley asked.

"An opportunity to make history—and a lot of money. You will be credited with the discovery."

"It sounds more like an opportunity to catch a bullet," Ashley retorted. "Have you considered the implications of screwing around with people whose power you can't imagine?"

"That's what I have you for, Ashley. Managing the implications of course—not catching the bullet."

"They're synonymous," Ashley contested. She met eyes with Dawson. "Well, if you weren't a few years from the grave to begin with, you've definitely got two feet in now. Have you any idea the mess you're in? At this point, either the Ahi or the Zoree would cut all our throats in this room just for the chance to tear you limb-from-limb."

"That's not lost on me," Wrangle admitted.

"Zoree?" Bankhart asked as he funneled the last of his addiction into his mouth.

"Just call them 'water people' so you can keep up, Jim. I doubt that's your first glass," Ashley sneered.

Bankhart shrugged. "Fine, *water people*."

Ashley awarded Wrangle her attention once more. The question that burned through her mind surfaced on her lips, "What made you do it besides the payout? You don't make the rank of maven by being a voracious scoundrel."

"That's high-talk coming from an assassin, Ashley," Dawson argued.

"Chaser," Ashley corrected.

"*To-may-toe, To-mah-toe*. You find members of our orders—you either kill them, or bring them to someone who will. Then you get paid."

The board members gasped at Dawson's accusation.

"Anyway," Bankhart interrupted, "Are you in or out, Ashley? It'll be worth your time."

Ashley scanned the room once more and took note of Gavin Mandrake. Mandrake's lilac suit was sharply tapered and his accessories were designer. His manicured hands suggested that he never participated in manual labor any day in his life. He scratched his left eyebrow with the spotless fingernails on his right hand. Ashley warily looked back to Bankhart, "I want protection if I do it."

Bankhart nodded. "Good. I can arrange that. President Mursten is flying in from Washington D.C. in one month. I presume you'll have the project streamlined by then. Get with Mandrake for the details."

CHAPTER 1: A MAN OF FEW WORDS

"This is Glenn Jackson with WKBT 9 news. We're here amongst the swaying palm trees outside of the Omicron Laboratory Facility in Honolulu. At any moment we expect the arrival of Air Force One on the private air strip behind me."

Glenn Jackson stood some thirty yards away from the runway he mentioned. An aged, portly man from Ghana, he was darkly complected with a bald head and square glasses. Behind Glenn there was a large building with a silver frame and black windows. The thick green grass surrounding the facility was just long enough to indicate the direction of the wind. Dancing palm trees elegantly lined the large round-about in front of the edifice. Adorning the sky-scraping roof was an underlined 'O' emblem that was conservatively designed, but nonetheless commanded awe.

"Upon his arrival, President Mursten is to be met by his personal security unit who will shuttle him to the inside of the Omicron Testing Facility. He has scheduled a visit with James Bankhart, founder and president of Omicron. President Mursten has also scheduled a tour of the facility. As you can see, there is already a heavily armed force waiting to receive the president."

The brakes howled and the plane taxied to a halt. Air Force One officially arrived at Omicron's runway. The boarding door was pulled open and a statuesque blond man emerged from the plane. He wandered into the bright morning sun and with a flick of his hand, a classic pair of Ray Bans opened—a suitable match for his spotless formal wear. He fished in his left jacket pocket and came up with a business card tweezed between his fingers. An eerie smiling face with an 'X' for one eye, and an 'O' for the other stared back at him. Mursten flipped the card over and read the back,

"'I don't like the world anymore,' said the moon. 'So, I'm attacking it.'"

On the ground awaiting the president was a security force powerful enough to win a small war. The rifleman at the bottom of the staircase was a Hawaiian native—a man of some 6'6". His stature was broad and excessively muscular. Resting in his capable hands was a military issue assault rifle. Like all the other soldiers, his uniform was urban camouflage, capped with a charcoal helmet.

Glenn Jackson continued his telecast, "President Mursten has just come into view after exiting Air Force One. He's making his way down the stairs now."

Maintaining a conceited gait down the narrow flight of stairs, Mursten was received by the large soldier. After a quick salute from Mursten, the rifleman led the way to a small but aggressive motorcade. Mursten was stowed away in an armored Escalade before the vehicles raced towards Omicron.

The president faced the man sitting across from him and removed his sunglasses. "Everything's done?"

"Done," the man in the black suit replied.

"The money?"

"Here," the man handed him a military grade attaché case.

"You're a man of few words, Dominic."

"I'm a man of necessary words. I say what needs to be said."

"I understand," Mursten smiled musingly. "I say what needs to be heard."

The cars filed into Omicron's garage via the back entrance. The large Hawaiian soldier opened the president's door.

"Thank you, Colonel," Mursten said as he exited the limo.

"President Mursten, we have a concern."

"Oh?"

"Omicron is hosting field trips today. That wasn't included in the security dossier."

"That could be a problem. Be at your best, Colonel. I appreciate your awareness." Mursten gave the colonel a hearty slap on the arm then went on to greet Omicron's representative in the auto bay.

"President Mursten! Welcome to Omicron! We've been waiting with great anticipation."

"Thank you, Mr…?"

"Mandrake, Gavin Mandrake," the man lisped. He flamboyantly stood 5'9" and strided effeminately when he walked.

"Mr. Mandrake, it's an unwelcome surprise that the field trips running today weren't included in the logistics dossier of my visit."

"I'm sorry, Mr. President. Is this of great concern?"

"When my men part their hair differently it doesn't go unnoticed. A field trip in-and-of itself isn't a concern. A major logistic deficiency is my concern. I trust there'll be no more surprises while we're here."

"Yes, sir! Very good, Mr. President," Mandrake cleared his throat. "Please, this way." Mandrake motioned toward the elevator that was beyond the long line of company cars.

Mandrake, Mursten, and the colonel all boarded the lift.

"The board is eager to meet you, Mr. President," Mandrake said as he gazed uncomfortably at the President and his colonel.

Mursten ignored the remark. "Tell me, Mandrake. Will Jim Bankhart be in his office today?"

"Dr. Bankhart will be present. Do you have special business with him?"

"That's between Bankhart and myself—isn't it, Mr. Mandrake?"

"Of course, Mr. President. Forgive my impertinence."

The elevator arrived at the destined floor. The doors swiftly opened and Mandrake stepped aside—allowing the other two men to enter Bankhart's office first.

The sun peering in through the crystal clear panes illuminated the white bamboo floors. A boomerang-shaped desk was adorned with a large flat panel computer monitor and black office accessories. The leather throne behind the desk turned around, exposing a stubbly executive with a salt-and-pepper crew-cut. The man was dressed in a gray sharkskin suit that was tailored to perfection.

"Jimmy, how've you been?" Mursten arrogantly hooted.

"Isaac Mursten, you'd think you were a president or something the way you come in here!" The man sitting behind the desk arose chortling. He buttoned his suit coat and made his way around the showy desk. "Hahaaa! That'll be all, Mr. Mandrake," the big shot dismissed his executive assistant after his physical reconnection with Mursten.

"Of course," Mandrake replied as he lost himself behind the elevator's pewter doors.

Mursten could smell the evidence of Bankhart's liquid-lunch on his sinful breath.

The soldier with Mursten took off his helmet, revealing a puzzle of scars across his sheared hairline.

Mursten spoke up, "Jim, you've met my personal bodyguard slash babysitter, right? He's Colonel Rick Rockland."

Bankhart looked at the two men, "Nope! I have not. Rockland, huh? Rick, Rick Rockland! That sounds fake!" Bankhart laughed. "I don't wish to be discourteous when I say this. You appear rather young for a colonel."

"33 and a colonel in the US Army—what a country!" Mursten gaffed.

Bankhart nodded with approval. "May I offer either of you boys some of the elixir of the gods? *Chivas Regal Royal Salute 50*—it aged in whiskey barrels from 1953 to 2002."

Mursten answered for himself and Rockland, "How can we say, 'no'?"

Bankhart fixed the highfalutin drinks in crystal double tumblers then handed one to Mursten and the other to the colonel. The exec happily indulged in his libation as he plopped down in his chair and pushed himself closer to his desk.

A sudden meddling interference— a crossed frequency as the colonel heard it— forced the computer's speakers to irregularly chirp. "That's been happening lately," Bankhart said as he killed the power to the irritating computer speakers.

"Lately?" Rockland made his way around to Bankhart's side of the desk.

"Yes," Bankhart answered the soldier who was now standing over his shoulder.

Rockland began tearing drawers open as if he were rummaging through his own office. He reengaged the power to the speakers and the chirping resumed. The inebriated Bankhart protested and rolled his chair away from the desk.

The speakers fell silent.

Rockland snapped his bulky fingers in Bankhart's face and flagged the exec back to his desk. Bankhart wheeled his chair closer to the desk. The truthful speakers chirped again. The cogs in the colonel's mind went to work. To Rockland's keen eye, the top button on Bankhart's jacket didn't fall as perfectly as the others did. Without warning, the colonel unholstered a switchblade knife from his belt.

The bumbling Bankhart tried to protest, but he was too slow.

Rockland guillotined the suspect button between the blade and his thumb. The button plunked to the desk and the maddening interference doubled in both intensity and frequency.

With a downward stroke of his knife, Rockland cleaved the button in two.

The chirping ceased.

"What the hell!?" Bankhart exclaimed.

The colonel seized the halved button. He exchanged the intrusive clothing accessory for a counter-surveillance device from one of his cargo pockets. He set the little box to the surface of the desk, prodded two buttons then shrugged. He looked up and said, "We're clear," to Mursten. "There's nothing else in this room."

"Some friends you have," Mursten scratched his forehead as he gauged Bankhart's response.

"No friends of mine. Resume or reschedule?"

"The colonel says, 'We're clear.' Resume."

"Good. Speaking of friends, Franklin, Jackson, Grant—are any in attendance?"

"We deal in bearer bonds," Mursten pointed to the silver and black attaché case. "Don't spend it all in one place."

"Fifty-million dollars I make no promises. You're lucky I like you, Isaac, I usually don't deal for less than one-hundred million." Bankhart opened the sturdy case and was pleased. "But it's not the money I need. It's the protection of the American Armed Forces."

Mursten tittered. "What?"

"I'm selling you the world. And for fifty-million—I'd say that's a hell of a bargain. Needless to say, I pissed some people off in the process. Therefore, I don't think I'm overreaching when I ask for your protection." Bankhart gingerly laid the case on his desk and reclined. "Is he in too?" Bankhart pointed to the colonel.

"He's the money," Mursten reported.

"Brilliant! My apologies, Colonel."

"Not needed," Rockland held up his glass.

"It must've been a complex process on a colonel's salary. May I ask how you secured such an amount?"

"No."

"But it's clean?"

"Doc, my money gets filtered like Fiji water."

"Good." The executive looked at Mursten in the most serious way he had since their reconnection. "How do you feel about war, Mr. President?"

"I don't want to be responsible for losing lives or losing a war we can't finance. It hasn't shown in *your* business, but we have mounting deficits that have been snowballing for some time now. Anyway, what's with this moon crap?" Mursten held up the business card. "You've gotta be hittin' something harder than alcohol and nicotine to come up with that. I'm starting to question whether or not this trip was worth my time."

"A rational explanation will come in due time. I asked you how you felt about war."

"Why?"

"We have a formula that takes chaos and brings order. It takes death, but it returns life. It may cost us money, but we'll make more. People will have to die so others may live. They will only live through our charitable hands."

Bankhart pressed his fingertips together and indulged himself in the idea. "Are you in?"

"*Oh*, I have a *long* list of questions."

"The tour of the facility will provide some answers. I want you to pay particular attention to the module hosted in the main laboratory by Dr. Ashley Ryker. She was so enthused to hear you were coming. She wanted you to see the project as much as I do. She's the one who arranged the field trips that pissed you off."

"Why'd she do that?"

"Now, now, Isaac. I don't want to ruin the surprise. You'll be impressed though. She's quite intelligent and a vixen to boot. I hope you see the same possibilities I do."

"May I ask you something, Doc?" Rockland interceded, arms folded.

"Anything! What's on your mind, Colonel?" Bankhart put his pompous glass down on the table.

"That Mandrake, you know him well?"

"He's a little fairy eager to please everyone. It works out when you're the boss. Why's that?"

"Did you tell him anything?"

"No, he doesn't know anything. Why?" Bankhart shifted worried glances between his two visitors.

"He asked if you and Mursten had any business."

"Really? What did you want to do? Did you want to see him?"

"Maybe through a scope," Mursten tittered.

"C'mon, Isaac, good help is hard to find!"

Colonel Rockland held up the listening device, reminding Bankhart of the evidence of an unwelcome listener.

"Well, I guess I'll have to start interviewing again," Bankhart sighed as he took the last gulp from his glass.

CHAPTER 2: EXPECT NOTHING LESS

At 10:00AM, a procession of clumsy school busses from Occam High School arrived at Omicron. Ethan Wright, Occam High's principle, disembarked the first yellow shuttle and straightened his sport coat. He was a man of some 5'11" with broad shoulders, short gray hair, and a clean goatee. He counted the procession of busses and noted eight had arrived—as expected. He raised his bullhorn and directed the students draining off the buses to gather at the front door.

"Ok, Ok, pipe-down and furthermore be quiet," Wright demanded as he approached the unruly teenagers. "It took just a shade under twenty minutes for a group of young adults to get off a bus and get quiet. You're a promising young bunch."

"Is this guy still talking?" one student muttered.

"Who wears a wool suit in September?" another student snorted.

"He has to *feel* important because he hates his life so much."

Another student joined, "I'd hate my life too if I could see my ass getting fatter and my hair getting thinner. I heard his wife is a fat slob too." His comment invited snickers from a large portion of the disorderly crowd.

"And I just heard Pat McNamara insult me *and* my wife!" The field-trippers hushed when the enraged principle's voice overtook their mindless chatter. "If McNamara was involved, I'm assuming Jordan Gannen and Akshad Khan were privy as well. Did I hear Tarsa too?"

"No, sir," a voice from the back declared.

"Good. Let's keep it that way."

"Fair enough."

"Why don't you other outstanding gents come forward, before I tailspin into a dimension of anger that will probably get me fired!"

Patrick, Jordan, and Akshad all stepped forward— obviously uncomfortable in front of the crowd.

"Please, tell me more about my fat ass," Wright derisively requested.

"I'm sorry, Principle Wright," Jordan Gannen said.

"You're sorry?" Wright laughed, "Your social commentaries are worthy of Thomas Moore," Wright commented.

"Who?" the boys chorused.

"If you weeds in this scholastic garden of mine paid attention in 10th grade literature, you'd know who I was talking about."

"Principle Wright, that's unnecessary," a pasty student with red hair and redder freckles came forward from the crowd.

"Unnecessary?" Wright stopped his pacing mid-stride and studied the sky. "What's unnecessary, Krissy, is a 17-year-old kid calling my wife a 'fat slob.' I know you're a little activist, but before you speak, know who you're advocating." The girl hung her head and lost herself in the snickering crowd.

"Gannen!" Wright called.

"Yes, sir?"

"To answer your question, 'Yes,' I'm still talking. Does that bother you?"

"No, sir!"

Wright moved onto the shapeless Indian kid in the baggy football sweat suit next to Jordan.

"Khan! I wear a wool suit in September! Do you have a problem with that?"

"No, sir," Khan replied feebly.

Wright pinched the baggy windbreaker Khan was wearing. "I didn't think you would. I'd like to remind you," Wright stuck the cone-end of his bullhorn in Khan's face, "You're wearing a sweat-suit!"

The principle continued to the surf-haired focus of the junior class girls—Pat McNamara. The chisel-jawed, gray-eyed rebel stood face-to-face with the principle. He ran his fingers through his wavy hair and sighed.

"McNamara!"

"What's up?" McNamara bumbled.

"You'll meet my fat ass on the football field at 5:00AM on Tuesday."

"Haha! Yeah right!" the defiant junior retorted. "No, I won't!"

"It's not negotiable!" Wright yelled. "I'll be letting your father know this afternoon."

"Fine. You're…weird," McNamara uttered then vanished amongst his peers.

"Ditto," Wright regained his composure and surveyed the class. "Ok, everyone, enjoy the trip and learn a lot."

Upon entering Omicron, a strong voice with a cheerful Aussie accent commanded the students' attention. "Welcome, everybody, to the Omicron headquarters! My name is Ashley Ryker and I'll be your hostess today." The svelte Aussie woman paused for a minute, basking in the

22

envious eyes of the girls and the wolf-whistling boys. "We'll start by giving you five minutes to buddy up with your closest tour-mates. So, *Ta* for now," Ashley waved with her spirited fingers.

Some students chattered while others aimlessly mingled. Most found their friends in less time than allotted.

Ashley began to speak again, "Well, it seems you've all found yourself in proper order. Let's get on with it, shall we?" She walked around the stationary group of visitors as she lifted a hand as a means of highlighting the grandeur of the area. "So as you all have probably guessed, you've found yourself in the lobby, also known as, 'the atrium.' It's a good place to start." She stopped her dramatic wandering and folded her hands before continuing her lesson. "The lobby was created keeping feng-shui in mind. We wanted to keep positive energy and appropriate balance in mind. The lobby alone is valued at over one-million dollars!"

The tour was typical—novel at first, but before long the trivial factoids of the architecture and the constant corporate-plugs were enough to drive the most courteous guest to madness. After an hour of hair-tearing tedium, the students found themselves in the spotless anteroom of the Omicron laboratory facility.

The tour guide proceeded, "On the opposite side of the glass behind you all, top scientists in the nation are currently working on the Neo-Exa project. The Neo-Exa initiative is an Earth restoration project that begins with the people and ends with a rejuvenated environment. This, ladies and gentlemen, is where the magic happens. We believe that we've discovered the method to reconstitute the Earth at a greatly accelerated rate."

The vacant students stared at her with empty eyes.

"In other words, we've found a way to reforest and rebuild the Earth very quickly."

"How can you do that?" Krissy, the little activist, blurted.

"Great question! Using cutting-edge technology developed here at Omicron, we've been able to enhance the photosynthesis to unprecedented levels! Imagine a world where a hardwood tree can reach fruition in a couple of days. You can practically see it growing!"

Ashley paused and sought a response from the sea of despondent students. She didn't get one.

She continued, "We have found that a mixture of the hemoglobin metabolites from the *Ahi* and the *Zoree*, you may know them as two of the '*Lost Orders of Exa*,' results in a formula for accelerated life processes. The formula also temporarily improves physical and cognitive performances in humans! We're ready to refurbish our troubled world and rebuild our sparse resources!"

"Excuse me!" one young man called out.

"Yes? Do you have a question?" asked Ashley.

"I do," he replied. A clean-cut student with tidy clothes presented to the front of the group. He wore a black and white long-sleeve t-shirt with acid-wash jeans. His buzz-faded hair was styled forward. Not a single strand of his black hair was out of place.

The hostess studied the blue-eyed student then smiled with approval.

A striking young lady, Harlie, appeared from behind the handsome young man. Her glowing mocha skin was framed by her straight black hair. Harlie's radiant green eyes were enhanced by her long eyelashes and smoky mascara. Keeping her polite, pearly whites visible, she stood next to Tyson.

The hostess returned her attention back to Tyson and asked, "What's your name?"

"Tyson, Tyson Lynd."

"What question do you have for me, Tyson Lynd?"

"Are you saying that we have the capability of rejuvenating the Earth at the expense of *blood* from certain demographics?"

Ashley hesitated. She stared deep into Tyson's wondering eyes. "I'm just going to go ahead and answer the logical follow up to the question when it's phrased like *that*. We don't advocate unneeded bloodshed."

"Who decides if the bloodshed is unneeded? *You?* Isn't the idea alone of replenishing the world with the blood of the Lost Orders cause for questioning?"

"Omicron won't let anything get out of hand. You do seem *particularly* worried, Tyson Lynd. Why are you so alarmed?"

"No reason. I'm not alarmed." Tyson wasn't a practiced liar. "Just a curious student." He held up a small note pad.

"Don't be coy," she argued as she adjusted her narrow glasses. "Yes, I get it."

"Get what?" Tyson asked, wondering why he said anything at all.

"You're an Ahi."

"Ahi?" Harlie asked as she looked up at Tyson.

"Don't be crazy!" retorted Tyson.

"I'm not crazy. It says it all over you. Your very nature, your superior forethought for your age, and your unusually confident stature are all characteristic of the Ahi—not to mention your long sleeves."

"I don't know what you're talking about," Tyson stepped back into the crowd.

"He *is* wearing long sleeves!" One student shouted. "He always does!"

"Why?" Another person hollered.

"Stop right there! Show me your forearms!" Ashley demanded.

"That's not necessary!" Tyson wondered how Ashley figured it out so easily.

"Excuse me!" A towering student with a golden faux-hawk shoved his way to the front of the crowd. "I may share Tyson's concern," The broad faced behemoth wore cargo pants and a long-sleeve t-shirt that his strong build filled well. He rolled his sleeves up and there were conspicuous markings on his large forearms.

"And you are?" The hostess inquired.

"I'm Vinnie Tarsa," he pushed his forearms together vertically and folded his hands together. The writing on his forearms read, *"Zoree"* in a vertical blue script with an argent outline. The mark was written in a bold and thick font. Vinnie continued, "I belong to the Zoree— the original water dwellers—the order of Exa that *normal* humans banished to the depths of the ocean." He glared at Tyson, challenging him, "and I'm not ashamed of *my* heritage or the waters where my ancestors dwelt."

"I never said anyone should be ashamed of what they are," Tyson rejoined.

"Sounds like you are," Vinnie noticed.

"I'm not ashamed!" Tyson corrected him through clinched teeth, surprising the rest of his classmates with the marked rage in his face. "We just don't brag about it."

"'*We?*' That's what you said, right, '*we*'?" Vinnie boldly winked and made a clicking noise with his tongue.

Vinnie was right. In his anger, Tyson gave away his long-kept secret. "All right, I'm an Ahi," Tyson reluctantly confessed.

"Will you show us your trace?" Ashley asked all too politely. "Vinnie was kind enough to do so."

The students debated amongst themselves –raising numerous questions.   "Trace?"

"Ahi?"

"Zoree?"

"What?"

"The Lost Orders! Aren't they just a local fable though?" Krissy yelled.

"*Aren't they just a local fable though*?" Jordan mocked. "Shut up, Krissy!"

"Bite me, Jordan! You're such an ass!"

Ashley's voice supplanted the class's nonsense, "Will you show us your trace?"

The students hushed and gazed at Tyson.

Tyson didn't have much of a choice in the matter. Not putting his forearms on display for the intrusive hostess would only be cause for further scrutiny. Tyson angrily squirreled away his note pad. He rolled up his long sleeves and horizontally stacked his right forearm on his left. Two separate designs on his skin became one word when his right arm rested on his left. The design read, "Ahi" in a horizontal, fiery red cursive script that was outlined in gold. The trace, like Vinnie's, was bold and thick.

"If that mark is genuine you're one of a rare breed, Mr. Lynd. *One-in-a-million*," Ashley looked more closely at his arms realizing it was the indisputable trace of the Ahi. "This is a unique experience. We have the two most volatile Lost Orders in one room." Ashley looked at both of them, "Neither of you two had known this about each other?"

"He neglected to mention it," Tyson argued.

"As did you," she asserted.

"And you're both born into your order? Neither of you we're 'baptized by fire,' so to speak?"

Vinnie was angered at the use of an Ahi expression to categorize his people. "I was born into the Zoree. There are no *baptisms* in my order."

"No baptisms, only killings," Tyson rubbed his chin and glared at Vinnie. "Did I say that wrong?"

"Gillings!" Vinnie snapped back. "People are gilled and welcomed into the Zoree territory. It's a great honor!"

The hostess tried to mitigate the tension in the air. "My mistake," she said. "I don't see any scars on your neck. I presume you weren't gilled either, right?"

"No, I wasn't gilled! And after someone is gilled, there are no scars if you did it right," Vinnie shouted.

"Ok," the hostess continued, "Tyson, you were naturally born into the Ahi order?"

"That's right."

One brazen student raised the question on everyone's mind. "'Gilled? Baptized by fire?' One, what does that mean, and two, what does it matter?"

Vinnie spoke up, "When you're gilled, you're neck is cut once on each side. You're then cut ear-to-ear. You're finally submerged in water until your last breath leaves your body."

"That's crazy! Why would you do that?" another student spoke up.

"It provides freedom in the Zoree territory and the infinite protection that the Zoree order can provide." Vinnie then looked at Tyson. "In the end you're still alive, unharmed and you're a Zoree. You're safe from the Ahi hot-heads like Lynd."

"But then you'll be just like Vinnie—soaked with Zoree ignorance," rejoined Tyson.

Vinnie stifled his anger and smiled boldly at Tyson, "Ms. Ryker, please forgive our rudeness. Please continue."

"Wait!" One student yelled out, "What's the fire baptism thingy?"

Vinnie took the liberty of answering the question. "You're drowned in lava instead of water. Is that right, Tyson?"

"No, it isn't. You're integrated in to the Ahi territory in the arms of an Ahi as you pass through the mouth of a volcano into our domain. It's the ultimate honor for an average human and in the end, like a gilling, you're alive and unharmed."

"That's cute! A hug protects you from smoldering elements. I think I'd rather be drowned!" Vinnie's comment drew laughter from many of the students in the group.

"Anyway," Ashley continued, "If Tyson and Vinnie wouldn't mind, I don't see any harm in giving the school a little extra bang for their buck. How would all of you like to see a real time, small-scale demonstration of the Neo-Exa initiative?"

"No, I don't think so," Tyson spoke up.

"Oh, come on, Tyson!" Ashley immaturely begged. "Please!"

The students in the group enthusiastically encouraged Ashley's idea.

"Come on, Lynd. Don't be such a bitch," Vinnie mocked him.

"How 'bout no, jackass."

"It'll only be once!" Ashley smiled, "Just once."

"Come on, Tyson!" His classmates jeered. "Do it for us! Come on!"

An athletic young man of Gabonese lineage muscled his way to the front of the crowd. It was Tyson's best friend

Jean-Claude Gionet. "Don't do it if you're not ok with it, Tyse." Jean-Claude advised as he glared at Ashley.

"Claude's right, Tyson," Harlie agreed.

Amidst the growing cries from his classmates, Tyson gave into their hysterics. "*Ugh*! Just once. It's against my better judgment."

"Great!" Ashley cheered, "I'll need Vinnie and Tyson to go into the anteroom where we will scrub up. I need the rest of you students to go to that door on the other side of the laboratory and find a seat in our screening room. All of our actions will be caught in digital high definition by our motion detecting cameras!"

Once the students had found their places in the theater, the screen and speakers burst to life. Ashley was on screen wearing a white laboratory jacket. "Earlier, I introduced myself as, 'Ashley Ryker', your hostess. I'd like to reintroduce myself as '*Dr.* Ashley Ryker.' I have joining me as you know, your classmates, Tyson and Vinnie. They are truly unique people. We have here a sample of each of their blood. As we'd expect to find from Ahi people, Tyson's blood is an orange hue, quite a transparent orange. His temperature is 200 degrees Fahrenheit—more than double the normal body temperature of an average human. It's proof that Tyson is in fact from the Ahi fire ancestry."

She then looked at Vinnie.

"Vinnie's blood remains an opaque blue in hue and his temperature is 49 degrees Fahrenheit. This temperature is approximately half of that found in an average human. It's proof he's from the Zoree water heritage. We have here on the table in front of me, a mass of the prototypical Earth surface."

The camera zoomed in on the experiment bench in front of her.

She continued, "This sample has been infused with the basis for monocot life with mitigated growth potential. In plain English, this means we're about to make little palm trees!" Ashley giggled like a little girl at the thought of it. "Now, please observe what happens when the extracts from Tyson and Vinnie's blood streams are combined with our special additive and irrigate our sample!"

Ashley dumped the contents of three vials into one. She placed the large vial into a centrifuge that mixed the samples. Ashley then prodded a button on the lab bench and flipped a switch. The combined blood leaked from a thin nozzle over the small land sample and left behind a smoky haze. The blood seeped into the surface of the test material and the smoke settled.

One-by-one, springing forth from nothing— there emerged from the surface little stems. Moments later they were bursting buds. Then tiny palm trees—radiant little trees. The colors of the dioramic plant products were especially vibrant. The three in the lab could hear the cheers and applause from the students in the theater room.

"That is Neo-Exa!" Ashley declared.

"I might just start selling my blood," Vinnie laughed. "If the price is right."

Ashley immediately cut the camera feed to the theater and replied, "Trust me, we'd buy it!" Ashley threw Vinnie a large roll of money.

She looked at Tyson and held up another roll of cash. Benjamin Franklin was staring Tyson in the face. "I'd expect nothing less from a Zoree," Tyson turned around and stormed off towards the exit.

"Where you goin', Tyse?" Vinnie shouted.

"Finishing what you started," Tyson replied with his back turned and a dismissing wave of frustration.

"Vinnie," Ashley said.

"Yeah?"

"There's more money in it for you if you can *our* hands on *his* blood."

"Really? You can't just replicate it with all the technology you have here?"

"If we could do that we wouldn't need the Red Cross. You can get the blood with or without his help. Worst case scenario, if he keeps refusing, you just need to spill it and we'll be there to collect it. It'll be less valuable to us and inevitably you though. Additional purification costs are quite expensive."

Vinnie called out to Tyson again, "This could be a good thing, Tyse! Think about it, man! We can bridge the orders! We can all get along again!"

"You don't know what you're getting yourself into, Vin!" Tyson shouted louder as he put more distance between them.

"The hell I don't." Vinnie smelled the roll of money and threw it into his other hand. He examined it again with his wide, greedy eyes.

CHAPTER 3: COINCIDENCES

Mursten awaited the colonel in the deluxe observation quarters that neighbored Omicron's main laboratory. Lying on a rich Persian rug was a red velvet billiard table. A crystal chandelier hovered from the ceiling and the walls were paneled with cherrywood. A complimentary wet-bar sat in the corner of the room below an LED television. Mursten looked up from the remnants of the experiment when the door's handle finally turned.

"Keepin' me waiting, Rock?" Mursten joked as the bulky soldier pushed through the door.

"Security needs checking, Isaac."

"What do you think? You saw all that, right?" Mursten asked.

"Yeah, blood-plus-blood equals plants. There's definitely power to be had for the people running the show…under the right circumstances."

"Do you think it's worth it?"

"In order to be worth it you have to know what you're getting out of it, Isaac. I don't know much about these orders except they're pretty touchy about their blood. You would need destruction, bloodshed, for it to mean anything to you. You need war and it has to be on time. You have to know the skirmishers and what they're capable of."

"True."

"How does the President of the United States catalyze a war between populations he seemingly has no vested interest in and sell it to the public?"

"We simply have to make the Lost Orders America's enemy."

"Americans will never go for it, Isaac."

"With the right reason, I think I can sell it to the public."

"I hope so. I put out fifty million dollars of my own money because I was promised a substantial, tax-free return."

"A young man with a degree from Harvard, I should've expected you wouldn't be satisfied with the fortune you already have," Mursten commented.

"I'll never go broke, but I still want more."

"I think it's time to talk to Bankhart."

"Me too," Rockland agreed.

The two men departed the ornate observation room and the security detail led the way back to Bankhart's office. "Where's our buddy Mandrake?" Mursten asked. The team approached Mandrake's office and Rockland knocked at the door.

There was no response.

The men in the security detail exchanged glances and kept walking.

"What do you think Jim knows about Mandrake?" Mursten whispered to his colonel.

"Only what you'd think he knows. He assumes that he's just a little fairy eager to please his boss."

"And what do you think?" asked Mursten.

"I'm not as convinced as Bankhart. Put your game-face on, Mr. President. It's time to play businessman."

The security detail barged into Bankhart's office. The exec's chair was turned around towards where the window used to be. There was no longer a window, but a paneless frame and cool breeze. A few moments passed. There was no remark. No sign of movement in the chair. No sign of life.

"Watch our six-o-clock!" Colonel Rockland ordered. His team turned around, ensuring no lethal surprises lurked behind them.

"What's going on?" Mursten questioned.

"You're not going to want to see this, Mr. President!" Rockland declared as he waved him back. Mursten grasped the nickel-plated .45 he kept tucked in the left-side of his jacket and slowly stepped back towards the door. Rockland assumed control of his weapon and two men from the security detail followed behind him.

"Bankhart?" The colonel called.

Mursten backed away.

The soldiers stepped defensively towards the suspicious chair. They inched closer, guns trained on the chair. The colonel broke the tension and wheeled the chair around. He maintained a perfect combat stance with his gun locked on target. His sights lay where an impending surprise's head would have surely been. The chair made the full turn and the men were shocked by what they saw.

"Jim!" Mursten screamed as he tried to overpower the men who were now dragging him away.

Rockland's brain ceased for a minute as he stared into the cold, dead, open eyes of the victim. The executive's once pristine suit was soiled with a combination of sweat and blood. His lip was fat, just like his edematous cheek. Rockland lifted the stubbly big-shot's bloody lip. Part of

Bankhart's tongue rested between his closed teeth, almost entirely bitten through. The sleeves on his shirt were wrinkled. A button on his cuff was missing and there was a combat dagger plunged inches into Bankhart's bloody forehead. A note was posted to the corpse that was written in blood. It read,

'Any excuse will serve a tyrant.'

Rockland inspected the dagger. There was a message etched on the blade with a small arrow pointing at the tip. The message read,

'This side towards enemy.'

Rockland laughed at the merciless little quip. "Security, get me a forensics unit with a DNA-test for the blood. Check on Dominic Veselev and Will Buxton the limo driver."

The colonel slowly surveyed the room, noting that the attaché case with his fifty million in bearer bonds was nowhere to be found. He meditatively brushed his hands over the desk's surface and analyzed every detail of the office. 'Who?' Rockland asked as he cursed to himself.

One of the men in the security detail reported to

Rockland. "Colonel Rockland! Mr. Veselev and Mr. Buxton are…"

"Dead?" Rockland guessed.

A forensics investigator interrupted, "Colonel Rockland, the blood is…"

"President Mursten's?" the Colonel correctly supposed again.

Mursten looked up, "What!?"

"I'm guessing it was taken from your emergency supply stock in the limo."

The colonel knew what happened. Not one detail escaped his honed eye.

The killer undoubtedly broke through the window. Perhaps he repelled, or maybe he had a wing-suit and crashed through the window. There was no other damage, nor any blood to bolster the theory of a sloppy entrance. The killer must have repelled and tactically broke through the glass. Bankhart tried to stand his ground, but an expert hooking punch and tongue-severing uppercut seated him back into his chair. The killer had the note ready on the blade of the dagger. He jammed the blade into Bankhart's head as the executive futilely struggled. The killer was too strong or too trained for Bankhart to have a chance.

CHAPTER 4: ARE YOU INSANE?

Occam High's field trip to Omicron ended the moment the school administrators found out about Bankhart's gruesome murder. The teachers rounded the students up, took a head count, and hurriedly left the facility.

The wobbling school busses destined for Occam High made apparent every pothole and bump in the road. Tyson was sitting on the window-side of his bouncing seat with a student he barely knew, but was hastily forced to sit with. The sun was bright in the student's eyes, forcing its way through the lightly tinted windows. The unused seatbelts clanged off the seats with annoying rhythm.

"Hey!" Tyson heard someone whisper.

His seatmate, Brendon, turned around and shook his head, agreeing to something.

"Cool, thanks," he heard the same voice say as his seatmate looked up at the bus driver. The driver's eyes were glued to the road and the oblivious chaperone was busy with a crossword puzzle.

Brendon swiftly jumped out of his seat. Vinnie appeared while low-fiving Tyson's now former seatmate. Vinnie slammed his back to the seat and faced Tyson. "Tyse, give me a minute to talk with you. First off, I'm sorry for earlier. I've known you since 7th grade. We got along fine until today."

Tyson halted Vinnie from speaking with an open hand, "Vinnie, you can't just…"

"Just give me a minute." Vinnie pushed Tyson's hand down and tried to bargain with him. "We had our difference today, the whole different orders deal, but this could be a good thing, man. All we have to do is sell some blood."

"Vinnie, what happens if the mavens find out?" Tyson angrily whispered. "Are you insane?"

"Our orders don't gotta know." Vinnie pointed at himself, "I'm not gonna tell anyone about this. Are you?" He turned his finger around.

"There's not gonna be anything *to* tell, Vin. I'm not doin' it!"

Vinnie pulled out the massive roll of hundred dollar bills. "Look, just for considering it, I'll split this straight down the middle with you." Vinnie took the rubber-band off the roll of money and grabbed half of the impressive stack of cash.

Vinnie noticed an eavesdropping student eyeing the wad of money with raised eyebrows.

"The hell you lookin' at, punk?" Vinnie snapped and the student immediately shied away.

Vinnie gave Tyson his full attention again and held the money near Tyson's face. "Lookit, Tyse, count it. That's twenty grand. That's your half. Twenty for you, twenty for me."

Tyson focused on the money, and then Vinnie, who was trying his best attempt at an honest face. Tyson was tempted. He contemplated the impressive payment. He rolled his lips back in his mouth and put a fist in front of his face, still making his decision.

"C'mon, Tyse, you and I can get paid just for being who we are!" Vinnie whispered ecstatically. "We're just people…" Vinnie finished his thought, "with more ability."

"And greater account*ability,* you need to learn that," Tyson decided.

"Why you gotta over think everything? Just use your instincts! Survival, that's what instincts are, man." He admired the money he was holding, "…and this," Vinnie placed the money in Tyson's nearly eager hand, "is just a means of survival. That's all."

"Vin?"

"What?"

"Did you even *once* think about why Omicron would pay you such an *exorbitant* amount of money for just one vial of your blood?"

"Dude, speak English, they're working on a project where our blood is a resource, plain-and-simple. Supply-and-demand. Limited supply," he directed his attention to the money in Tyson's hand, "and lots of demand. It's easy math, bro."

"Not as easy as you think," Tyson said giving the money back to Vinnie. "There's something more to it than that. So take what's yours, but keep in mind, you'll have to give what's yours too."

"Yeah, blood, my body will make more of that."

"I'm tellin' you, Vin, this project isn't worth it."

"Not worth it? Who else is gonna give you a pocket full of Ben Franks like this?"

"I'm not worried about all that." Tyson peeped out of the window.

The bus came to a hard halt and the groaning students began getting to their feet.

"I'll getcha one way or another. Are you gonna be at Jordan's party tonight?"

"I guess. Why?" Tyson asked.

"Because you're gonna see it my way, Tyse. I'll seeya tonight." Vinnie rose to his feet, dwarfing everyone who was already standing and then shoved his way to the front of the bus.

That night, Vinnie and Jordan escorted Tyson through the Gannen's massive great room. Hip-hop rhythms boomed from thousand watt speakers. Sloppy red cups were hoisted up in the air by all the partiers. The Occam High football players and friends of the team shuffled their feet on the unchaperoned dance floor.

"It's cool that you finally came to a party, Tyse." Jordan yelled over the music as he and Vinnie swaggered through the crowd of friends.

"Yeah, it's about time you came to one," Vinnie agreed.

Among those on the dance floor, Pat McNamara had a girl in each arm. A hazy purple smoke journeyed from Pat's mouth into the air where it plumed and finally disappeared.

The 72-inch LED TV mounted on the wall reviewed the week's sports highlights. Most of the attendees who weren't dancing were drinking around the enormous fire pit near the pool. Some were shooting dice and the rest were swimming or sucking face.

"Hey, Vin! Hey, Jordan!" the content partiers offered the party-cup salute to the two VIPs as they walked by.

Vinnie and Jordan showed the way to Harlie and her friend Vanessa.

"Hey, baby," Vinnie said as he leaned down and tried to kiss Harlie who shied away.

"Oh damn, girl! You still mad?" Vinnie gibbered.

"She didn't come here to see her cheating ex-boyfriend, Vinnie!" Harlie's best-friend feebly pushed his bulky arm. She narrowed her dark eyes on him and cast a disgusted expression at the galoot.

"Her loss, half of these girls are here to see me. So, I don't care either way!"

"Go away, Vinnie!" The girls chorused.

"Alright, fine. C'mon, guys," Vinnie turned to Jordan and Tyson and waved them on.

"Tyson can stay," Harlie spoke up.

"What?" Tyson asked.

"Only if you wanna," Harlie winked.

"Uh, sure."

"I see how it is, girl." Vinnie sneered. Vinnie gazed at Tyson. "We're all good, Tyse. It is what it is. If I can, I wanna talk to you later, just us. I wanna talk about what we discussed on the bus. How about an hour from now?"

Tyson shrugged just before Vinnie and Jordan lost themselves in the mass of inebriated partiers. Tyson didn't know what to say, the glamorous girl in front of him left him speechless. He opened the sport-bottle in his hand and took a dilatory slug of the lukewarm water. It tasted disgusting, but he couldn't come up with anything clever to say.

"Whatcha got in the bottle?" Harlie asked.

"Water," Tyson declared, awkwardly drinking from it again.

"I'm not the police, Tyson."

"Honest!" Tyson said, offering her a sip from the chewed up top. "I'll warn-ya it's disgusting."

"Haha! No, thanks. I believe you."

"I'll leave you two alone. I wanna talk to Jean-Claude. I think he's around here somewhere," Vanessa said.

"Claude's here?" Tyson craned his neck looking around for his best friend.

"Ya, but so is Harlie. So why don't you two talk for a bit?"

Harlie flashed her impossibly white teeth, "Sounds good to me."

Vanessa pushed Tyson closer and ambled away.

"Can I get you a drink?" Tyson asked.

"No, I don't drink. I just come to hang out with friends. Maybe talk to my new friend," she examined Tyson, waiting for a reply.

"Uh...me too."

"Good! I'm glad we finally talked today at Omicron."

"Yeah?"

"Yeah, but you didn't tell me much about yourself, Tyson."

"What do you wanna know?"

"Oh, I don't know!" she giggled and poked him in the chest. "Just tell me about you."

"What should I tell you about me?"

"Ok, I guess the lab seems like a good start. What was up with that lady trying to get you to show her your forearms?"

"I don't know." Tyson took another slug of the gross drink.

"Ya, you do," Harlie laughed. "C'mon, Tyson."

"Uh, that's a long story."

"I'm all ears," Harlie said politely as she plunked her little body down in the arm chair behind her.

"It's a *really* long story."

"That's ok. I don't have anywhere to be. Sit with me!"

Tyson smiled and did as Harlie asked him. Tyson was still ill-at-ease. Two things made Tyson nervous— his heritage and beautiful girls.

"So," she began, "tell me about it. What's with those tattoos of yours? The colors are so beautiful. The red is so unique, so bold. The gold around the word is so sparkly. But I didn't think you were the tattoo type."

"Thanks, I think?" Tyson swallowed the saliva in his mouth.

"It's not a bad thing," Harlie insisted. "You're full of surprises. How old were you when you got that?"

"I didn't get it."

"What do you mean?"

"It's always been a part of me, for better or worse."

The statement brought an inquisitive concern to Harlie's face. Her raised eyebrow told Tyson she doubted his sanity.

"For any Ahi, a trace is a part of their being, part of their identity. You don't have a choice. If you're Ahi, it's part of you."

"That's beautiful."

"It's not as cool as it sounds."

"So, you're an Ahi. What does really that mean?"

"Nothing much beyond what Dr. Ryker said at the lab," Tyson shifted in his seat nervously.

Sensing Tyson's growing discomfort, she changed the subject, "Did you get the sense that she didn't like me for some reason?"

"No, not at all!"

"Really? I felt like she looked at me weird."

"No, I didn't get that at all."

Vinnie wandered up to his two classmates in the armchair, "Harlie, I gave you guys the hour. I need to talk to Tyson."

Harlie huffed, but didn't answer Vinnie.

Tyson sighed and stood up cautiously, "Fine—fine. Lead the way, Vin."

"Byeee, Tyson," Harlie sweetly chirped.

"I'll see you soon?" Tyson asked.

"You bet! Sit with me in our next study hall."

"Ok, Tyse, let's go." Vinnie impatiently requested.

Vinnie and Tyson weaved through the oblivious party guests, dodging drunken arms and slobber-swappers. They trotted out into the large yard where they could be out of ear-shot.

"What's goin' on, Vin?"

"Tyse, forty grand!" Vinnie held up all of the money he had on the bus. "I'm doubling my offer."

"Vinnie, no amount will change my answer."

"Omicron wants Ahi blood. Trust me, that's gonna happen."

Jordan Gannen stumbled over to Tyson and Vinnie. "Yo, Vin, Lynd, we're about to start hittin' that good stuff! McNamara brought it! Get in here!"

"Oh word? Let's go, Tyse!" Vinnie exclaimed.

"No, thanks."

"What?" Vinnie and Jordan asked.

Jean-Claude appeared from behind Vinnie and Jordan. He looked at Tyson, "Dude, can we catch a ride home?" He asked as he drew Tyson's attention to Harlie and Vanessa.

"Yeah. What's wrong, Claude?"

"I can't be here. The stuff in there is a little too heavy for me to be comfortable with. I don't even want to be in the same house. I'll lose my scholarship chances. I heard Pat brought acid and who knows what else."

"Acid?" Tyson asked.

"Yeah, man. We should go."

"Nice!" Vinnie hooted as he bumped fists with Jordan.

Tyson looked back at Jordan and Vinnie. "I think it's time I left, guys."

"C'mon, Lynd! Stop sucking so much!" Jordan shouted.

"Vin, take what's yours, but, remember."

"Yeah, yeah, yeah, I have to give what's mine. Keep in mind, Tyse, my body will make more blood and so will yours."

"But your body can't rebuild the pride of your people."

"What the hell is he talkin' about?" Jordan laughed.

"Nothin', Jay. He's just preachin' or some shit."

"Think again, Vinnie. Taking the money was a mistake," Tyson warned.

"Shove the sermon up your ass and open your ears, Lynd! We're not kids anymore. I'm tryin' to get this to work and you're actin' like a fool, man!"

"C'mon, Vin! I'm goin' back inside," Jordan slurred.

"Fine," Vinnie agreed. "If you jerk-offs call the cops, I'm kicking all your asses on Monday—No exceptions ladies."

"Oh, yeah?" Jean-Claude staunchly held his ground as he stared down Vinnie.

"Yeah." Vinnie neared Jean-Claude.

Tyson defensively stood up to Vinnie with his friend.

Jordan grabbed Vinnie's arm. "Let it go, man. They won't call the police. They still wanna win the state champs as bad as we do. For now, they need us on the team and we need them. We need to think of the football team and drop this thing here."

"Fine." Vinnie turned away with Jordan. They were walking back to the Gannen house when Vinnie turned around one last time. "Omicron will have Ahi blood, whether you give it, or we take it, Lynd! Believe that! Sooner or later, it's gonna happen."

"They're not getting any more of mine. So save your breath, Vin!" Tyson rejoined.

"Oh yeah they are, Lynd." Vinnie told himself. "Yes, they are."

CHAPTER 5: I TRUST MY INSTINCTS

The door to the Pentagon's command center submitted to the forceful Colonel Rockland. He walked in purposefully, carrying his cap under his rigid left arm. The pampered chiefs-of-staff sat in deluxe executive chairs that surrounded the long stoic table. The flashing monitors on the wall depicted different scenes from the President's visit to the laboratory. The indistinct chatter and note-taking amongst the staff ceased when Rockland approached the table. The colonel perfected his posture and saluted everyone.

"Speak freely, Rick." The large old man at the head of the table nodded— approving of the colonel.

"Thank you, General Breca." Rockland eased his stance. "At 0800 hours we arrived at the facility. Our security measures completed as outlined in the report at your fingertips. We arrived at the car port five minutes after touchdown. On arrival in the car port, I informed President Mursten of the logistic error by the penman of the dossier."

"What error, Colonel Rockland?" Secretary of Defense Milton Seward asked. Seward was a hefty, round-faced man. He was also clearly in denial about his balding problem as his comb-over did him no favors.

"Nowhere in the dossier was there any reference to the field trip at the laboratory."

"Field trip? As in school trip?" asked Seward.

"Yes, sir."

"How many schools?"

"One school, Occam High, from Honolulu."

"Any persons of interest to us as a chaperone?"

"Not presently, but we're working on it."

"More on that later, let's get down to brass tacks." Seward adjusted his bland blue tie. "What can you tell me about the knife in Bankhart's head?"

"Jim Bankhart, the proprietor of the company, was an established businessman and active scientist his whole life. He achieved his MBA then a PhD in biochemistry from Yale.

He completed all of this in just six years time. He was a ranking member in a campus secret society with no criminal record. He maintained volunteer status throughout his years as a student, was a star athlete, and appeared to be an all around good guy. His net worth hovers around two-billion American dollars.

Bankhart was stabbed the day of President Mursten's visit. The dagger was characteristic of the combat daggers used by the Amity Militia in *Sarajevo, Bosnia*. On the blade there was a quote similar to one found on a Claymore. It read, 'This side toward enemy.' In addition, the *modus operandi* was somewhat consistent with the militia's M.O., but not conclusive."

"So, we can't assume it was the Amity Militia?" General Breca asked.

"I wouldn't, sir, not yet."

"Very well," Breca digested the thought as his fat thumb scratched at the cleft in his chin.

"Hold it!" Secretary Seward ordered. "We have an Amity dagger stuck in a guy's head, a similar M.O., and we're going to say it wasn't them? Use your head, General!"

"I didn't say it wasn't them. I said we can't *assume* it was them. I trust my instincts."

"Instincts? You've been a pen-pusher for how many years, General?"

"I'm sorry, Mr. Secretary? Does my time in Vietnam, Korea *and* Desert Storm not count?" The general narrowed his icy gaze in a challenging inquisition. "A combat-hardened veteran has instincts, a trait unattainable to an ivory-tower politician!" Breca shouted. "My instincts are to trust the young colonel."

"Thank you, sir," Rockland replied apprehensively.

"Very well, General Breca. Continue, Colonel Rockland," Seward muttered through his clenched yellow teeth.

"Thank you, sir. As I was saying we can't be sure of the identity of the assassin."

"What about the note, colonel?" asked Seward.

"The quote from Aesop justifies the assassination as a means to an end. The assassin thinks he kills to end killing."

"What of these Ahi and Zoree kids? What is the meaning of their heritage?"

"I have no answer for that, sir." the colonel lied. Rockland could tell Seward bought the story, but Breca suddenly didn't.

Seward pulled off his glasses and wiped them with a microfiber cloth, "Well then, all we've got about the murder is an alleged motive. They think they're killing to end killing?"

"Yes, sir."

"We have to figure out why the assassin, or assassins, decided they're preventing more killing by murdering what seems to be a lawful American entrepreneur."

"Exactly!" One of the men around the table added.

"We're not going to be able to figure that out until after the investigation." The general looked to Seward for his next question.

"Getting back to the note, it was written in blood?" inquired Seward.

"Yes, sir. It was written in President Mursten's blood." All of the men around the table were again paying undivided attention to the colonel. "The note read, 'Any excuse will serve a tyrant.'"

"I'm more interested in how the president's blood ended up on the note." Seward rushed Rockland along.

"As I'm sure you've read in the file, Dominic Veselev and Will Buxton were also found murdered. It's likely that they were in the way of the killer's message. They were the only people near the president's emergency blood reserve. There's a stock in Air Force One as you know and one in his limo. Air Force One was heavily guarded, but the limo was allegedly being guarded by Omicron's security personnel. They were nowhere to be found."

Secretary Seward sighed. "Fair enough, I suggest now we dismiss for the evening. Go home and go over your notes, gentlemen. Brainstorm. I want big ideas when I come in tomorrow. Is there anything else you can think of, General Breca?"

"Not really, like Milton said, go home, go over your notes and do a little research on your own. We've been in contact with the C.I.A. They're also analyzing details of the event."

Seward stood up, "All right gentlemen, dismissed, we'll regroup tomorrow at 0900 hours."

General Breca stood up; as did the rest of the men who were eager to go home. "Rick," he called.

"Yes, sir?"

"Walk with me."

"General, I've gotta get on the horn with Langley and find out what they know."

"It wasn't a question, Colonel. I *wasn't* asking. Come with me."

"Yes, sir."

The general and the colonel were the first out of the room, walking briskly ahead of the slower procession of men who drained out of the crisis room.

The brown doors that lead outside swung open and General Breca lead the way out of the building. "I have questions of my own, son. I was hoping you could help me."

"Yes, sir, I'll do my best."

"Speak freely, Rick. We don't have any suits with over-privileged occupants to show off for. I want to know why I suddenly doubt my instincts in trusting you."

"I beg your pardon, sir?" Rockland was taken aback.

"Why do I get the feeling you're screwing with me?"

Rockland didn't have a good answer.

The men were approaching the general's white Lincoln Towncar limo. Rockland held the door open for Breca, dismissing the old chauffeur that was standing there.

"I'll give you some time to think about that one, Colonel. I've known you for some eight years now...or at least, I hope I've known you for those years." The general took off his cap and sat in the limo. The colonel closed the door behind Breca. Through a barely open window, Breca sighed and said, "Good evening, Colonel," as the limo took off and disappeared into the distance.

CHAPTER 6: DAYBREAK

It was daybreak on Tuesday morning. The orange sun was just peaking over the horizon, warming the cool dewdrops that rested on the leaves of the palm plants. The sky was taking on its usual cerulean hue and the clouds were orange, much like the citrus fruits in the citrus groves that paralleled the freshly paved road on which Wright was swiftly piloting his sporty blue BMW Alpina B7.

Wright turned into the parking lot outside the football field where Pat McNamara was to meet him for his disobedience at the lab. There was no sign of Pat yet. Wright wasn't surprised. He opened his glove box and noticed a strange envelope was left inside. He broke the seal and read the note.

'Ethan,

I have been solicited by an Ahi friend to find the former Ahi maven, Dawson Wrangle and the acting Ahi Maven, Ellis Cohen.

Your loyal friend,
Victor Farrell'

Wright tucked the note away and noticed a dirty red Impala turning into the parking lot. Wright laughed to himself noting there was only one occupant in the car and it wasn't Pat. His smirk faded away and he drank the last of the coffee from his pewter travel mug. He unbuckled his seat belt and exited the car.

"Mr. McNamara," Wright asked, his tone and demeanor said so much more than what he articulated.

"I'm sorry, Mr. Wright. He just refused to get up." Alan McNamara was a nervous, long-faced man with a graying and scraggily beard. Alan walked around the Impala to greet Mr. Wright with a handshake.

"Please, hop in." Wright ignored the gesture, directing his attention to the beautiful blue means of conveyance. "Take me to him. I think if we talk on the way, you'll see that I'm not just a mean principle. I take an interest in young adults with potential who don't understand the gifts they have."

"Surely," Alan responded as he clumsily made his way around the car. "Your car is beautiful, Mr. Wright," Alan said as he sank into his seat and closed the door.

"Thank you, Mr. McNamara."

Alan admiringly looked the car over again. "Alpina B7."

"That's right," the principle confirmed.

"I'm not sure I understand…"

"Beg pardon?"

"On a principle's salary—I mean—I'm sorry. What a stupid thing for me to say!"

"It's not a stupid thing. A principle in a one-hundred-and-thirty-thousand dollar BMW raises questions. Aeronation Aviation did well for me. Seventy-thousand bumped one-hundred-fold," Wright offered.

"Haha! Not in this lifetime," Alan playfully contested. "Their only spike that big must've been some 80 years ago!" Alan chortled.

"It was more recent than that." Wright politely argued before changing the subject, "Please, help yourself to the glove box."

"Surely," Alan reached for the dashboard and opened the glove box. Alan examined his son's file and shook his head. It was a long list describing disciplinary actions for unacceptable behavior, consistent tardiness, truancy, drug use and declining grades.

Alan read aloud, "If Patrick put as much effort in his 'Skills-at-Home' elective as he did in his lunchroom protest today, he'd have a much better grade." Alan thought about the statement. "What does that mean?"

"I'm not one for disorderly behavior, but between you and me that was pretty funny."

"Please, enlighten me." Alan requested.

"Your son was displeased at the lunch menu selection that day at school. So, he hopped over the lunch counter to the prep table and threw together the closest alternative to chicken parmesan. I thought that might've been a forged signature on the referral." Wright glanced over at the astounded parent. "Look at the envelope paper-clipped to the back of the sheets on the left. Those are the referrals that I believed he forged you or your wife's signature on."

"Holy Hell! There's like twenty of them here."

"Twenty-three, actually. I understand we should have told you sooner, however your son wasn't my biggest problem. I know your son is better than this kind of behavior though."

"Thank you, Mr. Wright. My son *is* better than that behavior."

"Believe it or not, he's a lot like I was at that age those hundreds of years ago."

"You don't say. Hundreds of years ago, huh? I doubt you're that old." Alan laughed. "But I am curious. How is my son similar to how you were at that age?"

"I'll tell you when we have more time." Wright replied. "We'll need it."

"Ok," Alan laughed.

Wright and Alan arrived at the small bungalow that the McNamara family called home. Wright pulled the shimmering blue car into the driveway and his first impression of the home was that it needed work.

The men made their way inside where Mrs. McNamara unsurely greeted the principle. "Hello, *Mister*?" the tall and slim woman cocked her head to the side, waiting for Wright to tell her his name.

Alan interjected, "Eva, this is Principle Wright. Principle Wright, this is my wife Eva."

"Oh, I'm sorry! Principle Wright, how are you? I'm sorry for the circumstances under which we're meeting. I'm sorry Pat has caused you some grief at the school. He's not a bad kid he's just…misguided."

Wright smirked, realizing the irony in Eva's words. "No problem, I'm just here to help get him on the right track. In order to get him going we'll have to awaken him. Please, Alan, lead the way."

The men breached the door to Pat's room. Wright stepped over the pile of dirty clothes on the floor and looked around at the mess. An unclean fish-tank refracted the light coming in through the window. Various torn posters plastered the walls and the room reeked of marijuana. Wright turned around and noticed the closet with an off-kilter door. "Do you mind if I have a look?" Wright asked.

"Be my guest," Alan answered.

Wright opened the door and spread the hanging clothes. He fumbled around in the back of the closet, moving clean clothes, magazines and athletic equipment. Just as Wright suspected, the mess was camouflaging a shoebox. Wright grabbed the orange shoe box and showed it to Alan. "They always keep contraband in a shoebox," Wright sighed as he broke into the taped lid. Wright opened the box and showed it to Alan. "For an amateur, he's done well. There must be thirteen, maybe fourteen-thousand in cash here."

"What?" Alan scrambled over to Wright and peered into the box.

"And maybe another one-thousand dollars of various illegal street and prescription drugs."

"Mr. Wright, I had no idea!"

"I know. That's why I'm here to help, Alan."

"What do I do with it?"

"The money? Put it in a college fund. The drugs, we don't need to get your son arrested. We need to send him a message though."

"Agreed."

"The drugs are easily gotten rid of. You can secure them in a coffee tin with packing tape. Pack it full of used coffee grounds or foul-smelling compost soaked in ammonia. That'll keep animals out of it. Put it in numerous bags and throw it in the garbage. You don't want to drive around with it and you have nowhere to burn it. It's your only option really. If you turn it into the police, they'll rightfully ask questions."

"Ok, great. Good idea."

"Since that's taken care of for now. I suggest you wake your son."

"Indeed," Alan walked over to Pat's bedside and tapped his son's shoulder. He then shook the slumbering teen and said, "Pat, get up. Principle Wright is here." The sleeping teenager didn't budge. Alan looked at the principle. "See, he refuses to get up." He fervently shook his son by the shoulder. The half-sleeping teenager turned his body over and faced the wall away from the men.

"Mind if I try?" asked Wright.

"Please," Alan agreed as he threw his hands in the air as if to give up. Wright pulled a capped vial out of his pocket.

"What's that?" Alan inquired as he narrowed his gaze on the vial and crossed his arms.

"Spirit of Hartshorne." replied Wright.

Alan seemed all the more puzzled.

"You might have heard of smelling salts. It's what we used in my golden glove days when someone was kissing the canvas."

"You were a boxer?"

"Yeah, I don't compete anymore, but I still train. It keeps me young-ish."

Alan laughed as Wright waved the vial under Pat's nose and shouted in the slumbering young man's ear, "Get up, kid!"

Immediately, the young man was roused—startled awake. He was very surprised to see his principle glowering back at him.

Alan suddenly appeared concerned, "Mr. Wright, now that I think of it, haven't people died from that stuff?"

"The kid doesn't seem any dead-er to me." Wright glared at Pat, displaying all the fury he could possibly muster with his square face.

"What? Dad, what is this?" Pat all of the sudden realized how intimidated he was by his principle's angry face. Pat cut his commentary.

"Get your things and let's go," Wright demanded.

"Uh...you heard him, son. Get your things," Alan awkwardly demanded.

"Are you kidding me? This is bullshit!"

Alan, persuaded by Wright's fierce stare, corrected Pat, "Son, get your things."

"Shut up, just shut up!"

Wright hastily grabbed Pat's collar. "You have five minutes." Wright forcefully poked Pat in the forehead with his index finger. "Don't make me come back for you, kid. Do you understand?"

Pat was uncomfortable. He closed his eyes and shook his head, 'Yes,' completely afraid of the principle. He felt the principle let go of him and as he opened his eyes. Wright and his father were already out of the room and Alan slammed the door behind them.

After the awkward car ride, they arrived back at the football field at 5:45AM. "Pat, get your shoulder pads, mouth guard, cleats and helmet. Be back here in ten minutes. The locker-room is open."

The arrogant teenager rolled his eyes as he wearily wobbled out of the car. He slammed the door and made his way towards the gymnasium.

"Thank you very much for this, Mr. Wright. I'm sorry for the aggravation we've caused you and that he slammed your door."

"Don't worry about the door. But I'm not coming to wake up your son again. I need your support at home otherwise this won't work." Wright took the vial out of his pocket and gave it to Alan. "Don't worry, I have plenty more. I think you learned an easy way to rouse your son."

Alan laughed, "I'll do it right next time. For that matter, I'm just glad there is a next time. Is there anything else I should know?"

"Yeah, have some ice packs and heating pads ready at home. Day one hurts."

"All right, I'll keep that in mind. You be careful yourself, he's a tough young man."

"I'll take my chances," Wright laughed as he put his aviator sunglasses on. He then grabbed a black duffle bag from his back seat and got out of the car.

Pat showed up with his gear as Wright had directed and affixed his eyes on Wright. Pat had never seen Wright in a short sleeve shirt. The man who wore a suit that conferred no shape to him during school hours was in reality hiding a very strong frame with multiple tattoos and scars. Wright turned his head over until his ear touched his shoulder. A sickening series of pops chilled Pat to the bone. "You ready, son?"

"As ready as I'm going to be."

"Did the pot in your locker help?" Wright asked as he began taping up his thick fingers.

Pat let out a snorting laugh he was trying to stifle, "It smelt a lot like oregano and yard clippings when I lit it."

"Shame when that happens."

"Yeah, I could've smoked that."

"Oh and we found your stash."

"What! What did you do with my shit, yo?"

"Drugs destroyed. The money is going into a college fund your dad is setting up today."

"I'm not sure if you looked at my transcript lately...but spoiler alert...I won't get in! So thanks, dick."

"No problem." Wright stretched his neck to the other side, "I'm assuming that was a genuine thank you for not getting the police involved. I'm not one of your naïve teachers. The next time I find it, the cops find it too. Keep that stuff out of my school."

"Fair enough."

"Do you know why you're here?"

"Because I haven't graduated yet and you don't like

me—so you try to be a pain in my ass?"

"A swing and a miss."

"Because I called you 'fat' and admittedly that's not the case," Pat ceded.

"Flattering, but no."

"Whatever, Wright, you should just let me deal. I've got a good bank roll, a couple of ladies depending on the day and I'm having fun. I'm making more in a week than my old man does in two!"

"You keep going that way and you're gonna end up in jail or some morgue after a deal goes south."

"Mmmkay," Pat responded in a typical disinterested teenager's tone.

"Think about where you're at in life over the next two hours."

"Are we ready to get this over with?"

"You bet. Tire flips endzone to endzone—I'll be timing you."

"Are you serious? You know this exercise is for the big-ass lineman, right? I'm just a second-string receiver."

"It's your exercise now. Let's see some first-string effort."

Pat tucked his hands under the huge truck tire and bent at the knees like a runner when they set. The tire must've weighed two-hundred pounds. He had to move it one-hundred yards. Pat already knew he couldn't do it.

Wright blew the whistle from the sidelines and Pat let out a war-like grunt. He upended the tire and toppled it over. He screamed again and repeated the maneuver. He let out another yell and pushed forward. Flip-by-flip, and yard-by-yard his energy dwindled. He didn't make it but thirty yards up the field.

Principle Wright was still on the track that surrounded the football field 'skipping rope' as they called it in his military days. Pat saw him effortlessly jumping and shuffling his feet under the rope beneath him.

Wright noticed Pat had stopped short. He dropped the jump rope and hustled over to where the tire landed. Wright took the same position that Pat had taken when he began the drill. With a sharp grunt, he lifted the tire and flip after flip he kept a quick, efficient pace all the back to the starting point. The principle clearly bested Pat's time back to the endzone.

Wright flipped the tire over for the last time. "That was too easy. Next time we'll do the agility drills on the way back."

"O—ok."

After an hour and thirty-five minutes the principle blew his whistle. "You need to get ready and get to class, kid. 6:00AM tomorrow."

The teenager dropped what he was doing, rolled his eyes then without any 'farewell' he jogged off toward the locker room.

After readying himself for the day, Pat exited the gymnasium. As he walked across the street to the classroom building, he heard the rhythmic thumping of a car's sub-woofer off in the distance. The sound was getting closer. Pat saw a white Infiniti G37 coupe approaching with a roaring exhaust note trailing it. The big black rims stopped turning as the car came to a screeching halt. The tinted window rolled down and Vinnie sat inside with a swanky grin.

"Damn, son!" Pat admired the car as he rested his hand on the roof.

"Get in, man. Let's skip first," Vinnie said.

"Cool," Pat got in and slammed the door closed. "I *need* to get away from here."

"Why you here so early?" Vinnie asked as he turned down the music.

"Wright's been on my case lately. The dude showed up at my house this morning! He rifled through my shit and found my stock. Now, my dad is getting rid of my supply. He's putting my stacks in the bank or some bullshit."

"Oh word? That's crazy!"

"Yeah, he's been obnoxious because of that stupid field trip to the lab."

"That's so dumb!"

"I know, right. By the way, how the hell can you afford this?" Pat asked.

"You know me. I get mine."

"Cool, man. Let's get outta here."

Vinnie turned the music back up and revved his engine. He shoved the car into gear, peeled out, then sped off past the school. The students on the front lawn of the school swiveled their heads as the shimmering car that they all envied sped by, bass thumping.

CHAPTER 7: THAT'S COOL

Many windows welcomed natural light into Occam High's airy interior. The different cliques dispersed themselves amongst the numerous rows of metallic black lockers throughout the common area. One group of girls talked about their favorite overpriced caramel lattes. Other girls compared the playlists on their smart phones. The boys on the other hand were often slapping hands or laughing at the nerd that just fell on the floor.

The first bell rang and the students flocked to their homerooms.

Tyson glanced around the populated classroom and approached Jean-Claude who looked up from his studying.

"How's it goin'?" Jean-Claude greeted Tyson first.

"Same old, what about you?" Tyson sat down at the desk in front of his friend.

"More of the same."

"What are you studying?"

"Next unit for Chem." Jean-Claude closed his book and settled back in his chair.

"Is it hard?" Tyson asked flipping through the pages.

"Not really. It shouldn't be that bad."

"Sweet."

Jordan Gannen turned around to the two book worms. "There have never been bigger dorks on a football team. You're lucky the team needs you two, otherwise you'd probably get your asses kicked every day," he said with extra wide-eyed emphasis on the 'every day' part.

"That's a back handed compliment," Tyson said.

"I don't even know what that means," Gannen responded.

"Really? And you're insulting us?" Jean-Claude jumped in as he and Tyson laughed at their mentally inferior classmate.

"Yes, yes I am," Jordan concluded and turned around to the girl he was talking to before.

"I almost forgot, Tyse. Did you see this?" Jean-Claude pulled his cell phone out of his pocket and showed Tyson the internet headline. "Omicron has released a press statement about you and Vinnie."

"Huh?"

"Yeah, it doesn't mention either of your names, but it does talk about two students from Occam High with special 'heritages.'"

"What?" Tyson hastily grabbed the phone and read the article's headline.

"So, do you think I could ask you about that whole lab thing later on?"

"Uh...maybe."

"Cool," Jean-Claude decided.

"Tyson, please put the phone away," the homeroom teacher, Mrs. Welby, requested.

"Yes, ma'am," he said as he handed the phone back to Jean-Claude.

"Thank you," the portly lady with curly white hair responded. The mole on Mrs. Welby's upper lip bounced up and down as she took attendance. The teacher finished roll call and remarked, "So, we're missing McNamara...shocking." She inspected the room once more.

"Does anyone know where he is? Jordan, do you know where Pat is?"

The uninspired teenager looked over from the girl he was flirting with, shrugged his shoulders and shook his head 'no.' He swiveled back to the girl, made a snarky remark and she giggled while bunning her hair.

The teacher rolled her eyes. "Tyson? Do you know where he is?"

"No ma'am."

"*Yes, ma'am...No, ma'am*," Jordan mocked Tyson.

"Quiet, Jay," Tyson spoke up.

Mrs. Welby hobbled over to the phone and called another homeroom. "Is Vinnie in homeroom?" She listened to the response on the other end, laughed and replied, "No, McNamara isn't here either." After another pause, she responded, "Yeah, all right, thanks." The teacher hung up the phone and redialed another number. "Luann, can you tell Principle Wright that neither McNamara, nor Tarsa, were in homeroom this morning." After a longer silence the teacher laughed. "Shocking, right? Well, at least if he's not here he won't be mugging anyone in the halls," There was another pause and she said, "No problem," before she hung up the phone.

Before the second-to-last period of the day, Tyson ambled down the brightly lit corridor and entered the school library. He walked up to the circulation-desk where the diminutive, elf-like librarian was busy cataloguing her new books.

"Hi, Tyson!" The librarian smiled then continued about her cataloguing.

"Hi, Mrs. Lynch." Tyson replied as he signed into the study hall.

"When's the next game?" She asked as she shot Tyson a consenting glance.

"Sunday, 7:00PM."

"I'll be there."

"Great!" Tyson focused elsewhere and saw Harlie waving at him from a table on the far side of the library. Tyson hurried over to her.

"Hey, you," Harlie said as she flirtatiously winked. She pushed out the chair on the opposite side of the table with her foot, inviting Tyson to sit with her and Vanessa.

"Hey, Harlie. Hi, Vanessa."

Vanessa smiled at Tyson then looked at Harlie. "I've got to do that research paper. So, I'll catch up with you later, Harlie."

"See ya!" Harlie winked at her friend who grinned back and strolled to the computers on the other side of the library. "So, whatcha doin', Tyse?"

"I was planning on doing some of the next unit in Chemistry. Then I was going to do the week's Calculus homework."

"For the whole week?" Harlie gasped.

"Yeeeah?"

"That's...cool," Harlie giggled at how uncomfortable his response was.

"Kinda."

Harlie teethed her lip, trying not to laugh as Tyson clumsily opened his book and began reading. Tyson seemed excited about the pictures of the elements on the page titled, 'Alkali Metals.'

"Did you know that when water and cesium interact, the cesium explodes?" Tyson asked her.

"Um...I don't think I did know that." She put her index finger on her lips, still trying to stifle her laughing. "Thanks though, I'll remember that for the test."

"So," Tyson began. "What are you doing?"

"Do you reeeeeally wanna know?" Harlie leaned in towards him.

"Yyyyes."

"Reeeallly, reaaaaly want to know?" She squinted her eyes at him playfully.

"Yyyyes."

Harlie flagged him in with her index finger. Tyson leaned in and smiled naively, totally unsure of what to expect. He stared deeply into her green eyes. She loved the way he honestly looked and smiled at her. "I'm waiting for you to ask me out after you win on Sunday."

"How do I know that we're going to win on Sunday?"

Harlie backed away, "Really, Tyse?"

"Yeah, they're a really tough team!"

"Tyson, try again!" She was more annoyed than entertained.

"Oh wow, I'm sorry. Uh, do you wanna?"

"Wanna what?" She teased, closing her one eye and turning away as if watching a romantic train-wreck.

"Do you wanna go out with me?"

"Do I? Tyson, I thought you'd never ask, even if I asked myself out for you!"

Tyson's flush face took on its normal tone as it sank in that she *wanted* to go out with him. "How about we go to the school's pier after the game and do some star-gazing?" He offered with a confident smile, as if he asked her out without such obvious cues.

"I can't wait!"

The bell rang signifying the end of the study hall. Tyson got up from the table and grabbed his book bag.

"You comin'?" He asked.

"No, I have back-to-back study halls and my homework is done. I guess I'll just have to sit here and think about Sunday."

"All right, I'm sure I'll see you before then."

"I hope so," Harlie waved as Tyson left.

Harlie soon heard a familiar voice behind her. "Why you goin' out with that punk?"

Harlie turned around. Vinnie came through the back door and sat down with Jordan Gannen and Pat McNamara.

"You had your chance, Vinnie."

Vinnie laughed, "Yeah, word, I did, but why would I want a second chance, girl? You know I climb the ladder. Blam!" Vinnie pointed at his new scantily clad girlfriend, Luna, who was at the circulation desk. Luna was a tall, tan blond with an athletic and curvaceous body. Her attire didn't leave much to the imagination. She had a short denim skirt and a tight, low-cut shirt. "I wish I could say the same for you," he cackled conceitedly.

"He's cuter than you'll ever think about being," Harlie said, defending her choice in Tyson. "And he respects me."

"Men aren't *cute* Harlie," Vinnie said the word 'cute' with such disdain. "Dogs are cute, little kids are cute, you're cute, hell, some people think old folk are cute, but your boy Lynd, is just that…a little boy." He paused his mockery as if he were thinking, "So, maybe he is cute," he laughed "…a cute little boy."

"Shut up, Vinnie! He's more of a man than you."

"Yeah, I'm really wonderin' about that," he said as he

sat back in his chair with his arms folded, flaunting his muscular build.

"Just…shut up!" She turned away from the boys who didn't stop laughing. After a minute or two of indistinct chatter and laughter, Harlie had enough. "You're so annoying! Why do you even show up here if the only period you go to is study hall? Don't you have a convenience store to rob or something?" She seized her books and stormed to the far side of the library, turning around once more to express her anger.

CHAPTER 8: LOOKING FOR ONE OF OUR OWN

Rockland reported to the next scheduled briefing, storming through the doors in the crisis center as he'd often done in the past. Rockland greeted the men with a salute as he always did and was invited to sit down.

"How are you, Rick?" General Breca asked without his usual smile of appreciation for the Colonel.

"I'm well, General. How about yourself, sir?" Rockland maintained a good poker face despite his throat burning from the acid reflux caused by his nerves. He perspired profusely, but the sweat hadn't yet soaked through his uniform.

"We'll see," the general replied quietly with a sigh.

"Gentlemen," Milton Seward began. "We may have discovered a motive for the knife in the old man's head. We've gotten a report that fifty million in bearer bonds was stolen from Dr. Bankhart's personal safe."

"How good is the source?" asked Breca.

"He's very credible," Seward replied.

"Who is he?" Rockland impulsively asked. His nervousness began getting the better of his senses.

"Come again, Colonel?"

"Who is your source, Secretary Seward?" The colonel asked, clearly flustered.

"That information is on a *need-to-know* basis, Colonel. Right now, you don't need to know." Rockland could tell Seward liked to say that. Seward liked 'being in the know.' "When that information is available to the chiefs-of-staff, you'll know too."

"When's that?"

"Maybe today, maybe tomorrow...but what you do need to know is that fifty million dollars are missing, and it's likely Bankhart's."

"Likely? Not definitely?" General Breca spoke up this time.

"Correct, General Breca."

"If it was in his safe why can't we presume that it was his?"

"Right now, we're more concerned about whose

money it was before it was Bankhart's. We're toying with the idea that this was the result of a business deal gone very badly. It was possibly a power-trade in a sense. At this point, we're inclined to think that whoever killed Bankhart and took his money is the same person who gave him the money in the first place. Digest that info with the caveat that we're by no means sure of this."

The colonel's heart drummed and his forehead was damp. He deeply inhaled, calming himself as he touched his fingertips together and continued to listen intently. He recognized the new possibility of being accused of a murder he didn't commit.

"Very well," the old general replied as he scratched his forehead in thought. "It would be nice if you made your informant available to us, Milton. I would have questions of my own to ask him."

"Not yet, General, but soon."

"Do we have any idea at this point about the identity of the killer?" another man spoke up.

"We only have a potential idea from our source of information. Again, I will reveal his or her identity as soon as I possibly can."

"So…a potential idea from an undisclosed source is what we've got right now."

"That's correct, General Breca."

"We've got nothing!" Breca huffed and the men

around the table laughed. "Can you tell us anything else beyond it being a nationally headlined homicide? I mean, the best guess we've got is that someone walked into Bankhart's office, gave him the money, killed him and took the money back!"

"Something like that, General. We also believe that this valise the money was stored in was in one of our own military issued attaché cases."

"Was there a serial number on it?"

Secretary Seward began to intently flip through the papers in front of him. "Good idea, General, but unfortunately there's no information regarding a serial number."

"Of course, that would be too easy." The general said as he stuck a corn cob pipe in his mouth and puffed away.

Seward nodded in agreement.

Rockland saw this as an opportunity. He'd try to delay the investigation just long enough to make preparations for the next part of his plan. He might gain additional time to learn the source of Seward's information. Rockland knew that only he himself, President Mursten, and the killer would know the exact amount of money in the brief case. He continued to think. Of course Mursten wouldn't come forward about the deal. That would be pointless. And Mursten couldn't have physically committed the murder with Rockland having watched him almost all day. The informant must be the killer, unless he's simply an opportunist who took his money after Bankhart was murdered.

In an effort to control the situation, Rockland spoke. "I request that everyone attending the security detail that day who had an attaché case signed-out be responsible for presenting it by tomorrow. It seems like a long shot, but it's something."

"Well," The general nodded indeterminately, "At least it's the next step. It'll at least give us some direction in our pool of potential suspects."

Rockland had no attaché case officially signed out that day. The case that he gave Veselev was something he bought at an army surplus depot. The numbers were filed out when he bought it. The case wasn't traceable.

"Where do we go from here?" Rockland asked as he took a small breath of relief.

The men glanced around the table and began to chat.

Seward spoke up, "We have a key piece of evidence that may tell us exactly what time William Buxton and Dominic Veselev were killed. Frank, if you would," Seward gestured to the screen behind him asking the IT engineer to turn it to display mode.

Frank, the man behind the computer, accessed footage from the laboratory. Seward narrated, "Here we see one of Omicron's third story offices. However, look out of the window in the background," Frank enhanced the image from the data stream and Seward continued, "…and you can see that at approximately 10:40AM, one of our assets on the ground that day went into the car-port by himself." The footage clearly displayed the same style and color of camouflage the men were suited in during their security details at the laboratory. "Gentlemen, I think we can consider this more proof we're looking for one of our own. With that I'd like to conclude the briefing."

The men arose from their chairs and began their typical unhurried procession out of the crisis room. Rockland, unlike all of the other men, wasted no time. He stood up and made haste out of the room. He walked at a rapid pace through the hallway, beyond security, and out of the door to the outside stairs. He reached into his pocket, still trying to figure out who could've possibly killed Bankhart. Rockland pulled out a tracfone and was selecting a contact's number when he heard a powerful voice behind him.

"Colonel Rockland!" The colonel quickly slid his phone into his pocket. He turned around to investigate the voice that he thought sounded like law enforcement. General Breca was standing there, almost eye-to-eye with the unnerved colonel. Rockland was shocked that Breca had made it out so quickly. Rockland was more concerned about why the old general caught up with him.

Rockland immediately saluted. "Sir?"

"Put your hand down!" The general eyed Rockland with an expression that was equally as suspicious as his voice. "Who were you calling, Colonel Rockland?"

Rockland said nothing.

Breca repeated himself slowly and deliberately, "Who…were you calling…Colonel Rockland?"

"I was going to call my aunt, sir. My uncle isn't doing well. I wanted to find out what I could do—find out if they needed me there. You know, family stuff, the whole nine yards," Rockland replied casually as he gauged Breca's expression.

"Let me have the phone, Colonel."

"Yes, sir." The colonel never pushed the call button on the phone and he had no shady numbers saved to his contact list. At least, he had no shady names labeled. He had cleared the contact he selected in the phone when he slipped it into his pocket. Without hesitation, he handed over the phone to the general.

The general fumbled through the phone and realized no recent calls were made. Breca didn't investigate any further. "My apologies, Colonel Rockland." Breca was still unconvinced.

"No apologies necessary, sir."

"Give your dear family my regards." Breca coldly shoved the phone back into the colonel's hand.

"Yes, sir." The colonel saluted and the general barely

saluted back as he turned away from the colonel and strided off.

Rockland was already off and away when he heard the general's scolding voice one more time, "One more thing, Rock."

"Sir?" the colonel about-faced as the old general approached him again.

"Off the record, I like you, kid. You're the ideal image of an American soldier, strong, smart and gutsy."

"Thank you, sir."

"But, I just gotta say it. I don't know how you've managed to do all that you've done."

"What?"

"I'm not going to voice my instincts in the crisis room, but I'm also not going to delay the investigation for you anymore. If they didn't see through your little briefcase suggestion, they need the critical thinking practice. You're sloppy, kid. I suggest you tie up your loose ends and quit while you're ahead."

"Sir?"

"Do I gotta spell it out for you, kid? I'm betting that this fifty-million that Secretary Numb-nuts was talking about somehow belongs to you. I don't know why, but my instincts are telling me that there's something. Despite Seward's opinion, my intuition is usually right." The general crisply pivoted in his shined shoes and marched away from his mentee. "All the best."

Pride broken, Rockland sauntered back to his black Ford Raptor—wondering how much the general actually knew. He scanned the environment before he ticked away at his phone again.

The phone rang twice and was answered with a tranquil, "Yeah?"

"Eden?"

"Rock?"

"Yeah, it's me, Ed."

"Man! It's good to hear from ya!"

"How've you been, Eden?"

"Surviving, Rock, just surviving. How about you?"

"Barely doing that."

"What's the news, Colonel?"

Rockland sighed, "Things may get bad soon."

"Bad? How bad?"

"I'm going to have to cut my ties with the overseas operations."

"Ok, no problem. There's a ton of guys that want your empire."

"I know. That's not the hard part."

"I didn't think so. Do you need an out-of-towner to lay some people down?"

"Not yet. I need some information found first. Check out the news with Omicron Lab."

"I heard all about that."

"I was in charge of the security detail that day."

"Oh yeah?"

"I also lost fifty that same day."

"Thousand?"

"Million—and the geeks in Washington could possibly find my money before I do."

"Damn! I told you to quit while you were ahead! Didn't I tell you to quit while you were ahead?"

"I-know-I-know-I-know. I should've listened. They allegedly have an informant. Depending on whom this informant is and whatever the informant knows about me, they might be able to shut down the operation. Then who do you think goes to prison for a long time?"

"We're not gonna let that happen."

"Glad you're so optimistic, any thoughts?"

"Yeah, I talked to a friend of mine from back-in-the-day about it. They're thinking this… Ashley Ryker will be the new CEO of the lab. That's what it says in the news article I have in my hand. She's smokin' hot too. She's an Aussie I think. Let me see what I can get out of her."

"…or into her," Rockland joked.

"Hey man, in our business, input equals output."

"Do what you gotta do, man, and do it well."

"Done-and-done."

"I owe you one," Rockland said thankfully.

"No, you don't. It's the least I can do after our time in Afghanistan."

"You're a good friend, Eden, thanks."

"You got it, Rock. I'll catch ya later."

CHAPTER 9: IT'S NOT OFFICIAL

About 5,000 miles away from the colonel in D.C., Ashley Ryker was leaning up against her car in a remote location some twenty miles outside Honolulu. Her straight golden bangs wisped gently in the breeze. Her smooth and tanned skin absorbed the sun's rays keeping her comfortably warm. Like her hair, her short gray skirt rippled in the breeze and her untucked shirt did the same.

Ashley ripped open the envelope she found on her desk earlier that day and a little business card fell out into her hand. She read the all too familiar quote from her many years as a chaser.

"'I don't like the world anymore,' said the moon. 'So, I'm attacking it.'"

She knew it was Bankhart's original message to Mursten. Ashley flipped the card over. Surrounding the eerie smiley face on the front of the card was a message. It was written in small, neat, uppercase print that she read to herself,

"I'M STILL INTERESTED. IT'S YOUR PROJECT— SO I EXPECT YOU ARE TOO. 11:00PM TWO WEEKS FROM NOW—TUESDAY—AT THE FREEWORLD CAFÉ IN WASHINGTON DC."

Ashley supposed the message was from Mursten.

She reached through the window and put the business card in her glove box. She then waited for her portion of the money from the silver attaché case that was stolen from Jim Bankhart's office. She turned her face away from the sun and saw a silver convertible swiftly approaching from the distance. The car was pursued by a bellowing exhaust note and a trail of dust from the stony path that the vehicle capably tackled. Ashley recognized the sporty auto as Mandrake's BMW M3. The car harshly braked and the engine was left running.

Gavin stepped out of the car, leaving behind the façade that was known to everyone around the laboratory. He wasn't the sweet, effeminate go-to-guy who took care of secretarial tasks. It was the real Mandrake that was meeting

Ashley in the secluded area. Mandrake rounded the front of his car holding Rockland's attaché case. He wore white pants and a sharply tapered sport coat that hid a Glock in a shoulder holster. He hurled the attaché case straight to Ashley, who adeptly caught it.

"Your cut," said Mandrake in a crisp masculine tone. It was his real voice.

"Fifteen million?" Ashley asked as she opened the case towards Mandrake.

"Every penny of it," Mandrake said as he studied how carefully she opened the briefcase, "Don't worry, hot-stuff. I didn't put a Claymore in there, although the thought had occurred to me."

"Good choice on your part," Ashley argued. The open side of the briefcase was facing Mandrake. He would've suffered as badly from the explosion as she did.

"Apparently it was. By the way, your planning was piss poor. Your logistics sucked."

"Rough day at the office, Mandrake?"

"Someone hit the big shot before we did."

"What?"

"I took care of the limo guys, but someone got to Bankhart first. I wasn't the one who knifed the bastard."

"Then how did we strike pay dirt?" Ashley fished in the briefcase and came up with a one-million-dollar bearer bond.

"Your guess is as good as mine, Ryker. Someone apparently had no use for fifty-million dollars. I thought for sure you double crossed me until I saw the money."

Ashley remained silent.

"But anyway, congratulations on your new job as the next head of the company," Mandrake didn't mean a word of it.

"It's not official yet," Ashley said.

"Official, no, obvious yes," Mandrake argued as he buttoned his sport coat. "You'll be getting the call at any minute." He cleared his throat and reassumed the effeminate charade he deceived everyone with. "We'll, Dr. Ryker, it's been super nice having done business with you. Now, if you will excuse me, I have business elsewhere to take care of. *Ta!*"

Ashley watched the assassin make his deceitful way back to the car. Suddenly, she heard the chime of her cell phone. Her smart phone then danced around on the dashboard. She reached in through the window and exchanged the attaché case for her phone. She answered it by the second loop of her ringtone.

"Hello?" Ashley said nervously.

"Is this Dr. Ashley Ryker?" The chipper voice coming from the earpiece asked.

"Yes it is."

"Ashley! Wonderful! I have big news for you, you

intelligent young lady!"

"Really? May I ask who this is?" Ashley pretended not to recognize the unmistakable voice.

"Ashley, it's Dr. Ray! Raymond Sankar! How are you?"

"I'm fine. May I inquire about this big news?"

"You may, as soon as you get here. When can we expect you?"

"Let me check my schedule." Ashley took a moment to breathe and break from her act.

"Very good, I'll wait."

"I can be there in about thirty-five minutes— if that's alright."

"That sounds just wonderful!"

"Great, I'll see you then."

CHAPTER 10: WHEN SOMEONE WILL NEED IT

Wright steered around the winding roads and through the varying groves of citrus trees. The football field was soon in his sight. Wright noticed there was a small black car already in the parking lot. Somebody was leaning against the car reading. As Wright drew closer to the car, he realized it was Tyson.

Tyson looked up and saw the fancy car swiftly gliding by on the road that paralleled the parking lot. The principle pulled into the lot and halted next to the little Volkswagen.

"Hey, Mr. Wright. Nice ride!"

"Thank you, Tyson. I'm surprised to see you here."

"Coach Martin said that you two talked yesterday and that you might have a use for me. He said Pat was going to be here, but I haven't seen him yet."

"Right, yeah he's supposed to be here in ten minutes." A thoughtful silence came over Wright.

"Is everything all right, Mr. Wright?"

"Everything's fine. We can definitely use your arm after his warm-ups. If you want you can join him, but it's very strenuous. It's actually punishment."

"Sounds great, I'm up for a work out."

"Great, get suited up and be back out here in fifteen." The same thoughtful silence came over Wright as he paused again. "I was wondering are you in his chemistry class?"

"Yeah, he's in my class."

"How's your handwriting?"

"These are my notes actually." Tyson handed him the notebook he was reading out of as he waited.

Wright turned through the pages of the notebook admiring the immaculate writing. "Impeccable! Are you using these tonight?"

"No, I'm working at the garage tonight."

"Do you mind if I borrow them then leave them with Dr. Viola tomorrow morning? They'll be waiting for you in chemistry when you go to class."

"Not at all, please do."

"Great! Get ready. The locker room is open. We'll be getting started soon."

Once Pat arrived, he approached Wright. The principle didn't acknowledge him. He just kept jumping rope.

"So are you going to just stand there jumping and wasting my time or am I going to get a work out in?"

"McNamara," Wright was still shuffling his feet over the whipping jump-rope.

"Yeah?"

"Run."

"For how long?" Pat threw a disobedient hand in the air.

"Until I get tired!" Wright screamed

Pat promptly bolted off.

Minutes later, Pat suddenly stopped. His cheeks were desperately flushed. He bent at the waist and retched before spilling the green and yellowy-orange contents of his gut all over the freshly cut grass.

Wright approached Pat from the sidelines. "I'm not tired of watching you run yet, McNamara!"

"Well, I am tired, dick!" Pat yelled as he threw up again.

"Your act is pathetic, McNamara! You sprint a 6:23 mile and you look like death!"

As Tyson approached the field, he grabbed the athletic drink out of his bag and ran to the aid of his disobedient teammate. Pat's mouth was so dry he couldn't even thank Tyson. He rested a hand on his Tyson's arm and handed him the drink back. One last time, his mouth gaped and the green suspension plopped into his previous pile of vomit.

"Th-Thanks," Pat said taking in heavy breaths.

"Don't mention it. Do you need more?" Tyson asked.

"No, it'll just come back up."

"Push up position!" Wright demanded.

"C'mon, Wright! I'm dying over here!"

"Push up position!" The voice was louder and more deliberate this time. "This is your break-time. You're doing bear-walks all around the field."

Pat complied, but the demand from the exercise was too taxing. He fell flat on his face— landing in the mud. He didn't mind the dirt on his face. Lying down, muck or not, felt so much better than the punishment. Pat didn't care that he was able to taste the mud that covered his face. He was just too tired to care.

Tyson again helped Pat to his feet.

"Principle Wright, will you please give him a break?" Tyson asked. "I don't think he'll take much more of it before he has a real problem."

Wright seized Pat by the collar and stood him up, "Stand up and face me like a man!"

Pat shook the haze, scoffed, and glared at Wright.

"Get hydrated then get ready for more. This is you learning that I don't deal well with your shit!"

Pat had no wise comment.

Tyson helped Pat to the bench and Wright ran off to the track. Tyson was tending to Pat when he looked up and saw Wright's swift pace around the track. "Holy damn," Tyson commented.

"Dude, he's literally going to kill me one of these days!" Pat said once he finally caught his breath.

"You'll be all right. Today he's just breaking you down, trying to get you to listen."

"I get it. I'm listening and I'm ready. I just can't do anymore of this."

"Then when you get the chance, tell Wright that you're listening. Just tell him anything that lets him know he got through to you. It probably helps if you don't call him a dick."

"Yeah, I guess." Pat raised his flushed and dazed face. He stared at the lawn-tractor depot not too far off in the distance, just on the other side of the parking lot. "Why don't they ever bring the oil drums inside the utility shed?"

Tyson casually looked off towards the depot. "Are you ok, man?"

"Yeah, I'm good. I just wonder if that's dangerous to leave out."

"I don't know. I guess you never know when someone will need it." Tyson supposed.

Wright approached the boys on the aluminum bleachers. "Are you ready, kid?"

"I'm ready," Pat got to his unbalanced feet.

"Good, glad to finally hear it."

"Tyson, are you ready?"

"Always."

"Pat's going to jog around the field and you're job is to stay with him. I'll be right there with you in the golf cart. I dumped two ball bag's worth of footballs in the bed. Lead him with every pass. Make him run for the ball. If he drops it or can't catch up with it, he'll do twenty pushups...Begin."

After the day's last bell, Wright sipped from the water he had on his desk and peeped out the window. He scanned the campus grounds, but there was nothing unusual going on outside. There was only a lawn full of teenagers ready to get on with their afternoon. He wheeled his chair about and focused on the doorway. Pat was standing there.

"Sit down, Pat."

"Thank you." The teenager responded uncomfortably, trying to take Tyson's advice from earlier.

Wright let out a breath and nodded in satisfied approval. Wright reached into his briefcase where he kept Tyson's notes. "You're welcome," Wright said as he pulled the green notebook out and dropped it on his desk with a pensive sigh. Wright stared at the young man who was unable to look him in the eye. "Look at me, kid. It's time to man up. We both know you're ready to."

The teenager nodded, but still looked elsewhere.

"No, look at me." Wright snapped his thick fingers and pointed at himself.

Pat did as he was told.

Wright continued in a level voice "You impressed me today—barring the fact that were still calling me a 'dick' this morning. I have to look past that. That's just par for the course with you. But after I collared you today, you really reigned it in."

"I'm sorry," Pat replied.

"So, like I said, barring all that, you cut back on the huffing, the rolling of your eyes, and the overall attitude."

"Thank you, sir."

"That being said, you pissed me off the other day when you hopped in Vinnie's ride and took off to *God-knows-where*."

"Yes, sir."

"How was the chemistry class you didn't go to?"

"I wouldn't know, sir."

"I appreciate your honesty."

Pat nodded.

"Tyson helped you out today. He was there for you. He helped you. You fell down and he helped you to your feet. You did push-ups, he did push-ups. Your failure to catch the ball was his failure to throw the ball. Do you understand?"

"Yes."

"He took responsibility for what he did. It was his fault too when you didn't catch the ball."

All Pat could do was remain quiet and nod.

"You can learn a lot from that kid. You have a chemistry assessment tomorrow worth a large portion of your grade this semester. Did you know that?"

Pat nodded.

"Have you taken any notes?"

"No."

"I didn't think so. You proverbially 'dropped the ball' on this one kid. Do you know how many pages of textbook material the assessment covers?"

Pat woefully shook his head 'no.'

Principle Wright exhaled again, "It covers 107 pages."

"Oh man," the teenager sunk his head.

"Yeah, '*Oh man*.' How are your grades in chemistry?"

"I don't know."

"You have a 'D', McNamara. This assessment could easily pull you down into the failing range, or it could pull you up to a 'B-.' That'd be a damn good start at getting an 'A' by the end of the semester."

"I'll try to study tonight, but 107 pages. I mean, I haven't even begun to study. It's hopeless." Pat contested.

"Yeah, probably."

There was a moment where the principle gauged Pat's reaction. Finally, there was a genuine sorrow in the teenager's face, a fear of failure.

Wright continued, "But, your friend Tyson consolidated those 107 pages to 21 pages of exquisitely written notes. Notes he got while at Dr. Viola's lecture. He's a clever kid, very helpful pneumonic devices. Do you understand?"

"Absolutely! I take those notes home, study them, do well tomorrow and prove that I've gotten the point!"

"Not exactly. I'm personally making sure Tyson gets these back tomorrow bright-and-early." Wright held up the notes. Pat's smile faded away, he was left with no detectable expression. "You get to study the notes, here, with me, for as long as it takes."

"Then we're gonna be here a while, Mr. Wright."

"It won't take that long. I'm about to prove to you how smart you really are."

"What? How?"

"Push up position."

Pat did as he was told and Wright slid the notebook under Pat's face. You read, you feel the pain. You feel your ignorance and the weakness leaving your body. Tell me when you're done."

After thirty minutes, Pat decided he was done. He'd fallen on his face several times and shrieked often from the pain. Between pained grunts, Wright quizzed Pat with two questions from each page. Wright was satisfied with Pat's progress.

"Get to your feet, Pat."

"Yes, sir."

"You'll never forget this information. Your dad is about to give you the keys to the car. Today, you'll drive home and learn to seal a driveway. Your dad left directions at home. He wants to talk to me and today is the best day for it. You can wait for him outside on the bench near the front door. It's nice out, enjoy it. Outdoor work is a great way to clear your head. It's a great way to start the next day over. A sealed driveway is smooth. There's no fissures from weathering merciless storms. You get it?"

"Yes, sir."

"I want the rest of your career here, and beyond here, as smooth as the driveway when you're done sealing it. I really don't like coming down on students. It's not why I'm in this business. I'm here to guide young minds. If we can do that amicably from now on, I think I'd like that."

The teenager agreed with a bob of his head. "Me too."

"I'll seeya tomorrow, Pat."

"Thank you, Mr. Wright." Pat respectfully reset the chairs that they moved for the study exercise and left.

Minutes later, the principle again eyed the doorway when he noticed a figure standing there. It was Alan.

Wright stood up politely, "Please sit, Mr. McNamara. I hope today wasn't too inconvenient for our meeting." Wright ambled around the desk, shook Alan's hand and shut the door. The men sat down on opposite sides of the desk.

"As a matter of fact it's quite convenient. I appreciate the ride home and the sealed driveway," he chuckled.

"Absolutely no trouble at all."

"I brought you a coffee. I owe you at least that much." Alan handed Wright the cup.

Wright laughed, "Thank you very much, Mr. McNamara."

"Please, call me 'Alan.'"

"Of course, Alan." Wright continued, "I know we are both fully aware of the purpose of this meeting. You somehow figured out that I have an answer to a question you may have about your son."

"Precisely," Alan agreed. "I double-checked my facts. I was right about Aeronation Aviation. That investment you told me about...you did make that investment 80 years ago."

"Give or take," Wright answered. "I knew you'd figure it out after I let that slip."

"No foolin'?"

"No foolin'," Wright confirmed.

"And you said, he's too much like you were at that age...'*those hundreds of years ago*.' You *actually* meant it."

"Yeah," Wright mouthed. "Loose lips, I guess," he grinned.

"About my son..." Alan continued as the principle concentrated intently at his visitor. "My son is as unique as you are?"

Wright put his cup down, "He's extremely unique."

"You also know who his biological mother and father are?"

Wright looked down mournfully.

"Were?" Alan inquired.

Wright nodded.

"Please tell me, what exactly is Pat?" McNamara asked, seemingly annoyed that a man that his adopted son has known for three years knows more about his seventeen-year-old than he did. "Is he a fire-breather?" McNamara paused then posed the next question. "Did he live at the bottom of the ocean? Can he fly? Can he control people or things with his mind? Does he know about whatever he can do?" McNamara's eyes welled up as he began his next question, "More importantly, is he capable of loving two average human parents?"

Wright leaned back in his chair. "I'll answer those questions one-by-one in the exact order you asked them. No, to the fire. No, to the ocean. He can have the ability to fly if you let him. God, I hope he can't perform mind-control. And the answer to the last question as to whether or not he loves you and your wife is unequivocally, 'yes.'"

"What population does he belong to?" McNamara asked leaning forward in his chair.

"He's a very typical, 17-year-old *Avia*."

"An Avia? As in 'avian?' My kid is a bird kid?" Alan asked.

Wright laughed at the expression 'bird kid.'

They both did.

"That's one way of putting it. Nevertheless, he isn't necessarily a quote 'bird kid.'

"How's that? Won't there be a day where my kid catches a north-bound wind and takes to the skies?" Alan inquired, drawing another laugh out of Wright. "That may sound ridiculous to you, Principle Wright, but to us average humans it's a concern. I feel fairly abandoned and ignorant."

Alan was clearly frustrated, "My question was sincerely submitted with humble validity, Mr. Wright!"

"I wasn't laughing at you, Alan. It's just in all my years, you hear the same question asked so many different ways and you're taking it very well. I just found the phrasing funny. To answer your question succinctly, 'no.' He won't just one day take to the sky. It's impossible."

"How's that?"

"First off, he doesn't even know that he's an Avia."

"True."

"Now, presume he did know for some reason."

"Ok."

"Think of your son as a highly intelligent mouse."

"O…k?"

"The Avian ability is the cheese. He wants the cheese on the trap, but he knows it's dangerous. He knows there's a trap."

"How?"

"Sheer pain and Avian instincts always prevent anyone from learning on their own. It prevents them from trying to steal the cheese, a sense about the trap and the impending danger that comes with it."

"I know you're trying to help me, Mr. Wright. But I just don't follow."

"If your son tried to deploy his wings on his own, he'd die. You get a sense of imminent doom in addition to excruciating pain. It's never failed. Only an elder Avia can guide a young Avia to deploy his or her wings."

"Really?"

"Really. You also can't exploit other Avian ability until your wings have been deployed for the first time. The only Avian capacity he'll have if he never deploys his wings is the lengthy lifespan."

"It's that simple?" Alan asked.

Wright nodded. "It's that simple. At least to answer your question of whether or not he was going to one day take to the skies without knowing he has the ability to. Whether or not you inform him of his blessing or curse is totally different. That's a much harder question."

"Why? We can't just forget about it?"

"One day, whether he breaks his wings or not, assuming no lethal external accident happens to him, he will turn 170 years old and feel as if he's still just 17 years old. He won't know why he is that old or why he is still in incredible health."

"170 years old?" Alan sunk his head as his son had done in the same chair no more than forty minutes before.

"He will only know that he has long out-survived his family, friends, elders, and more concerning to him, people that he remembers being fifty years his junior. They will be younger than him, but they will have aged far more than he did."

"Are you serious?"

"Completely, it's incredibly haunting. An average lifespan of a millennium is an unbelievable curse if you have no one to share it with, a wife, a friend, a sibling, or anyone whom you truly love."

"A millennium?" Alan gasped.

"That's right. For the 'mainstreamed' Avia, that typically means relationships last no longer than an average human lifespan. If you're unbelievably lucky, a relationship will last seventy-five years. That's not even close to ten percent of your son's expected lifespan. Your son may even live significantly beyond 1000 years. We have relative longevity in my family as well. My grandfather died when he was 1407 years old. My grandmother was 1410 years old."

"That again explicitly confirms my question. You know because you're an Avia."

"That's right." Wright shifted his weight in his chair as he studied Alan's face.

"Forgive my impertinence, but you appear to be on the older side of middle-aged."

"I'm 759 years old. Is that what you were asking?"

Alan just nodded. Taking in the answer that the principle had given him was difficult.

"To put that in perspective for you, assuming the average age a human reaches is 70 and the average lifespan in my family is 1300 years, I've aged forty-some equivalent human years."

"So, you're still something of a fairly young man yourself, a very old, youngish man." Alan sipped from his coffee, It was very difficult to wrap his mind around the facts he was confronted with.

Wright laughed. "Very good, Alan. Haha! I'm a very old, youngish man," Wright paused for a moment and quickly wrote something. "To put it into perspective, your son hasn't even aged one human year equivalent. Your son is a very young, young man. Avia age normally for the first twenty years of their lives and after that, they approximately age relative to Avia life expectancy.

Alan asked his next question. "So, I'm not likely to see Pat age very much in my lifetime?"

"Not very likely, no."

"Why do Avia age the way they do?"

"Even we don't know that," Wright admitted.

Alan sighed, "How do I know when to tell Pat?"

"You'll just know. It may be sooner, it may be later. You're his dad. Adopted or not, he's your son. I know you love him very much and you'll do what's right for him when you figure out what's best. Unfortunately, I don't even know when it's the right time. Yours is a pretty unique situation."

CHAPTER 11: I'M NO MURDERER

"Gentlemen, we have a lot of new and intriguing information today," Seward announced. Rockland perked up, thinking that this would make his to-do list much simpler. He nodded and gave Seward his full attention. "When our source contacts us again, he will testify in court against Bankhart's murderer. We believe the killer is one of our own. As a matter of fact, the suspect is someone in this room," Seward decided.

Two federal agents came through the door.

The colonel snapped at Seward in surprise, "What?" The colonel's shock got the better of him. He felt the intense eyes devouring him from every side of the table.

"You're surprised, Colonel?"

"You might say that." Rockland sweat profusely as he wiped his forehead.

"Do you know something we don't, Colonel Rockland? If so, please, enlighten us." Seward stared into Rockland's nervous eyes.

"Of course not!"

"I think you're lying, Colonel Rockland."

"Why's that?" There was a pause in the air, an uncomfortable silence. The men around the table looked to Secretary Seward for the answer. Secretary Seward tilted his head as if he were insulted by the question.

"Because you're the only murderer in the room, Colonel Rockland," Seward replied in an unperturbed tone. "You killed Jim Bankhart and you stole the same fifty million dollars you managed to supply that day at the lab." General Breca looked down and away from the table, angrily shaking his head. All the heads at the table immediately swiveled towards the colonel. Seward continued his accusation, "You were trading money for power. Things went to hell and you left the lab that day—a murderer!"

"I'm no murderer!" The colonel vehemently protested.

"Yes, you are a murderer, Colonel. And believe me when I say, 'We will figure out how you acquired such an amount of money in the first place.' Agents" Seward held an open hand towards the colonel—requesting that the agents carry out the arrest. "Please," Secretary Seward said, emphasizing his melodramatic motion.

One of the two agents, the older of the two, came from behind the colonel and began to speak. "Colonel Rockland! My name is Agent Roy Sifter. This is Agent Devin Jennings. It's my duty to inform you that I have a federal indictment for your detainment."

"The official reasons?" Rockland delayed as he cupped his face in his hands.

"You're being accused of the murder of Jim Bankhart and grand larceny in the first degree—in the amount of fifty million dollars."

Jennings looked at Rockland, "You have the right to remain silent—"

Sifter put his hand on the disgraced colonel's shoulder.

Rockland had no intention of wearing handcuffs out of the crisis room. Sifter grabbed Rockland's right hand, his left hand still on the colonel's shoulder.

Rockland's survival instincts kicked in and he stood up immediately. With his foot on the wheeled-base of the chair, he drove the armrest into Jennings' groin. Rockland then reversed Sifter's weak police hold. Rockland took control as he wrenched the older agent's wrist until it cracked. He pulled the man in closer and drove his shoulder into the agent's sternum. Sifter immediately hit the floor, writhing in pain from his collapsed rib cage and broken wrist.

The men at the table all pushed away so as not to be harmed by the impending melee.

Jennings quickly straightened himself up. He drew his service pistol, pointing it toward the aggressive colonel. Rockland wrapped-up the agent's hand with the gun in it and sunk his stance. He thrust his elbowed into the agent's ribs and wheeled him over his shoulder. Jennings crashed to the floor.

Both agents lay there cursing at the intense pain.

"Jesus Christ!" Seward shouted.

Rockland claimed the gun off the floor, checked the ammunition and readied it for firing. He grabbed Frank, the computer operator, and scrambled for the door. Rockland reestablished his one-hand grip on Frank's lapels as he drove Frank backwards towards the locked down door. Rockland trained his sights on the security panel opposite the door. He fired three shots that fried the console, killing the lockdown mechanism. Rockland lifted Frank into the air and heaved the little geek into the doors— breaking them open.

"You can't run forever, Rockland!" Secretary Seward yelled.

Rockland made a break for the entrance, but was immediately tackled by a massive security guard when he reached the doorway. The guard was an acquaintance that the colonel had always been fond of named Felix.

Rockland and Felix crashed to the ground. Felix drew his arm back then tried to strike the colonel in the face. Rockland craned his head out of the way. A loud cracking noise was subsequently heard as the large guard's fist fractured under the force of the missed attack. Rockland secured the guard's arm in a Kimura hold. "Sorry, Felix," Rockland shouted just before exercising the damaging technique. Rockland torqued Felix's arm and the sound of the joint coming out of its socket preceded Felix's scream. Rockland violently threw his elbow across the man's face and finished their encounter. Rockland snapped himself to his feet, but no longer had the weapon in his hand. He dropped the gun when he was tackled and there was no time to search for it.

Rockland ran out of the room into the long corridor where another guard, 'Mel' according to his nametag, awaited him. Mel waited with a locked and loaded stun gun. The colonel furiously accelerated towards his next obstacle. Mel prematurely fired the stun gun's spear-like electrodes. Only one electrode hit Rockland. Without the other electrode connecting, no current would be generated.

The colonel ripped out the electrode that hit him in the chest. Mel swung a desperate fist at him. Rockland weaved the attack and sunk his fist into the guard's abdomen. Rockland pushed the doubled-over man into the wall then drove a powerful knee into his chin, immediately dropping him to the floor.

The colonel ran the familiar route that he usually took when he simply walked out of a briefing. The colonel rounded the corner and was met by a team of six men with assault rifles. "You move, you die!" the commander of the unit yelled as he brandished his Heckler & Koch MP5 in an experienced combat stance. "Put your hands behind your head and kneel!" The colonel was trapped. He could only do as the commander with the machine gun instructed. The men forcefully cuffed the colonel and he was detained for a murder he didn't commit.

CHAPTER 12: SETTING A PRECEDENT

It was 7:00PM on a warm and clear Sunday night at Occam High School. The stadium lights were bright. The aromatic grass was freshly cut and the tide of the nearby ocean was strong. The mighty breaking of the potent waves was audible to all in attendance at the football game. The billowing spectators were excited for the game that would decide which of the two competing teams would make it to the playoffs in Kapaa—the field nearest the lively Mount Kilauea.

The onlookers hooted as both teams rushed onto the field in their boldly colored uniforms. Occam High donned their striking black and gold uniforms. The visiting team from Maui wore white and orange.

The teams were eager to play and the crowd was ablaze. Winning this game then clinching the championship in Kapaa meant a year's worth of bragging rights, a series of parties and universities scouting talented players at their school.

As always, Tyson was Occam High's starting quarterback. Jean-Claude, the state's premier running back, was the man Tyson could hand the ball off to when he needed it to be run up the field. Also on the starting line was Vinnie Tarsa, the number one receiver in the state—and the last person in the school that Tyson wanted to share the field with.

The visiting team was the favorite to win, but Occam High was ready for a war.

Tyson looked to the sidelines and saw Harlie with the dance team. Win or lose, after the game tonight, he was taking her out and that was all he could think about. He waved to her and she blew him a kiss. Tyson wasn't quite sure how to respond for fear of looking dumb. Luckily, Jean-Claude was there to get Tyson's head out of the clouds.

"It's time, bro! Let's go!" Jean-Claude exclaimed.

Tyson turned and ran to the coin-toss at centerfield with Jean–Claude. Tyson looked back at Harlie and waved one more time.

"C'mon, man! Game-face! Focus!" Jean-Claude slapped the back of Tyson's helmet.

The crowd was roaring and the announcer on the sidelines began introducing the rosters. "Ladies and gentleman, boys and girls, tonight we're hosting the great state of Hawaii's high school football playoffs sponsored by WKBT news 9. I'm Glenn Jackson and I'm happy to be here with Occam High coach, Daniel Martin. Coach Martin, you've been here ten years. The team has consistently performed better every year under your direction and you have three players that the NFL coaching union already discusses. What's your secret?"

Coach Martin wiped his cottony mouth and answered the question. "You've gotta come in and set a precedent. You've gotta do a little better every time. Before you know it, a little better every time turns into more and more tally-marks for the 'w' column and that's exactly what we're going to do tonight. We're going to win this game and take our season to the championship at Kapaa."

"Thank you for your time, Coach Martin. We're looking forward to your team's performance. Coaching the Maui Wavebreakers is Coach Jonathan Hale. Coach Hale, you're the favorite for today's game. You obviously have your fair share of ranking players in the state—both offensively and defensively. Tell us, beyond your seven select players, what makes you the favorite tonight and how will being the visiting team affect your team's performance?"

"Coach Martin hit the nail on the head about setting a precedent. We've been the precedent for the past decade. We've consistently taken our season to the championship for the past ten years and that's what we're doing tonight."

"Thank you, Coach Hale."

"You got it, Glenn."

The coach left and the reporter looked back into the camera. "WKBT news 9 is sponsoring tonight's event, as well as bringing you exclusive side-line coverage. I will be calling the play-by-play and the senior-class president, Nick Buckland, will be providing color commentary." The reporter graciously recognized the student and touched his shoulder, "Glad you're here, Nick. Try not to steal my job!"

After a laugh worthy of an oily politician, Nick replied, "Thank you, Mr. Jackson! It's an honor. I'm really excited about the game!"

"Me too. The air is electric! It's gonna be a good one." Glenn looked back into the camera "We'll be back with the excitement after these messages."

The players went back to their benches after the coin toss. Occam High was receiving the ball first. After the usual pre-game rituals; a team 'hands-in', some helmet slapping and jumping around, the teams took their positions. The players were ready for the kickoff.

The Maui Wavebreakers kicked the ball to the Occam High Razors with a loud intimidating team roar. The ball soared high through the evening air and traveled all the way down field. Jean-Claude received the ball, aptly catching it then furiously running up the field. His head was in the game and he was focused only on winning. He weaved through the opposition. His feet pounded away as he quickly put a lot of distance between himself and where he began. The Wavebreakers' players were closing in on him. He saw an opportunity to try to run through an opposing player and make it toward the endzone. With a loud battle cry, he met the player full force with the loud crashing of helmet-to-helmet, shoulder to chest contact. Jean-Claude handily dropped the player to the ground. The time Jean-Claude spent regaining his footing was just enough time for the enormous captain of the Wavebreakers, Chris Meany, to crush Jean-Claude under his ridiculous body mass.

"Try again, fool! Try it again, Vala-*dick*-torian! Haha!" Meany taunted as he let his girth crush Jean-Claude.

"Man, *no-means-no*! Now, get the hell off me!" Jean-Claude pushed the galoot off of him.

"What a start!" Nick Buckland exclaimed. "That was a hard hit from 255lbs of the meanest of meanies, Chris Meany. The Senior from Maui High stands 6'5" and is attending UCLA next year."

Glenn Jackson took over. "What a start indeed! Junior class valedictorian Jean Gionet, AKA the Jean-Bomb, 5'10" 165lbs, puts sixty yards behind him and moves the Occam High Razors into a good starting position for the offensive drive. Occam High favorite, Tyson Lynd, will be taking the field to lead the Razors towards their formidable visitor's endzone.

"You all right, Claude?" Tyson said as he helped his friend to his steady feet.

"Yeah, it hurt, but I'll live."

Tyson and his linemen walked up to the line of

scrimmage, where the next play would start. "Hiiiike!" Tyson yelled at the top of his lungs as he dropped back with the ball in hand. He looked at both sides of the field. Vinnie Tarsa was wide open for a pass, but Tyson made a bad choice and went to a two-man covered Pat McNamara for the long throw.

The opposing player nearest Pat, cut in front of him and lunged into the air. Making Tyson look like a fool, he intercepted the ball before it reached Pat. Gravity pulled the player swiftly to the ground and he began running up the field. Occam high's offensive linemen tried to stop him, but he proficiently spun around or overpowered them. The showoff dive-rolled into the endzone.

"Avi 'The Wanderer' Caspit, 5'11' 200lbs, with an impressive performance, taking it to the Razors after an interception on the first offensive play," Reported Nick Buckland.

"Interesting nickname, Nick," Glenn commented.

"Interesting indeed! Having lived in seven different countries since his birth in Tel Aviv, it's no wonder why they call the promising sophomore, "The Wanderer.""

Tyson cursed and looked at the ground, walking slowly over to the bench where he knew the coach was waiting to scream at him. He looked up and saw the Wavebreakers showing off with a much-practiced endzone dance.

Coach Martin grabbed Tyson's facemask and began his predictable rant. "What the hell was that? I thought you wanted to go to the championship, not watch it from work!" Coach Martin pointed at the opposite sideline, "I know that sweet new gal-pal of yours is on the dance team. I saw you waving to her at warm-ups. Why don't you give her a reason to be here? I want this win, so do you and so does she! I know your mom and dad are here. I got a chance to talk to Bob before the game. At least give them a reason to be here! I know Honolulu PD keeps the SWAT team busy. He's finally here so at least try to impress him!" Tyson saw Harlie with the dance team and his parents Bob and Laura in the stands. "See them. See all of them...give them a reason to be here!"

The coach was done with his rant and he slapped Tyson's helmet—Coach Martin's way of dismissing the player he was reprimanding. Tyson nodded and ran to the bench.

"You wanna tell me what that was?" Vinnie asked as he irately took off his helmet.

"Bad judgment call," Tyson mumbled barely opening his mouth.

"Yeah it was. Quit being a hot head and throw me the damn ball. I'm the one that puts yards behind me after the catch." Tyson found it difficult to control his anger. This time Vinnie was right although Tyson didn't want to admit it.

"Fair enough," is all Tyson had to say.

After another kick off from the visiting team, Jean-Claude received it again, but didn't make it as far up the field. The Wavebreakers felt the momentum of their early lead and took it out on Jean-Claude.

"Jean-Claude Gionet gets hit hard again!" Buckland announced. "C'mon, Razors, help your teammate out."

Tyson's line took the field again. "Hiiike!" Tyson yelled as Akshad Khan snapped the ball to him. Tyson fell back and saw that Vinnie was wide open again, but he really didn't want to throw it to him. He handed the ball to Jean-Claude to run with as far as he could. After a short gain up the field, the player's on Tyson's line came back to him to decide the next play.

Vinnie walked up to Tyson and spoke very slowly, pausing between each set of words in his statement. "Getchya-head...outta-your-ass. Throw me the damn ball when I'm wide open! The hell is the matter with you?" Tyson looked away as Vinnie continued ranting and the rest of the team jeered at him. "The Jean-Bomb can't carry the whole team the whole game! It's like there is no fire in you at all." The last statement wasn't like the other ones at all. It was scathing. "So get your mind off my ex and in the game, bitch!"

"Just get yourself open again, jackass," Tyson snapped as the group broke and they took back to the line.

"Hiiike!" Tyson yelled. Tyson was tackled before he could throw the ball, losing the short yardage that Jean-Claude gained on the last play.

Coach Martin was on the sidelines throwing his hat to the ground and cursing.

Again, the players on Tyson's line began coming back to him including Vinnie. Tyson motioned for all the players to get back to their spots so they could start the next play immediately.

While the players were lining back up, Jean-Claude advised Tyson. "Dude, I don't know what you and Vinnie have got going on right now because you haven't exactly been up front with me lately. But you need to put that away and throw him the ball. We need some points. We need this win."

Tyson acknowledged his friend and began the next play. Again, Tyson yelled, "Hiiike!" The players scrambled up the field and Tyson had time to decide. Pat was covered so he took Jean-Claude's advice. He yanked his arm back and sent a perfect spiraling pass to Vinnie. Vinnie expertly jumped into the air and pulled the football into his body as his feet reconnected with the freshly cut grass beneath him. He juked and maneuvered around the opposing team then ran through Chris Meany—sending him to the ground.

"Blam, son!" Vinnie yelled after he collapsed the towering Chris Meany— taking the ball all the way to the opposite endzone. Vinnie jumped up onto the crossbar of the up-rights and began to do chin-ups, "This is what I do!" Vinnie shouted and the crowd cheered Vinnie's famous chant. The game was about to be tied and Vinnie dropped off of the cross bar. He looked into the stands then pointed to Luna.

"This is what I do, *beeyatch*!" Jordan yelled as he slapped Vinnie's helmet.

"Seven days a week, partna!" Vinnie hooted.

"This is what I do!" Akshad yelled as he and Vinnie chest-bumped.

"Ain't nothin' to it!" Vinnie bragged.

"Vinnie 'Swag-Juice' Tarsa *does what he does* as the crowd cheers his famous line, 'This is what I do!'" Glenn Jackson observed. "What charisma!"

The game finally ended. Occam High won 49-28. The players and fans from Occam High School scuttled onto the field. They were all shouting over the person next to them.

"We won!"

"Kapaa!"

"Go, Occam High!"

Tyson spied Harlie, running towards him, calling his name from the other side of the field. Tyson ran toward her smiling until she finally skipped right into his arms.

"You played so awesome!" She said resting her head on his chest.

Just then, Vinnie purposefully bumped into Tyson as he walked by. "Watch yourself, Lynd."

Tyson looked unbothered as he stood up straight and wrapped his arm around Harlie. "Vin, where are you goin'? It's not like you to avoid celebrating yourself after a win, jackass!"

"Shut up, Lynd. I've got business to handle. I'll get at ya later, fire-freak!"

Tyson and Harlie wandered behind the gym and strolled out onto the school's pier. At the edge of the pier, they found their place on a bench. Tyson wrapped his arm around his desirable Harlie and dragged her closer to him. The full moon watched them from afar and the stars danced amongst the clouds over the ocean. Harlie pecked him on the check and rested her head on his shoulder. As the deep horizon dragged Tyson's attention away, Harlie tugged at Tyson's sleeves. She pulled them up his forearms.

"What are you doing?" Tyson asked.

"I don't want you to hide who you are from me." she admitted. "You're my Ahi."

Tyson didn't protest.

"Can I tell you about a dream I had?" she asked.

"Of course."

"It was the night before the field trip to the lab," Harlie recalled. She grabbed Tyson's hands and brought him on a journey into her mind.

"There was a dark apartment. It was miles outside of Honolulu. A television reporter's message was broadcast to a murdered man who lay slumped over the armrest of his blood-stained recliner.

The reporter on the TV was Glenn Jackson. He said the same thing that he did during the next morning's broadcast. I remember it word-for-word. Harlie's face was marked with a hypnotic tunnel vision as she repeated, 'This is Glenn Jackson with WKBT 9 news. We're here amongst the swaying palm trees outside of the Omicron laboratory facility where at any moment we expect the arrival of Air Force One on the private air strip behind me.'"

"Harlie?" Tyson snapped in her dazed face.

She spoke again. "Upon his arrival, the president is to be met by his personal security unit who will shuttle him to the inside of the Omicron Testing Facility. He has scheduled a visit with James Bankhart, founder and president of Omicron. President Merling has also scheduled a tour of the facility. As you can see, there is already a heavily armed force waiting to receive the president."

"Harlie!" Tyson shook his seemingly hypnotized girlfriend.

She jumped. Tyson startled her.

"How do you remember all that?" Tyson asked. "And word-for-word no less!"

Harlie put her index finger over Tyson's lips. "There's more. The TV set in the apartment flickered and the image of Glenn Jackson faded then reappeared sporadically. The shimmers bounced off the bleeding corpse in the arm chair. The being that was responsible for the murder walked back into the room. The dull sputtering of the old television set erratically illuminated the killer's face. With each flicker of the old screen, the small apartment that housed the dead body was momentarily visible. The wavering luminescence from the television conferred brief visibility to the bland coffee table in the center of the room, the gray short fiber carpet, the light brown love seat, and the matching recliner that the freshly murdered man occupied."

Tyson lost himself in Harlie's vacant stare.

"A small, athletically-built woman, an assassin by occupation, walked toward the mirror on the wall with her head down, eyes glued to the drab carpet. She raised her face to the mirror as the inconsistent shimmers from the TV reflected off of the surface. She considered her dark hair, narrow eyes, and thin nose as forgettable. She regarded the features as an occupational convenience. If less stood out about the assassin, she would more likely live to kill another day. She looks kinda like me." Harlie smiled. "I think she's kinda pretty."

"Harlie?"

Harlie didn't respond. Her smile faded as she continued retelling her dream to Tyson. "The woman grasped her forehead and sunk her fingertips into her skin as the worst headache she'd ever felt kept pounding away, torturing her. The assassin hadn't quite felt like herself of late. An essence had taken over her body some time ago. It integrated itself into her being and had kicked her out of her own mind.

She gazed into the mirror sensing her comeuppance for an emotionless life of cold calculations. Factoring wind ratios for appropriate bullet travels, estimating velocities of a moving target before triggering a detonator, approximating her window of escape before pulling a trigger— these are the cold calculations the veteran assassin made without remorse.

The assassin strained her weary and unsure eyes as the mirror told her about a tear that trickled down her cheek. 'So this is what they've felt like?'

The assassin's mouth began to move, but it was no longer her own voice being expelled from her full lips. 'Perhaps, my dear, we can't forget how good you were at your job. Only certain people you killed knew of your presence and their impending death.' The voice was gravelly and as menacing as the message.

'Couldn't you have granted me the same courtesy?' The woman scoffed. 'Maybe you could've tried a more subtle, clever approach.'

'Oh I don't know if I'm as clever of a killer as you, my dear.'

'How clever is a woman when she's begging for her life?'

'Let's not be coy, Riley. You've been a great harbinger of death. You make life so...'

'Miserable?'

'No, Riley, shorter.' The being's unsettling laugh rang in Riley's ears. 'I'm getting tragically bored. No one has died in this room in some thirty minutes and I'm not sure that I have much use for you anymore.'

'Please, no,' she pled having done the maddening math in her head with the quotient being her untimely demise. The tears, an unfamiliar feeling to the assassin, flowed down her face.

The gun that ended a life minutes ago lay in her right hand. Her fist clenched more tightly around it. Her knuckles lost color and she continued pleading, 'No, No, No! I beg of you!' Her arm slowly rose and her body quivered with unmitigated fear. The assassin was in the midst of a feverish struggle within herself.

'You're making this somewhat difficult, Riley! The sooner you relax and accept your fate the sooner we get through this...ugly business.'

She exhaled, began to sweat and cried uncontrollably. It was at this time she came to the realization that her resistance was futile. She succumbed to her fate. The gun rose to her head and the essence mocked her, jamming the silenced Sig-Sauer P226 into the side of her head repeatedly.

'Where do you want it?' The demon's ashy laugh again chilled her to the bone as he dragged the cold metal barrel across her full lips. 'I know! Let's play a game! I'm not going to shoot you in the face. Instead, we'll have some fun.'

The assassin, still crying and cursing the spirit, faced the grimy mirror. She looked deep into the eyes that were no longer hers, seeking the beast responsible for this torturous insanity. Her once beautiful blue eyes were as black as a moonless night, but when the light from the shimmers caught them just right, they took on a purple hue.

'Let's play catch! So, we're going to switch hands.' Against her will, the assassin tossed the gun from her right hand to her left. The demon forced her to bend her arm at the elbow and jam the gun into the left side of her head. 'Do you think we can catch the casing before your body hits the ground?' The assassin wept for whatever life the essence hadn't scared out of her. 'Ok, so get ready, because here she comes!'

'Who are you?' Riley asked.

The pistol recalled the same silenced song it sang some thirty minutes prior. The spent casing ejected out of the pistol. The woman with a bullet already in her brain reached out and grasped the spent shell out of the air. Another moment later and her body fell in the center of the apartment floor. The contents of her veins leaked out of the side of her head, mouth and nose. The crimson color running from her face mingled with the fibers of the carpet beneath her. Her again blue eyes were wide open, as if staring at the last thing she ever saw, the brass casing that lay in her small palm."

Tyson snapped in Harlie's face and shook her again, "Harlie! Come back to me! Please!" He pled.

She was still vacant. Tyson wiped her mascara away with his sleeve. He forked his fingers and pulled her lower eyelids away from her emerald eyes. On the glassy whites of her eyes, there were three vertical lines. They were thin black lines. "Harlie!" Tyson said into her ear.

Again, she was startled awake.

"Are you ok?" Tyson asked.

"I think," she said. "That's been happening a lot more lately. *Deja Vu* on steriods," she nervously smiled.

"Describe the dead man in the chair."

"He was a gaunt man. A strange-looking man. He had an odd skin tone. He was kinda blue-in-the-face with thick lips."

A look of worry came over Tyson's face, "Do you know his name?"

"Dawson Wrangle."

"What!?" Tyson exclaimed. "Are you sure?"

"I don't know *who* he is," Harlie added. "I *know* his name was Dawson Wrangle."

"Who's Riley?" Tyson asked her.

"My mother."

CHAPTER 13: VERY GOOD CHOICE

Ashley Ryker entered the Freeworld Café, a private Washington D.C. lounge. Ashley expected the president would be incognito given the nature of their meeting, but not a single person in the lounge appeared to have a frame half the size of the king-sized Isaac Mursten.

All of the furniture, the sofas, loveseats, low and high-top tables, as well as the seats at the java bar were earth-tones. The floor in the main room was composed of a meticulously clean, multicolored slate. The lighting was dim. The oblivious customers kept their noses in their books and lips on their mugs.

Ashley noted it was nearly 11:00PM. "How did he get to where he is without being punctual?" She thought out loud.

"Who's not punctual, dear Ashley?" an older man inquired from the high-top table right behind her.

"Bravo, I didn't recognize you," Ashley admitted.

"I don't know what you're talking about, Ashley." The man smiled a toothy smile, a wicked grin. "Now, why don't you join me for a bit?"

"I'm impressed. Not a single person in the lounge knows they're in your company. Even your voice is so…different." The man's voice she was referring to was gravelly and rough. All-in-all, it was entirely different from Mursten's youthful voice.

Ashley looked at the man's stature and was suddenly worried that she wasn't talking to President Mursten at all. But then how would the man in front of her know her name? Possibly from the news, she concluded. "Are you worried about someone finding out you left?" she whispered.

"Not at all."

"And how is that? How are you not worried?" She was now reprimanding the odd man across the table in a soft whisper.

"Because I never left," He answered as he sipped from his coffee. Ashley looked confused. She still didn't know if she was talking to the right individual. This man might be some creep toying with her. Her nerves were still getting the better of her. She regained her wit after having thought for a minute. The ominous man across from her smiled as he put his coffee cup down on the table.

"You still haven't figured it out, Dr. Ryker?" He asked in his unsettling voice. "Maybe I should've said, 'because Isaac never left.'" Ashley squinted her eyes as she continued trying to piece together a mental puzzle, unsure of whether or not she had the right pieces. The man spoke up again, "I'm considering not doing business with you at all. You're a good scientist and decent hostess, but back at the lab I mistakenly assumed you were a formidable chaser the way you outed that Ahi kid."

Ashley again remained silent. The president knew she was a scientist and publicist for the laboratory, but how did this man in front of her know she was a chaser?' "Who are you?" she asked.

"The one you're scheduled to meet."

"But you're clearly not the president." She was still confused.

"Why can't I be both?"

"Only Keaka can be in more than one place at a time."

"Your point?"

"You're not a Keaka." Ashley blurted out without thinking.

"I'm not?" The man raised his bushy eyebrows.

"Are you? You are!"

"It took you long enough to put that together especially for a chaser. Don't make me reevaluate my confidence in you."

She examined him not believing a word of his admission, but everything about him indicated he was a genuine Keaka. "No, that's impossible."

With each passing second, she was more convinced that he wasn't lying.

A waiter in his early twenties approached the old man and Ashley. "May I warm up your coffee, sir?"

"Please," he pushed the saucer that the cup rested upon toward the waiter.

"For you, miss?"

"Irish coffee, please."

"Yes, ma'am, a very good choice."

"My boy," the old man called after the waiter had turned his back to retrieve their order.

"Yes, sir."

"The lady and I will be making our way into the observatory."

"Very good, sir."

The old man got up to his feet and walked away from the table. He was about 6'1" and frail, not at all like the large, athletic president.

Ashley warily followed him as he ambled past the other rooms that were occupied. He opened the French doors that lead to the observatory and gestured for her to go in first. There were plenty of tables in the room, but very little light. There was a small replica of the Hubble telescope in the center of the room. The walls in the observatory were adorned with plastic luminescent stars as well as a glow-in-the-dark mural of the solar system.

"Who are you?" asked Ashley.

"For now, you can call me, 'Ephraim.'"

"For now?"

"For now," the odd man confirmed.

"Why did we come in here?" Ashley asked as she closed the doors. She still had trouble believing that the body in front of her housed a Keaka, the most wicked of the Lost Orders. "I need to know who I'm speaking with. I want some proof of your order."

Ephraim sat down and his withered upper eyelids met the bags under his eyes.

"Great, fall asleep, perfect," Ashley huffed.

"He's not asleep," the wicked voice hissed, apparently coming from nowhere.

"What the hell?" Ashley looked at the wall behind her, where she thought she heard the voice was coming from, "What do you mean?"

The doors opened and their waiter walked through

with the drinks in hand. The waiter began to speak in the same gravelly voice that was just coming from Ephraim and his eyes were a radiant red. "What the hell do you think I mean, chaser? He's not asleep." The waiter put the drinks down in front of Ashley.

"What?" Ashley shook her head, closed and reopened her eyes.

"He's dead." The waiter licked his teeth with a depraved emotionless expression. "It'll make more sense after you've had a few Irish coffees." The waiter laughed an unusual laugh, an evil laugh, and left the room as he hummed a menacing melody.

Ephraim raised his withered eyelids when the waiter left the room. "What did I miss?"

"Wow!" Ashley paused for a moment, "That's not normal."

The door opened and the waiter politely popped his head in the room. "Ok good! I did bring you the coffees! I honestly couldn't remember. Isn't that the damndest thing?" He remarked.

"That *is* weird!" Ashley dismissed the waiter who caught onto her frustration then withdrew himself from the room and closed the door. Ashley turned to the bizarre man next to her. "Ok! You're Keaka. I get it, test over, let's get down to business."

"It's about time, Ashley. I've been growing weary of your arrogance. You're lucky this ugly old bastard I'm occupying is the only dead one in the room. Do you get what I'm saying? You're useful to me, but you're not that useful." The threat left Ashley uneasy, but it made her very compliant. "You're right though, my dear. We do need to take care of our business."

Ashley just nodded her head, not to test his temper again. "What now?" Ashley asked in a less challenging tone. She raked a strand of hair behind her ear and waited for an answer.

"Omicron already needs Ahi and Zoree blood. I just need it sooner."

"We need a war."

"Precisely the realization that got Jim Bankhart killed, precisely the point of *your* Neo-Exa project."

"Why did it get him killed and why didn't it get me killed?"

"It hasn't gotten you killed, *yet,* my dear. I'll keep you that way if you stay useful."

Ashley knew there was no point in asking if it was too late to say, 'No, thank you' and promise to stay out of the way of the intimidating Keaka. She asked the only logical question that she could think of asking. "How do I stay useful?"

"We need blood. We need Ahi and Zoree blood. I

need you to find the blood, the bodies that house the blood, the Lost Orders, and keep the people bleeding. As long as the people bleed, you stay alive."

Ashley was too nervous to speak. She was fighting back the tears from what she felt was a certain death sentence. She was trapped in a deal with the devil from which there was no escape. Finally, the words found their trembling way out, "How might I do that?"

"What makes you different than Bankhart?" Ashley shook her head, maintaining her alleged ignorance. "You're a chaser. You understand the orders and what makes them tick, or I was hoping you do. You can find these people and bring them to fight." Ephraim slammed his old frail fists together hard enough that his brittle joints cracked. "That sounds fair doesn't it? You don't mind a little bit of bloodshed. It wasn't too hard for you to plan the dispatching of Bankhart."

"I didn't kill, Jim."

"You didn't push the knife through Bankhart's skull, nor did Mandrake. But you had no problem making sure that the killer had the necessary window of opportunity to take care of business." He pointed his old arthritic finger at her, "Yes, *you* took care of the logistics behind it. You had no problem allowing a comparatively innocent colonel take the rap for a murder that he didn't commit. You took your part of the money from the arrangement—and the promotion that

140

came with his death." The Keaka in front of Ashley paused for a moment, basking in her fear and disgrace that she tried her best to hide. He began speaking to her again. "And when you think about it, one dead body isn't that much different than one million."

Ashley was losing the fight with her conscious that was brought on by the embodied evil in front of her. Her pride began to burn and her eyes puffed up as Ephraim spoke his unsympathetic words. Ashley got up from the lecture in ethics she was receiving from the wicked thing before her, tears rolling from her eyes.

Ephraim began speaking again, lifting his shiny red eyes towards the woman standing before him. "Stop crying. Everyone is broken at some point."

Ashley sought life-preserving advice from the wicked being that she expected would soon take it. "What do I do next?"

"We'll, you want to stay alive. Don't think I'm the only one that you have to worry about."

"What do you mean?"

"You sent a fearsome man to prison for something he didn't do…and took his money!"

"Yeah, he's in prison," Ashley reminded him in an irritated tone.

"People escape from prison, Dr. Ryker."

"Not this one. It's maximum security, armed guards,

141

both inside and outside. He's not going anywhere. Besides, if he did escape, he's not going to find me."

"Ashley, as sure as you're born, he will escape and he will find you."

"Right," Ashley rolled her moist eyes at the far too cliché warning.

"He's a highly trained American soldier. He doesn't kick in doors with his guns in the air, shoot first and ask questions later."

"Mmmkay…"

"He'll be meticulous. He thinks. He sees the big picture. Don't underestimate a man like Colonel Rockland. It'll be the last wrong estimation you'll ever make, a painful misestimation."

"Whatever," Ashley looked at her watch. She seemed unthreatened by the prospect of the colonel escaping. The only thing that scared her was Ephraim, the man warning her.

"In the interest of preserving your almost valuable life, I suggest you find a way to make his stay unbearably uncomfortable."

"Like?" asked Ashley.

"Use your imagination. You're a crafty girl. Ask your buddy Mandrake. He has friends on the inside of the joint. Now, get out."

Ashley angrily stormed out of the room, upset that

Ephraim didn't say anything she felt was useful. Ashley thought she was done with her supernatural business partner for the evening.

As Ashley walked towards her white Lexus LS, she suddenly heard Ephraim's menacing voice again. "I almost forgot. You will be hearing from me soon, my dear." The ugly odd man was right behind her and she didn't know it. The voice startled Ashley and caused her to drop her keys. She stumbled into a black Chevy Tahoe with tinted windows that was parked next to her car. "Don't worry. I'll be more pleasing to your beautiful eyes next time."

"I can't wait," Ashley said sarcastically as she picked up her keys. "Who shall I be looking for?"

"Find the most handsome man in the room and ask for 'Mara.'"

"Who's Mara?"

"I am."

"No, you're Ephraim."

"Can't I be both?" Ephraim rhetorically called upon the same justification from earlier. "Wear your best clothes. We're going to dine in a very dignified restaurant. We're going to dine at the Komiama Block." The old man turned around and walked away.

Ashley clumsily jostled into her car and pressed the 'push-to-start' button. The dazzling instrument cluster came to life. Despite Mara's warning about the colonel, it wasn't the colonel that instilled unshakable fear in her. Mara terrified her. Ashley examined herself in the rear-view mirror before driving away. One minute after she left, the black Chevy Tahoe she was parked next to also left the parking lot.

CHAPTER 14: NICE WORK

From about eight feet away, Wright could hear the rhythmic bass from the hip-hop beat that was repeating in the Pat's ear. The thunder crashed overhead and the angry rain hammered the green field. They looked up at the sky and then at each other. Wright blew the whistle and Pat up-ended the tire. Flip-by-flip, through the rain that soaked his hair and the mud that splashed his clothes, Pat made his way towards the endzone where Tyson was standing.

Pat was beginning to wake up, his eyelids no longer felt heavy, his legs not as wobbly. His arms felt strong and his motivation was high. He wasn't disappointed in himself anymore. He couldn't be happier than doing what he was doing. He felt the taxing task becoming easier with each practice. With every flip of the tire, he felt stronger and more determined to flip the tire again. The music pounded away in his ear as he neared the opposite endzone. The wind harshly blew and the refreshing cool rain splashed in his face. He could hear Principle Wright motivating him as he closed the distance between himself and the endzone.

"That's right, kid! That's right! Do it!"

With a final flip, he cleared the goal line and let out a big satisfied yell.. A resonating "Yeeeeah!" echoed off of the bleachers and the school's buildings. The sweat dripped out of every pore and the rain streamed down his face

Tyson slapped Pat on the back and blew the rain of his own face. "Nice work, Pat."

"How'd that feel, Pat?" Wright asked.

"Pretty damn good."

"You know, not too long ago, you would have said I was crazy if I told you that you could've done that by now."

"That's for certain."

"We're going to get even more out of you next time. Get hydrated, it's Tyson's turn."

Tyson assumed the starting position confidently with his hands on the slippery tire. In Tyson's eyes there was strong determination—a fire roaring within him. This determination could also be seen in his confident grip on the tire. His cleats were dug as firmly as possible into the soaked ground beneath him.

Wright blew the whistle and Tyson raced up the field, flipping the tire at a consistent pace with sharp coordination despite the inclement conditions. He made short work of the training exercise. A hazy cloud of smoke rose off Tyson's shoulders as he straightened himself up.

"So it's true?" The principle asked as he approached Tyson, feeling the ambient air heating up, studying the haze over Tyson.

Tyson nodded and averted his eyes.

"Tyson!" The principle snapped. It was the first time he ever raised his voice at Tyson.

Tyson immediately straightened his posture and nervously smirked at the principle. He wasn't sure what to say so he just waited and listened. Wright took off his unneeded sunglasses and draped them on his shirt collar. He put a hand on Tyson's soaked shoulder. "Don't ever be ashamed of who you are."

"Yes, sir."

"Get yourself a quick drink. Do five laps with Pat and then we're doing it all over again."

"Yes, sir."

Tyson ran over to the bench where Pat was sitting, "Wright is a pretty cool guy."

Pat smirked. "You know, I never in a million years would have thought about agreeing with that statement."

"But now?"

"But now, I agree. I kinda feel bad about being such a dick to him these past few years." Pat thought and corrected himself, "No, I really feel bad now."

"There is always a chance for a fresh start and a time for a new beginning. Wright knows that. That's why he's out here with you."

"Yeah. It seems so." Pat pensively agreed.

"What are you thinking?"

"I'm thinking I have something I need to say to Principle Wright. I'll wait till we're done with our laps."

"Did you need me to get lost while you talked to him?"

"No, it's ok if you're there. You were there when I insulted him and his wife. You can definitely be there when I apologize for it. Hell, I probably need you there."

"Ok cool," Tyson laughed.

After their laps, they returned to Wright who was in the middle of a concerned phone call.

"What happened?" Wright asked, "Is she ok?" The concern grew on his tired face. The boys noticed he shut his eyes like one would when processing bad news. They didn't know how right they were in reading the expression on his face.

"Maybe we should back off a little bit," Tyson suggested.

"Yeah, definitely."

Tyson and Pat were throwing a football when they heard the principle speak again, "Penicillin and sulfa derivatives." There was another pause. "Dr. Gionet?" After a final pause, they heard him again. "Thank you very much!

I'm on my way!" Wright stowed his phone away and ran off. "Sorry, boys, I gotta go! Do what you gotta do. Whenever you're done with all of this, please put it away and lock it all up." He tossed Tyson the keys to the equipment shed.

"Principle Wright, can I tell you something?" Pat asked.

"Sorry, Pat. I can't right now. Definitely keep the thought and the next time I see you, tell me then. I am interested, but my wife needs me."

Wright ran toward the bleachers, grabbed his damp duffle bag then handily hopped the surrounding fence. He waved a 'goodbye' before getting in his car and speeding away.

"That can't be good," Tyson said.

"I wish I knew exactly where he was going."

"He's going to the hospital in Honolulu. Dr. Gionet is Jean-Claude's dad. That's where he works."

"Do you know where it is?"

"Definitely, I can take you there after school. It's on the way to the garage that I work at."

"Really? That would be awesome if you could bring me. I can put my bike in the team's shed."

"Yeah, no problem, I'll leave my car parked right over there." Tyson pointed at his VW.

After getting dressed for school they made their way

over to the classroom building together. As they approached the street, they heard the familiar thumping up the road. Coming from the distance at a deliberately excessive speed was Vinnie in his glorious white Infiniti.

"That's Tarsa's car, right?" Tyson asked Pat.

"Yeah, it's a wicked sweet ride," Pat answered as he approached the curb— expecting Vinnie to slow down. The Infiniti screamed by and raced into the distance. "Huh?" Pat watched the car speed off down the middle of the road to the dismay of the drivers in the oncoming lane.

"It's my fault he blew you off."

"Eh, don't worry about it, Tyse," Pat said as he realized he would rather be hanging out with someone that didn't judge him for maintaining direction in his life. "I'll catch up with him later. Tell me about that gorgeous girl you're seeing."

"Oh, Harlie? She's just awesome." Tyson had a smile on his face.

"Yeah? I knew she was a good one. Vinnie never treated her right."

"No?"

"No. I think he laid hands on her before."

"What? Like hit her?"

"I think he may have. I don't know for sure. She's a nice girl though and you're a cool guy. So, you two are good for each other." Pat smiled.

149

"Thanks. You know, it seems like every time I hang out with her it gets easier. To be honest, with past girlfriends I've had, that wasn't exactly the case."

"Yeah, I think that's true of a lot of people. What's next for you two?"

"The night before the championship game in Kapaa we were planning on visiting Mount Kilauea."

"That's cool, using that volcano people thing to your advantage, huh?"

"It's a secret I wish I could've kept, but at this point I can't fight it. Everyone knows anyway which still pisses me off to no end. I do hate talking about it though."

"Oh yeah?"

"Well, I'm going to see if I can catch Harlie and Jean-Claude before classes start."

"All right, cool, man. Thanks again for everything." Pat said.

"No problem, I'll see you after classes." The two bumped fists then went their separate ways.

When Tyson arrived at homeroom, Harlie was already there waiting for him with Jean-Claude. She sprung from her chair and threw her arms around Tyson when he got to his desk.

"What's the word?" Jean-Claude asked as Tyson sat down.

"Pat and I were doing some football drills this morning with Principle Wright."

"Wright? Really?" Harlie asked.

Jean-Claude interceded, "Yeah, Tyson's been leaving me here to study by myself every morning while he goes and gets his football on with the principle and Pat. Jerk didn't even invite me!"

Tyson laughed, "You know Wright would be cool with it, Claude."

"Why so early?" Harlie asked.

Tyson straightened up in his chair, "It started as a discipline thing for Pat, but he grew to actually liking it. He feels that the extra workout in the morning is going to help improve his work and focus in school. He wants another chance. I think he'll really make something out of it."

"Yeah, I think he will too," Jean-Claude agreed. "I like Pat."

"Good for him," Harlie added.

"Yeah there's just one thing that concerns me," Tyson said.

"Vinnie?" Jean-Claude guessed.

"You know it."

"He's a jerk," Harlie said.

"Yeah. He's probably going to give Pat a hard time for hanging out with me. He's going to try to drag him back down."

"Misery loves company." Jean-Claude adjusted his glasses. "Speaking of this Vinnie thing, you've got to get me up to speed on what's going on. I can't believe you kept such a big secret from me man. I mean, I should have guessed there was a reason why you always wore long sleeves."

"Next time we hang out I'll bring you up to speed. I'm actually lucky enough to take this beautiful girl with me to Kilauea when we go to Kapaa." Tyson said as he tilted his head twice in Harlie's direction. "If you want, you can come along. I can fill you both in there."

"*Nah*, not with ya'll love-birds... I wanna be able to hold my lunch down," Jean-Claude laughed.

The bell rang and everyone made it to their homerooms. Harlie said, "Bye" to Tyson and Jean-Claude then ran to catch one of her friends she saw outside of the homeroom.

Students started filing through the door and making their way to their seats.

"Hey, Mrs. Welby," Pat said as he walked by. The teacher's face lost color as if she had just seen a ghost. In all her years as his homeroom teacher, Pat never once greeted her.

"Good morning, Patrick," she replied in a suspicious, yet justifiable voice.

After everyone made their way to their seats, the teacher took a quick head count. "Oh wow! Everyone's here," the teacher remarked. "I guess miracles do happen!" she said as she filed the attendance record. She placed the envelope in the tray on the wall below the phone then closed the door.

"So what did you and Harlie talk about?" Tyson asked Jean-Claude.

"She came in and asked where you were."

"Then what?"

"She was telling me about her friend Vanessa."

"Oh really?"

"Yeah, I think she is playing the match-maker game," Jean-Claude said.

"The whole 'my friends gotta date your friends' thing?"

"Yeah, something like that. You know girls," Jean-Claude folded his arms and sat back in his chair.

"Are you considering it? Is she your type?"

Jordan turned around from his chair and interrupted, "What's with the questions? Are you jealous? Is someone gonna steal your boyfriend?"

"And another attempt at wit from the witless," Tyson jeered.

"Shut up, Lynd," Jordan laughed.

Jean-Claude resumed speaking when Jordan withdrew himself from the conversation. "You know, maybe I'll talk to her or something. She's pretty cute and I talked to her a lot at Jay's party the other day."

Jordan faced them again, "Another one after we kick asses and take names at Kapaa next weekend—keep it open, guys."

Jean-Claude nodded, "Maybe I will if you keep your drugs outta my face."

"It's all good, man. No drugs at the next one. Pat's done dealing I guess," Jordan shrugged and swiveled back to his homeroom sweetheart.

Jean-Claude looked at Tyson again, "I've always been kinda reclusive I guess. I think it's time to start meeting people. So, the short answer to your question is 'maybe.'" Jean-Claude finished his statement remaining deep in thought. He was no doubt over-thinking something that didn't need to be stewed about.

"Cool," Tyson said.

"By the way, you gotta fill me in before we go to Kapaa. You at least owe me that."

"Yeah," Tyson said as he pinched the bridge of his nose and focused on the homeroom teacher who was ready to make the day's announcements.

Later, Tyson and Jean-Claude sat down to their favorite table in the library. Tyson checked his schedule, confirming that Harlie should be there, but there was no sign of her after fifteen minutes.

Jean-Claude went to one of the book bays to find a text for a paper he was writing when Vinnie walked into the study hall. The egotistical Vinnie sat down with some Senior classmen at the table right behind Tyson. "Sup, fire-freak?"

"Nothing, you scaly prick." Tyson turned around, "Why are you bothering me?"

Their classmates at nearby tables gawked at the drama unfolding.

"Why shouldn't I bother you, freak?" Vinnie challenged with an angry expression as his fists clenched and his face grew red. "Ahi are the reason we hide who we are. And I tried to make everything square with you man."

Tyson spoke up, "You're bothering me about something that Zoree were responsible for over six *billion* years ago?"

"You Ahi need to die, man. I'm serious... like just stop breathing." Vinnie's angry facade had become a bothersome gleam defined by a psychopathic rage in his eye.

"Slow up, Vin. You're taking this way beyond words," Tyson would not back down from the bully at the next table.

"How's my ex-girlfriend?"

"Leave her out of this, Vin. Your problem is with me."

"C'mon, Lynd, how's she doin' it for ya?"

"She does it good," Tyson said, sitting back in his chair with evident satisfaction on his face. "...better than your mermaid mom." Tyson arrogantly smiled and folded his strong arms, dittoing Vinnie.

Vinnie slammed his fists and stood up. He flipped the table he was sitting at out of his way. "You," Vinnie pointed at Tyson with the irate veins popping out of his neck, "just pushed this beyond words."

"Why? Because I told you how good your father's wife was?" Tyson scoffed. Vinnie grabbed the table in front of Tyson, lifted it up and threw it in the direction of the onlookers. The gawkers immediately scattered as the table crashed to the ground.

"Let's do this!" Vinnie shouted.

Tyson shrugged as he started to stand up.

Vinnie didn't wait. He threw his fist at Tyson's face. Tyson barely slipped the blow. Vinnie pressed closer throwing another fist. Tyson wasn't in a position to attack while he dodged Vinnie's non-stop flurry. Vinnie pressed towards Tyson. Tyson backed up towards the wall as Vinnie still swung away at him. Tyson realized a very swing-able chair would soon be in arms reach. Tyson inched backwards slapping each fist away as Vinnie picked up the pace punch-after-punch.

The chair was finally in grabbing distance. Tyson knocked away the final punches of Vinnie's fierce attack that he was intending on tolerating. Tyson grabbed the four-legged lifeline. In a spinning fall, he effectively ducked

Vinnie's blows as he struck Vinnie behind the legs, taking the galoot's feet right out from under him.

"Holy crap!" he heard a student shout as Vinnie yelled and fell to the ground on his back.

Vinnie immediately recovered. Tyson was also on the ground and he didn't expect Vinnie to recuperate so quickly. After the initial contact from the chair, it didn't seem like the attack really phased Vinnie. It just made him angry.

In midst of the skirmish, Tyson noticed there were no teachers trying to break up the fight, but Tyson wasn't surprised. No one would want to get in the middle of a fight where the smaller kid was 6'2" and a very strong 180lbs.

"You're dead, Lynd!" Vinnie scrambled to get on top of Tyson, drawing his fist back. He repeatedly attempted to strike the elusive Tyson. Tyson kept dodging the blows until Vinnie grabbed him by the collar and slammed his head off the ground. Tyson let out a pained grunt that was cut short by a forceful fist hitting him in the jaw.

Pained, Tyson immediately saw the follow-up fist coming towards his face. He screamed out in anger as he forcefully blocked the attack. Tyson grabbed Vinnie by the shirt and punched him in the neck. The severe blow hurt Vinnie, but didn't stop him. Tyson chopped Vinnie's stabilizing arm and the galoots face fell on Tyson's rising fist. Again, the blow didn't stop Vinnie. Vinnie kept swinging away as Tyson evaded all the blows he could. Vinnie and

Tyson both ate inconsequential blows that bloodied their faces and stained the library carpet. Their differing blood hit the floor around them and a haze rose off of the floor.

Vice-Principle Mike Bromers, a retired fire-fighter and Occam High's wrestling coach ran into the library as soon as he heard about what was happening.

"Mike! Please, stop them!" a frightened Mrs. Lynch cried out.

The vice-principle ran over to the skirmish and seized Vinnie around the shoulders. Vinnie, in his rage, shook the vice-principle's grasp, "This is far from over, Lynd! Maybe I'll be seein' you at Kapaa, or maybe I won't!"

Tyson seized Vinnie's collar, "You keep playin' with me and I'll be the end of you. Believe it." Tyson fired back.

"Oh yeah?" Vinnie laughed and turned around as he threw a tightly-balled fist at Bromers. The vice-principle handily evaded the blow and quickly seized Vinnie's arm. He yanked Vinnie off of Tyson and immediately subdued him on the floor with a wrestling arm-lock. All the spectator's eyes lit up at his display of power.

"Whoa! V-P Bromers just totally went 'Jason Bourne' on Vinnie's ass!"

"Haha!"

Tyson pushed himself off of the floor, also surprised. He didn't want to try Bromers' temper with any remarks aimed at Vinnie. Tyson just backed away and wiped the blood off his face.

The spectators gasped over the violent conflict and the smoke that rose around the two bloody classmates.

The vice-principle forced Vinnie to his feet and turned around furiously, "My office in fifteen, Lynd! Clean yourself up!"

"Yes, sir." Tyson consented before he went back to gather his books up off the floor.

"Mrs. Lynch, don't worry about the mess. That's an awful lot of blood on the floor. I'll clean it up myself," Bromers proudly declared.

"Thanks, Mike. That'd be great. I've got a lot to do and blood just grosses me out...especially so much of it!" she cringed.

"It's no trouble," he grinned. Bromers turned around to the rubber-necking student body, "Everyone, the remainder of the study hall will be completed in the auditorium," he announced. Bromers then steered Vinnie towards the door.

"Tyson," a female voice called from one of the aisles, breaking his train of thought. Tyson looked around. He wasn't sure whose voice it was. It definitely wasn't Harlie's voice. "Tyson" the voice called again. Vanessa walked towards him with Jean-Claude.

"Are you all right?" Jean-Claude asked, slapping Tyson on the shoulder.

"Fine, thanks," Tyson again wiped away the blood from his face. His non-bloodied hand responded with a friendly slap on Jean-Claude's arm.

"Damn, son! I didn't know you could do that. Where'd you learn to fight like that?"

"Long-story, Claude."

"That was an impressive defense, quick hands!"

"Thanks, man."

"Did you hear?" Vanessa interrupted.

"Hear? Hear what?" Tyson sighed.

"Harlie is packing her stuff at her locker. She wanted to know if you can take her to the hospital."

"Yeah, absolutely!" Tyson answered nervously. "Is she all right?"

"She is, but I don't think her father is."

"What happened to him?"

"He was in an accident. I think it's pretty serious." Vanessa clenched her worried teeth.

"Oh man! Where is she now? Still at her locker?"

"I think so."

Tyson ambled over to Mrs. Lynch behind the library desk. "Mrs. Lynch, I'd like to sign myself and Harlie out of this study hall. I'm taking her to the hospital to see her father. There has been an accident."

"Sure thing, Tyson," the sympathetic librarian responded as she marked her initials on a sheet and asked Tyson to sign it.

"Can I use your phone?"

"You bet." She handed Tyson the phone, "Are you all right?"

"Fine, thanks. Will you dial, Mr. Bromers?"

"Sure! By the way, congratulations on making it to the championships at Kapaa. I'll be there."

Tyson politely nodded and awkwardly forced his response, "So will I...I hope."

After justifying himself to the Bromers over the phone, he got the permission to sign himself out, assured that there would have to be repercussions for hitting Vinnie with the chair. Tyson sanitized his hands and signed the sheet. He seized the box of tissues on the circulation desk and tried to wipe away as much blood as he could.

Tyson bolted out the door and found Harlie in her locker row. Her tears and emotions prevented her from packing her book bag. Her anxious arms tremored as she tried to jam the heavy calculus book into the bag.

"Let me take care of that," Tyson insisted as he grabbed the last of her books and stuffed them it in book bag. Harlie faced Tyson, noticing his battered face. She bawled at the sight of the blood that he missed when he cleaned himself.

"Oh my God! What happened?" She looked at him with her puffy eyes and started to cry again.

"Me and Vinnie had at it. Don't worry he got his too." Tyson threw her book-bag over his shoulder and she gave him a grateful hug.

"I'm sorry." Harlie said as she clung to Tyson, expecting that she might not even get a chance to say, 'bye' to her father. "Thank you for bringing me," she sniveled.

Tyson pointed at the exit, "I parked by the football field. Let's get to your dad." They hurriedly made their way to Tyson's car. "Is it the hospital in Honolulu?"

Harlie nodded trying to convince herself that there might be hope for her father.

Once they arrived, Tyson scrambled around to the passenger door to help his distraught girlfriend out of the car. Holding her hands, he did his best to provide her some comfort before she went inside to see her father. "Don't worry. I've got your stuff. I'm going to go back to school and take care of everything. I've got to bring Pat back here at the end of the day. I'll call work, tell them I can't make it tonight and stay with you. I'll see you in two hours or so."

Once the school day was over, Tyson eagerly waited for Pat in his car.

"Hey, Tyson!" Pat opened the car door. "Are you all right?"

"Yeah, I'm good."

Pat examined Tyson's face, "You know for as many punches as he threw, you didn't do too badly. You're giving away what, 50, maybe 60 pounds of 'roids to him?"

"Steroids?" asked Tyson.

"Hell yeah!"

"Like what? Deca-durabolin?"

"Not anymore. I used to sell him Deca when I dealt. Now, he uses some weird stuff. To be honest with you I don't know what it is, but despite all that you got your blows in too. You're an impressive fighter."

"I did all right considering. Are you ready to go?"

"I hate to ask, but do you care if we stop at one of the local farmer's shops on the way? Apologies are always easier with flowers I've heard."

Tyson pulled out of the parking lot and accelerated towards the hospital. "Yeah, it's no problem. I better get some myself. Harlie's dad was in an accident so I'll be at the hospital tonight too."

"Wow! That sucks!" Pat exclaimed—eyes wide open and shocked.

"Yeah," Tyson let out a weary sigh.

"My dad knows Grayson. He's a good guy. Is he going to be all right?"

"I really don't think that it's looking too good."

"Oh damn! That really sucks," Pat again offered his teenage sympathy.

"Yeah it does." In an effort to have a somewhat less bleak conversation Tyson changed the subject. "At any rate, what did you think of the quizzes today?"

"You know, they're a lot easier when you do a little bit of studying."

"Yeah, they are," Tyson laughed.

"I felt good about all of them. It's crazy. In such a short time Wright made me realize how stupid it is to not try."

"If you have a gift, why not use it?"

"There's so much more that I already wish I had done differently. 17 years of my life is over and I really haven't done much with myself." Pat peeped out the window at the beautiful palm plants and palm trees that lined the sides of the smooth roads they were traveling. He returned his attention to Tyson and continued his thought, "But those days are gone and they're not coming back for me."

"Eh, don't worry. There's plenty of time left to get it right"

"Yeah, maybe," Pat eye's wandered aimlessly and again he found himself staring out the half-downed window.

The two of them reached the front desk at the hospital—flowers in hand. A physician finished writing his orders on a notebook computer then looked up from his work and greeted them with a compassionate smile, "Can I help you boys?" He politely ignored the bruises and cuts on Tyson's face.

"I'm trying to find Mary Wright," Pat said, "or her husband Ethan if you happen to know where he is."

The doctor nodded and focused on Tyson. "Same person?" he asked.

"Actually, no, sir. I'm looking for Grayson McGrath, or his daughter Harlie McGrath."

"Ok, so Wright and McGrath let me see...I'm not sure where the clerk is, so bear with me as I browse her computer."

"Sure thing," Pat replied.

The doctor was intently searching the database while his misbehaving shirt cuffs frequently got in the way of his typing. After a minute or two, he informed them that both patients were in the intensive care unit.

"Our ICU down here was full it seems. It's been a busy couple days. They're both actually on the thirteenth floor's auxiliary intensive care unit under Dr. Gionet, lucky for them. He's probably the best doctor in Hawaii. But that poor man has been up and down between the two ICUs and the ER all day! I was just finishing up my last order for the day. I have to go up there quickly anyway so I'll take you there. This way."

"Great, thank you," Tyson said.

"No worries."

They wandered onto the elevator and made light chat about their schooling, their football team and the doctor's duties around the hospital. The doc was an emergent-care physician with a specialty in pediatrics. His name was Dr. Matt Morehouse and he had just finished a twenty-two hour shift.

"Are pediatric emergencies frequent, doctor?" Tyson asked.

"Common enough. Maybe we'll get one kid through the ER doors for every four or five adults some days. From nasty bike accidents, allergic reactions and other 'boo-boos'— all the way up to violent crimes. Kids aren't immune to the very real dangers that we only associate with adults. Yeah, sure kids fall off their bikes, but they shouldn't have to worry about violent crimes and things of that nature."

Pat and Tyson nodded in agreement with the doctor's sentiment. He was very engaging and exceptionally sharp despite the bags under his eyes.

Dr. Morehouse yawned as the elevator doors opened, "All right, boys, this is the floor." They got off of the elevator and followed the doctor.

Everyone in the hallways greeted the charismatic doctor, having small pleasant exchanges with him.

"All right. You, sir," the doctor said touching Tyson's shoulder, "want to be in this room here. And you, sir," he said to Pat, "want to be four doors down on the right."

"Thanks, Doctor. It was a pleasure," Tyson said shaking Dr. Morehouse's hand.

"Indeed it was. Good lucks, boys." Morehouse shook Pat's hand after Tyson's. He then walked through the door that was labeled 'staff only,' leaving Pat and Tyson to deal with their respective crises.

CHAPTER 15: A LOT OF RUNNING

Rockland lay in the prison cell he was confined to during his trial— thinking about his prospects. He would likely receive a sentence of twenty-five years to life without the possibility of parole. The informant who was to testify against him wasn't named as of yet. Rockland knew the wheels of justice weren't turning correctly, but through various loop-holes and clauses, the prosecutors were able to stifle his rights. About the only thing Rockland knew was that he was being held at a maximum security prison just outside of Washington D.C.

It was a very unruly block where Rockland was placed. Obscenities and threats were shouted from every direction. He stared up at the dark ceiling above him, thinking about how much he already missed his freedom. He was surrounded by cold cinderblock walls and the front of the cell was cage-like, with very little space between the bars. He could barely hear himself think over the noise beyond the cage.

A seemingly deaf guard occasionally paced the corridor. He kept an emotionless expression as he surveyed the malcontents of society—assessing possible threats.

Rockland sensed that there wasn't very much time before he would again call upon his survival instincts. The colonel had two cell mates, both sketchy thugs that relentlessly glared at him. The first of the two men was a large, darkly-complected man with corn-rowed hair. His name was Bruce. He was 6'3" and built like a football player. Prison tattoos uncivilly bedecked his body. He had the Egyptian eye tattooed on the back of his neck and a tattoo on the side of his neck that read,

'Sphynx.'

His biceps were enormous and smirched with scars that told Rockland a lot about his cellmate. Rockland could tell that Bruce was a careless fighter with a propensity to fight armed men.

The second of the two cell mates, Owen, was another sizeable man. Owen had a light complexion, shaved red hair and memorial tattoos all over his arms. Apparently, a lot of his friends were dead. On his bicep was a tattoo of a pair of crossed boxing gloves above a four-leaf clover. Around the tattoo there was writing that read,

'Put up or shut up.'

While the tattoo suggested to Rockland the man was a boxer, the lack of calluses on his hands—his knuckles specifically—revealed the tattoo was a lie.

The colonel stewed on how bleak the outlook for his future was. "Twenty-five to life," he thought out loud. He let out a depressed sigh and rolled over to face the wall.

"Without the possibility of parole." Rockland heard a disturbing gravelly voice say.

"Who said that?" He asked, searching for the imperceptible source.

"Me." The voice answered. "They can't hear a word I'm saying to you, but they can hear you. So, be careful."

"Quiet down, new blood," Owen complained.

"Who are you?" Rockland whispered at the wall.

"Just a friend, that's all. A friend that could be very useful to you right about now."

"How's that?"

"Life without possibility of parole—doesn't mean without possibility of escape."

"Ok, I'm already losing it. Jesus, I'm talking to a shadow!"

"New blood! Didn't you hear the man tell you to shut up?" Bruce yelled.

"I can help you and you can help me. There will be a point very soon where you have to make a choice, either me or misery." The wicked voice continued.

"I'm living in misery already. Do you hear them? That's who I live with. These are my cellmates."

"Good, the choice won't be hard then when it gets worse."

"Worse? Worse than life without the possibility of parole?"

"Your cellmates are fairly calm for murderers—for now anyway."

"I can handle them. Hell, if I slap them around it might get me some time to myself in solitary. So thanks, but no thanks."

"When things get worse, call into the shadows for Domovoi, I'll be waiting for you."

"You'll be waiting for a while." Rockland arrogantly declared.

"I doubt that entirely." The voice laughed maniacally and faded away into the shadows.

"Whatever, I must already be out of my mind." Rockland turned away from the wall he was just conversing with.

"You don't hear too good, son." Owen stood up and cracked his neck.

Rockland smirked.

"Answer me, newbie! I said, 'you don't hear too good!'" Owen shouted.

"I hear just fine. I rolled over in my bed. You're really going to be a little bitch about that?"

Bruce wind-milled his burly arms, apparently getting ready for a scrap. Owen neared Rockland. "I got six years in here, new blood. I don't get told, I tell. I'm telling you to quit with the noise. Get it...bitch?"

Rockland rolled over to face the wall again, predicting the next step of the escalating situation and already comfortably prepared for it.

He wasn't disappointed. Owen seized the back of Rockland's jumpsuit and yanked with all his might. Rockland kicked off the wall and he threw himself into his antagonist's face. When Rockland rolled over, he seized Owen's soft throat with his closest hand. While he dropped off of the bunk, Bruce was standing within perfect striking distance of the falling colonel. Rockland gritted his teeth and with the force of all his weight behind him, he tried to put his fist through the back of Bruce's head. The blood streamed down Bruce's broad face and his head snapped back. The merciless force knocked him unconscious. Rockland landed behind Owen, turning the front choke into a tense sleeper hold.

"You're dead! Let me go, asshole!" Owen howled in as demanding of a voice that he could muster.

"Have it your way, old blood." Rockland pushed the inmate into the wall and awaited the next feeble attempt. Owen turned around, his arm cocked way back. He foolishly telegraphed his next move to Rockland who predicted the menace was going to swing at his face. When Owen let his amateur hand fly, Rockland ducked the blow. Rockland seized his attacker by the back of the jumpsuit and drove a damaging knee into the attacker's kidney. Owen let out a wide-mouthed, blood-curdling howl and fell to his knees. Rockland grabbed the back of the defeated attacker's head and slammed his face into the cold, callous floor. The persistent nuisance painfully joined the other cellmate in a gruesome unconsciousness.

"You!" the nearest guard exclaimed. "On the ground now! Get on the ground!"

Rockland faced the guard on the other side of the bars. The man drew his service pistol on Rockland and made his demands again. The colonel kneeled on the ground and put his hands behind his head. "On the ground, scumbag!" the guard hollered again.

Rockland didn't say anything. He dropped from his knees to his chest. A heavily suited up riot squad stormed through the cell door and secured the colonel's hands and feet in restraints.

Rockland was indifferent to the situation. On one hand, he would be placed in solitary confinement for administering such a savage beating. It was however likely that when he was placed back in the general prison population, he would probably have to face more aggressive pests, or maybe friends of the men that he had just overpowered. The colonel's cellmates were taken to the on-site emergency ward to be treated for the severe wounds.

Unsure of why he too was brought to the unit, Rockland was also taken to a separate wing of the medical ward. The doors to the medical ward opened and the colonel was now being escorted by three of the prison's largest guards. The guard's aggressive tempers paralleled their obnoxious size.

Rockland's hands were strictly bound in front of him with handcuffs that had no chain between the cuffs. His feet were bound by a chain that was double-wrapped around each ankle. A long chain connected his handcuffs to the chain that was around his ankles, limiting his potential for motion even further. Rockland inched his feet along as he was escorted passed the nurse's station. The nurses watched in awe at the size and defined build of the handsome colonel. They indulged themselves as they stared at his strong frame and masculine face. One nurse turned to

173

another and whispered something in her friend's ear—immediately causing her to blush.

The guards directed Rockland to an open room where there was a stunning female physician waiting for him. The elegant physician had porcelain skin, medium-length straight red hair and perfect teeth. Her bright blue eyes were framed by her fashionable glasses and her thin nose was stylishly pierced. The nose-stud was a trifle rebellious, yet somehow contemporarily professional. Rockland liked it.

"On the scale, please," she said as she looked up from the clipboard she was holding. He didn't say anything. He did as he was told. With effort, he got himself up onto the scale. "An iron-clad 273 lbs." She said as she wrote down the results on her clip-board.

"How tall are you, Richard?"

"6'7'"" Rockland shifted his gaze from the wall in front of him to the average sized physician.

"I believe it!" She nervously laughed, trying to make herself more comfortable with the intimidating goliath in front of her. In her fear, she held her breath, a cute little quirk under the circumstances. It was an idiosyncrasy Rockland had seen in many men's faces just before he sent them to their maker. Rockland gave her a small smile to ease her visible discomfort.

"Don't be nervous," he whispered. "I'd never hurt you."

"Thank you." She cleared her throat, "Um, any allergies?"

"No."

"Any medical conditions we should be made aware of?"

Rockland just shook his head 'No.'

She adjusted her glasses. "Will you please have a seat upon the examination table?"

Rockland complied.

"May I take your vitals now, please?" The doctor asked in as polite of a tone as she could.

Rockland shook his head 'yes' and the doctor put an oversized blood pressure cuff around the his arm and got the readings she needed.

"Wow, you're blood pressure and your pulse are both very good! They're especially good for having just had to defend yourself and for being such a sizeable man."

Rockland appreciated the fact that she didn't assume that he just bullied his cellmates. "Thank you," he said apologetically as he stared into her gentle eyes.

"You must do a lot of running?" she guessed.

"I do."

"And your teeth are immaculate, what's your secret?"

"Lots of toothpaste," Rockland replied.

The doctor blurted out a loud, awkward laugh. "I'm sorry." She balanced her temperament, effectively deadening her charming personality, "I'm now going to administer this sedative. It's standard protocol after there has been a fight in a cell."

The colonel sighed with his eyes locked on the floor. It was clear that any protest was just going to give them more of a reason to sedate him. The physician sterilized the injection site and carefully inserted the syringe into his deltoid. "You'll start feeling that shortly. We have a gurney just outside the door that we're going to ask you to lay upon. That is how we will have to transport you to your new unit."

"Let's go, Rockland!" The largest jailer, a man of some seven feet, demanded.

Rockland again noticed that he was a spectacle for all of the eyes in the medical ward. He lowered his head then propped himself up on the gurney and slowly laid down. As they wheeled him to his new unit, he felt the sedation. The lights over his head were blurring until the luminescence of the individual lights ran together. He turned his head to the side. The walls were just a gray blur. None of the otherwise discernible features of the walls were evident to the colonel. He began to willingly slip into unconsciousness. He eventually succumbed to the powerful hypnosis of the sedative.

CHAPTER 16: BAD DECISIONS

Tyson entered the hospital room to find a motionless Harlie sitting alone. Her hand mercilessly squeezed her forehead and her eyes were cast upon the floor. Tyson gazed at Harlie's ill-fated father in the hopeless hospital bed. He quickly deduced that Grayson would not be alive very much longer. The man laid there with tubes in his mouth, IVs in his arms and numerous dressed wounds. His heart monitor indicated a slow heart beat and the screen said, 'Bradycardia' in the bottom left corner. Tyson's eyes began to well up when he felt a lump in his throat.

Before he approached Harlie, he took in the terribly unsympathetic room. The scuffed tile floors, the colorless walls, the aged ceilings—it was all very insensitive.

Tyson dried his eyes and with a firm grasp on the flowers, he knocked gently on the door. Harlie wiped away the tears from her cheeks, stood up and walked over to Tyson. She wrapped her arms around him in her fondest embrace. He held her tightly in his arms and allowed her to cry out whatever tears she had left. She was tapped out, too tired from the stresses of the day. She had cried all that she possibly could for one day.

"It's ok if you need to let it out," Tyson said, "We all cry. You've even got me going a little bit." Tyson assured her as he held her close to him.

"I've been crying all day. At this point I'm more apt to

177

fall asleep standing right here." She stood there in Tyson's tight embrace, realizing how comfortable she was. His body temperature was so much higher than an average human's. He emitted comforting warmth.

Tyson walked over to the hospital bed with Harlie. They sat down in the two chairs by the bed, hoping, praying for some life-saving miracle that would make life all better again.

"What time did it happen?" Tyson asked.

"Around 11:30 this morning."

"He was in a car accident?"

"According to a witness report, a seemingly drunk driver in an SUV was seen. He ran a red light like a madman and struck the driver's side door. And now, my dad, and this…" Harlie gestured at the bed, speechless, and frustrated. She began crying again.

Tyson grabbed her hand. Unsure of what to say, he just listened to her.

Between uncoordinated breaths in all her angry tears she managed to choke out, "Why? They drink, they get behind the wheel and then they take my father from me! God damn it! He worked hard his whole life! He has always been a moral, faithful man. Why do bad things always happen to good people?" Harlie bit her quivering lip until it leaked a drop of blood. "They still haven't found the bastard."

"I'm so sorry, Harlie. I don't know what to say. I'm kind of bad at this."

"Bad at what?"

"Well, talking for one, being comforting for another, I wish I knew what to say." Tyson's small reversion into his charming awkwardness made Harlie smile.

"You're doing just fine." She wrapped her arms around him again, only tighter. "Thanks for being with me."

"I'll be here as long as you need me."

"See, you're not as bad at it as you think you are."

Tyson smiled politely. Harlie snuggled up against him as she cast her dampened eyes sadly upon her father.

While Tyson stayed with Harlie, Pat slowly inched towards the room that Mrs. Wright occupied. It seemed to him that he practiced his apology a thousand times in his head. He stepped cautiously towards the door, now considering a new possibility. He wondered if Wright would be mad he showed up to the hospital. Granted, over the past couple weeks they really came to good terms. Pat was trying harder in school and Wright had eased up on him when he'd see Pat harmlessly carrying on in the hallways.

A simple, "C'mon, Pat, get to class," had replaced getting berated in front of anyone in the student body who would listen to the principle's sarcastic rants. Pat was unsure of what he was doing now. *'Of course he'll be mad. I'm getting disciplined, that's why we're on the football field at 6:00 every morning.'* Pat thought to himself. He turned around to walk the other way, but an average-sized, sharply-dressed doctor was standing there looking up at him. On the doctor's lapel there were pins of an American and a Gabonese flag.

"I'm Dr. Jean-Luc Gionet," he said with a thick French accent as he smiled politely.

"Oh, you're Jean-Claude's dad? Tyson's friend from Africa! You're his dad!"

"Right, what brings you here, young man?"

"Bad decisions I think, Dr. Gionet."

"Is that right?" Dr. Gionet chuckled at the response. "Bad decisions *often* bring people to the hospital—they're usually my patients."

Pat couldn't help but laugh with the amiable doctor. "My case is unique. I think."

"How's that, now?"

"Well, if you hadn't guessed by lookin' at me—I'm kind of a punk."

"Punks don't bring flowers to their principle's wife when she's ill, Patrick. You're no punk."

"You know who I am?"

"Of course I do. I go to all of my son's football games. You've been on his team for some time. Through Jean-Claude, who knows through Tyson, I know what's going on with you and Principle Wright. You're really doing the right thing. Now, don't 'punk-out' and leave. That's the easy way out. Go in and say what's on your mind to Principle Wright. Wait a little while for his wife to wake up and apologize. She'll hopefully be up soon, but I can't guarantee it." The doctor winked and turned around. He went to a medicine cabinet, selected a syringe and walked towards one of the patient's rooms.

"Thank you, Dr. Gionet." Pat smiled a nervous smile.

Dr. Gionet smiled back, "Don't mention it, Pat. You're a good kid. Don't forget that."

It wasn't often that Pat was called, "a good kid." He turned around with a new feeling of confidence and approached the room where the principle and his wife were. Just as Tyson had done, he had stood in the doorway, before entering. He too noticed that the room was industrial. Everything was metal, or on cold, ugly, metal supports. He noticed the woman in the bed. She was sleeping peacefully. She had an IV in her arm, but she was stable and would be transferred to the general ward soon.

Pat knocked on the door gently and civilly cleared his throat. Wright was at the window-sill contemplating the bright city below. The principle turned around, eyes wide as a big smile ran across his face.

"Pat?" Wright asked.

"I'd like to first apologize if I'm intruding, Principle Wright." Pat again began thinking that he might have crossed the line.

"Nothing could be further from the truth. We could really use the company." Wright smiled. The principle walked up to the teenager and welcomed him into the room with a hearty hand-shake. Wright began speaking. "I've gotta confess, kid, I didn't expect this."

"I know, but I wanted to tell you this morning at practice that I'd look forward to a chance to apologize to you and to your wife." Pat nervously cleared his throat. "So, I'm sorry for what I did to you both. I'm sorry for the stress I've caused you these past few years. I'm sorry for the disgusting, cowardly insult to your wife. I heard from a new close friend, 'There's plenty of time left to get it right.' I want to make everything right.'"

"There's more time left than you know. And I know you're going to get it right. You've already begun getting it right." Wright added as he pulled up another chair, "If you have nothing better to do, you're more than welcome to stick around. If you have things to do, I won't be insulted if you have to go about and get things done."

"I've got my homework done. I don't have anywhere to be. I'd like to stay and apologize if I may."

"I'm impressed. It sounds like you've got it figured out, son."

"Not all of it." Pat awkwardly smiled as he sat down in the chair that Wright was offering him. "I'm ready to learn though."

A few hours had passed. Wright and Pat had talked the entire time about everything there was to talk about. There were no awkward pauses. There was no conversing that was uncomfortable or forced. They shared a lot of laughs and Wright had even told Pat that of all of his referrals he laughed at about six of them.

"Which ones did you find funny?" Pat asked the principle enthusiastically.

"C'mon, Pat, I can't encourage delinquent behavior."

"Mr. Wright, I'm done with all that now! I swear I'm done with all of that. I'm ready to start over. You gotta tell me! Please! Which ones did you find funny?"

"When you went over the lunch counter and made yourself some food because you didn't like the lunch menu that was kind of funny."

Pat laughed. "It is kind of funny looking back on it. C'mon, Mr. Wright, you've enjoyed some of my other work."

The two heard a knock at the door. It was Alan. Wright stood up and welcomed him in with a handshake.

"Let me get you a seat," Wright offered as he walked over to the unoccupied side of the room and grabbed a chair. He easily picked up the bulky piece of furniture and set it down behind the man who just entered.

"Thank you, Ethan," Alan replied as he sat down cautiously.

"Dad, I'm surprised to see you!"

"I know, son. I'm surprised I'm here too. It's necessary though, I need to be here."

"It wouldn't have been a problem, Dad. I could've walked home or gotten a ride with Tyson."

Alan glanced up at the principle.

"Now?" Wright asked Alan.

"If I may,"

"Absolutely," Wright walked over to the door, he caught the nurse's eye and asked for ten minutes of privacy. The nurse noted the time as well as Mary's condition and approved. Wright closed the door and blinded the observation window.

"What's going on, Dad? Is everything ok?" Pat swiveled around, shifting glances between the principle and his father.

"I hope so. I have something to tell you Pat that may come as a shock to you."

"What's wrong? Is Mom ok? Are you ok?"

"Mom's fine. I'm fine. Everyone is ok."

"Then what's the matter?"

"There is some news you may take as bad and other news that I'm hoping you think is the most awesome thing you've ever heard. You're a unique kid, Pat."

"What's this about?" Pat asked defensively.

"It's about a special bond that you and Principle Wright share. I unfortunately don't share that bond with you. I'm not quite sure how to say it." Alan hung his head.

"What?" Pat asked, still on guard, "Please, Dad, look at me. What are you trying to tell me?"

Alan looked up and noticed that Principle Wright was standing behind Pat.

Wright's confidently folded arms were surrounded by graceful white wings that wrapped around his body and draped to the floor. The bright and elegant wings found their way out of Wright's shirt collar. With a loud snap, Wright spanned the wings the length of the room.

Pat turned around, "What the...hell?" Pat's mouth gaped open as he nearly drooled in his incomprehension. His young brow furrowed and he sat there stammering in his disbelief.

"I'm sorry...Aaron," Alan said.

"Aaron?" The young man crossly inquired. "Damn it! Explain it to me now! Words! Please! I can't take anymore of this code-speak! And what's with the 'lookit Birdman is behind you' routine? What's goin' on?" He turned around to face Wright, "What are you?" After a moment of silence he

185

concluded his rant with a long exasperated sigh as he slammed his head back in his chair.

Principle Wright began to speak. "The short version is you were adopted as an infant, by Mr. and Mrs. Alan McNamara. You were renamed 'Patrick.' Your biological parents were killed serving their order. The order I belong to and the order you belong to."

"Order! Order?" Pat threw his maddened hands in the air, "What?"

"You, Aaron, and I—are Avia. The McNamaras are wonderful people who came to the rescue of a forsaken child. You were born an Avia that wasn't given a chance by a series of unfortunate events that rendered you parentless. Your adoptive mother and father gave you the chance that you deserve. They love you just as much as your biological parents did."

A tear of disbelief trickled down Pat's cheek as he turned his tearful face to his father. "Is it true, Dad?"

"Yes, it is true. I'm sorry, Patrick." Alan said, also with a tear careening down his long face. "You're still Patrick to me. You're still my son. You're still Patrick McNamara." Alan paused to think. "And Principle Wright is correct, I love you very much, son." Alan put his hand on the confused teenager's shoulder. The hand on his shoulder turned into a paternal embrace.

Pat couldn't be mad. He didn't feel lied to as many teenagers would in such a situation. He felt protected. He felt closer than he ever had to his father. He also felt disappointed in himself. He was saddened by the grief he had given them in the past despite what they had done for him. His mind was teeming with thoughts he couldn't yet define and questions he couldn't answer.

Wright spoke up, "You *can* have it both ways on this one, kid. To your parents you're Pat. To me and your order, you're Aaron. Your family and your order will always accept you. And when you're ready, there is still a lot more I'd like to tell you." Wright paused to gauge Aaron's response.

Aaron nodded slowly.

"Alan is still your father and you're still a McNamara. You'll always be Patrick to him."

"Did my biological parents have a last name?"

"They did." Wright replied.

"What was it?"

"Now's not the right time, Aaron. I want you to think of yourself as the McNamara that you are. It'll help you sustain your mental health."

"Somehow that makes sense." The mind-blown Aaron agreed.

The room was silent. The bewildered young man sat there in his chair thinking about the astonishing truth and unable to stop staring at Wright's wings. Principle Wright turned and looked out the window at the night sky.

"Do you like to watch the birds outside, Aaron?" Wright asked.

"Nothing makes me happier."

"I thought so." Wright peeked over his winged shoulder and smiled then gazed thoughtfully into the night sky.

Despite its dispassionate décor—or lack-there-of décor, the hospital room did afford a beautiful view of the clear Honolulu evening. Stars blazed vividly and the orange moon had an impressive robustness. Beyond the city lights, the peaceful surface of the ocean was visible. The room remained quiet for some time before the silence was again broken.

"You said you had more to tell me when I'm ready," Aaron began. "Just give me some time and I'll return when I'm ready if I may. I might as well find out more about this blessing or curse tonight. I want to get all the surprises out of the way. There is someone I need to talk to though."

"Take your time, son." Alan encouraged, again embracing his adopted son.

"All that you need." Principle Wright added as he completely turned around from the window. "There's an exquisite balcony at the end of the hall through the double set of doors. The view is unbelievable...and for what it's worth, it may make everything go down a little easier."

Aaron left the room silently. He needed to talk to Tyson.

Aaron walked down the hallway as a thousand thoughts still flooded his mind. With each step he took, another question presented itself, *'What were my parents like? Who were they? What does it mean to be an Avia? Who is the man he calls Principle Wright? What new responsibilities did he have? What benefits are there to being an Avia? Would he ever meet more Avia? Were there any other Avia that he went to school with?'*

He closed in on the door where Tyson was with Harlie and her critically injured father. He walked into the doorway and saw Harlie resting her head on Tyson. They had exchanged their separate chairs for a hospital 'love-seat' and turned out the lights. The previously unsympathetic hospital room was made somewhat romantic by the natural evening light.

Aaron knocked on the door softly—rousing Harlie from her sleep and getting Tyson's attention. Aaron beheld the dazzling girl he had unintentionally awakened. "I'm sorry, Harlie. I'm sorry for everything that's happened. You don't deserve such difficulty."

"Thank you, Pat. That's sweet. With Tyson here though, well, he has helped make this dreadful situation less painful."

"I can believe it. And for what it's worth, I'm sorry for how much of a jerk Vinnie has been."

"I know, Pat. You're a good guy. Please stay that way. Don't let Vinnie get through to you ever again."

"You bet! I'm done with all that."

"Good."

"And I hate to ask, but I was wondering if I can be a jerk and borrow Tyson for about twenty minutes? It won't be any longer. I'm really sorry, but I just need him for twenty minutes."

Harlie lifted her weary head and looked at her handsome boyfriend's face "It's no problem at all. I've been selfish. I've kept Tyson here all day. I'll understand if you need to go home too, Tyse. I appreciate you being with me for all the time you have been here."

"Don't worry," Tyson said to Harlie. "I told you that I was staying with you tonight and I meant it, but I gotta see what I can do for Pat."

"That's Tyson—saving the world one person at a time." Harlie kissed Tyson's cheek and took her weight off of him allowing him to get to his feet.

Tyson walked over to his friend, "It's been quite a day," Tyson said as he spied Harlie who was now laying down on the love-seat. She was petite enough to fit her entire body on the small piece of furniture. Tyson watched her lay there for about a minute as she closed her eyes and drifted off to a sleep that delayed the bad news she was sure to get at any time.

"You said it," the young man in the doorway agreed.

"What's going on? Did you apologize to Mrs. Wright?"

"No, not yet, she hasn't come to."

"Really? Is she going to be ok?"

"I think so."

"Then what's wrong?" inquired the concerned Tyson.

"Can I talk to you outside on the balcony?"

"Yeah, sure, lead the way."

The fluorescent light of the hospital hallways was very bright and their eyes adjusted slowly, almost painfully, to the excessive luminescence.

"They have a terrace we're allowed to go out on?" Tyson asked.

"Yeah, apparently they do. Principle Wright told me it was just outside of those doors at the end of the hallway."

"That's cool. I'd like to get outside for a little bit."

The two boys made their way to the end of the fluorescent hallway. Tyson grabbed two water bottles off of a courtesy cart that had single-serve refreshments on it. They walked down the hallway and opened the hospital-green doors that separated them from the impressive hovering terrace.

They walked outside onto the airy balcony. The terrace was a large semi-circle that extended about twenty feet from the main building. It was styled with contemporary, weather-resistant furniture. The furniture on the balcony was pastel colored. There were numerous planters with rich colors and densely populated flower beds. The boys walked to the balcony edge and rested their arms on it as they eyed the city below them.

"What's on your mind, Pat?" Tyson smiled at his friend. "Are you ok?"

"Can I ask you something?" Aaron had a hard time meeting eyes with Tyson.

"Sure, anything." Tyson handed his friend one of the bottles of water.

"Anything?"

"You bet." Tyson nodded his head.

"What's an Ahi? What does it mean to be an Ahi? Is that what the tour-guide at the lab called you, an Ahi?"

Tyson irritably huffed. "Maybe this question would've been better suited for another day, Pat," Tyson sighed then turned around and walked toward the door that lead back inside.

Just as Tyson was about retreat back inside, the confused teenager called out to his otherwise sage friend, "I just found out I'm an Avia."

Tyson immediately stopped then cautiously wandered back to Pat.

"What did you say?" Tyson's nose unflared, his brow

furrowed and the frustration appeared to have gone away.

Aaron wasn't quite sure what to say. He didn't know if what he just said was a good or bad thing. He swallowed a dilatory gulp, cleared his throat and restated what he had just shouted to his friend. "I, uh, just found out that I'm a…Avia. What does that mean? Is that good or bad?"

Tyson hugged Aaron. "That's the best news I've heard in a long time!"

"Tyson, why are you hugging me?"

Tyson released his friend from the hug, realizing he had only made him more nervous. Tyson reassumed his relaxed stance, again resting his half-folded arms on the balcony's balustrade as his friend did. "You're a good ally to have in a surely unstable time to come. It's fantastic news that you're an Avia. You're going to find out though that we're in the midst of a potentially chaotic time as far as the Lost Orders of Exa are considered. So what does it mean to be Avia?" Tyson rubbed his hands together. "It means you can fly, bro."

"What?"

Tyson thought about the situation at hand and made an assumption. "So Principle Wright is an Avia, huh?"

"How the hell did you figure that out?"

"Something that the principle said to me on the football field got me thinking. Now that I think of it, the way he didn't care that I was an Ahi. That combined with the fact that you're finding out now. He was waiting to tell you, that is why he has been disciplining you." Tyson thought for another minute and said, "Can I ask you something?"

"Anything."

"Anything?" Tyson asked with a quiet ironic laugh, shifting his gaze from the beautiful view back to his friend.

The bewildered teenager shook his head 'yes' and waited for Tyson's question.

"How do I say this without making you uncomfortable?" Tyson thought out loud.

"Just ask. I can't get any more confused. I couldn't feel any weirder than I do now. Yesterday, if you told me certain people can fly, I would've given you the number to the local drunk-tank. Now, I don't know what to believe. Even you, Tyson—a kid I know I can trust—you're telling me I can fly. It seems so…"

"Ridiculous?"

"Yes!" Aaron laughed out of a combination of frustration and weariness.

"I'm not trying to sound insensitive, but I'm forced to assume that you were adopted. Is that correct?" Tyson paused for a second realizing how personal that question was. "If you don't want to answer that, I'll understand," he said as he made an apologetic hand wave.

Aaron just nodded and remained silent.

"Ok then," Tyson said, choosing his words more carefully and trying to deliver them more sensitively. "May I ask if Pat is your real name?"

"My name is supposedly, 'Aaron', and again, how the hell did you know I was adopted?"

"It's simple logic. Let's sit down in those chairs and we'll talk about it. I do know a little bit about your order. I'm no expert, but I think it's just enough to help ready you to go back in there to talk with Principle Wright."

Aaron followed his friend to the wooden Adirondack chairs that were separated from all the other fashionable furniture on the terrace.

"Would you be more comfortable if I called you 'Aaron' or 'Pat'?"

"You can call me 'Aaron' when no one else is around and 'Pat' when we're at school—at least until I feel comfortable enough to tell other people about it. Honestly, I do like the name 'Aaron' better."

Tyson could tell that Aaron was feeling the very same feelings that almost drove him back into the hospital five minutes earlier. He was feeling uncomfortable about others not understanding his heritage. The feelings alone of the heritage stirred the soul. It was an uncomfortable feeling at first.

"Trust me, man. Here-and-now I'm tellin' ya, you'll never be totally comfortable with it. In the Avia territory, it'll be different. Being amongst your own is entirely different. You asked me what it means to be an Avia." Tyson resumed the conversation where it was cut short.

"That's right."

Tyson cleared his throat, "The Avia are the oldest order. They're a very noble order. They're also *not* terribly numerous."

"Why's that?"

"Your order is possibly the most blessed, or perhaps the most cursed of all of the orders. It all depends on how your perspective. Most of the people in your order see it as a curse, but your biological mother and father saw it as a blessing no doubt." Tyson studied Aaron as he sat there. Aaron's eyes closed as he reclined as far back as the Adirondack chair would allow.

Aaron reopened his eyes and focused on his friend. "Why am I so blessed?" He asked with a sarcastic upward inflection in his voice. He changed his demeanor and his tone to reflect the day that passed, "Or why am I so cursed?"

"An Avia lives on average about one thousand years."

Aaron's jaw dropped and he felt a chill run up his spine. He shook his head in disbelief saying, "You've got to be kidding me! That's impossible!"

"It's about as impossible as a human budding wings and flying, right? Let me remind you, Aaron—you can do that. Principle Wright will show you how. And I'm sorry I'm

196

the one that has to tell you, but the human idea of impossibility doesn't apply to anything for you anymore." Tyson took a pack of gum out of his pocket and offered a stick to Aaron, "Gum makes life a little easier."

Aaron laughed as he took a stick. "So, if Avia live the longest, shouldn't we have the largest population?"

"That's where the blessing versus a curse thing comes in."

Aaron raised an eyebrow, a cue for an explanation from Tyson. "I'm listening."

"Avian adults think about their lives before they have kids. Only few of your people love the idea of the excessively lengthy lifespan. Few people consider it a blessing and reproduce. A lot less than one percent of your population reproduces. Many of them kill themselves after a while."

"*Awesome*," Aaron scoffed then paused for a minute—contemplating the therapeutic sounds of the not too distant ocean, the view of the orange moon and the bustling city he could hear below them. "How do you know all this?"

"As you reminded me a few minutes ago, I'm an Ahi. It's the Ahi principle to know a little bit about every order."

"Oh? Well, what else is out there?" Aaron softly kneaded his temples, trying to relax.

"This isn't too much for you? Don't you want a break from it?"

"I might as well do some listening. It's easier than research." Aaron looked at his cell phone and realized they had been out on the terrace for almost thirty minutes. "Oh man, I'm sorry! I should let you get back to Harlie. We've been out here for a while."

"It's no problem." Tyson assured Aaron, "I'm sure she's long gone dreaming the rest of the night away. She needs her sleep. I don't think tomorrow is going to be a very good day. I'm going to need to be there for her the whole time. So, I'm free now and I can talk if you want to know anything else."

"I'm all ears," said Aaron.

"There's a lot out there and I'm not even close to knowing it all. What I do know about is the Zoree, the Ahi, the Avia, La Tormenta and the depraved Keaka. There may even be more that I don't know about."

"Tell me about your order first," Aaron insisted. "You've been here telling me about myself. I'm listening if you want to tell me about yourself. I know it almost drove you to leave me out here. So, if you don't want to I'll understand."

"That was a jerkish thing of me to do and I'm sorry. It's unfortunately one of the Ahi's worst flaws. At times, our anger gets in the way of our thinking."

"That's a human trait, that's not unique to your order," Aaron supposed.

"The Ahi were born to be thinkers first and doers or speakers after that. Anger renders us completely thoughtless and very violent when stirred to anger. A Zoree from the water heritage, like Vinnie, is a doer or a speaker before thinking, but nothing will get him so angry that he's rendered thoughtless."

"That's only two of the groups you mentioned."

"Well, you know about as much as I know about the Avia," Tyson confessed.

"La Tormenta was the next order you mentioned."

"They're also a rare breed, scarce as the Ahi. The Tormentan territory is believed to be in the area of the Valdes Peninsula in Argentina. They're very charming and often very attractive. It's been said that thunderstorms happen when a Tormentan male satisfies a woman."

Aaron scrunched his face. "That's…interesting?"

"The Zoree and La Tormenta have always been allies. Even before the chaos, back in our previous Exa, they shared the same home."

"What's this 'Exa' you mentioned?"

"Exa was the land where all of the orders dwelt in harmony. An apocalyptic war destroyed it. We refer to it as, 'The day the moon attacked the Earth.' The result was chaos. From chaos there came Earth, or 'New-Exa' as we call it."

"Who's in charge of all this?" an intent Aaron asked.

"The mavens are the overseers of certain orders. Some orders don't have mavens. As far as I know, the Avia have not chosen a maven, but a king. As I hear it, they serve as watchers and information sources for the mavens. It's a very important position. I've heard their leader is a triord."

"Oh, what's a triord?"

"It's a person with the capability of three-orders. It's considered a victory amongst the triord's first order and failure by the orders whose abilities were acquired."

"Like an intense game of capture the flag with super powers?"

Tyson shrugged. "That's not a bad way of thinkin' about it. There are diords as well and different kinds too, such as the Azoree. They're both Ahi and Zoree."

"That's crazy! What about that last one you mentioned?" Aaron asked, curious about the name he couldn't make heads or tails of. "Keaka?"

"The Keaka are the vilest and most despicable creatures to ever roam this otherwise fair planet."

"Really?"

"Keaka are shadow-dwelling, spirit-hijacking parasites. They get in your mind, integrate themselves in your body and make you do horrible things. They can do this to more than one person at once, but I don't know how. They abandon you after they've used you and leave you to suffer the consequences of their actions no matter how horrible. If you're lucky, they force you to kill yourself after their inhabitance."

"Whoa, that's heavy!" Aaron thoughtfully traced the front of his hair line with his thumb and forefinger.

"We don't know much about the Keaka. We only know there are two common motives for their evil ways. Some of them love power, especially a scheming rise to power. Others just enjoy crippling the world. The Keaka wait in the shadows for a soul they can overpower, or a dead body they can inhabit. They have no community. Their home is in the shadows. As far as we know, every Keaka is out for itself."

The boys heard the door behind them open. Harlie was standing there in the moonlight, nearly asleep. "Hey, I just woke up," she said. "Wow! It's incredible out here. Do you mind if I join you guys?"

"Not at all, I'm sorry I kept him so long," Aaron said. Harlie wearily looked at Tyson.

"You can sit here," Tyson got up out of his chair to offer it to Harlie.

Jean-Claude came out of the door behind Harlie.

"Hey, Claude!" Tyson said.

"What's goin' on?" A preoccupied Jean-Claude greeted his friends as he pulled up a chair.

Harlie gently pushed Tyson back into the chair, the scent of her shampoo danced under his nose. "You're too much," she said. "You've done so much for me. I just wanted some air."

Tyson glimpsed at his best friend, "I'm sorry, Claude! I know that we were supposed to hangout today."

"No problem, Tyse. I knew you had to be here. Life happens. I was just dropping off my dad's dinner—he forgot it at home. Am I intruding? I can bounce if ya want."

"No way," Tyson and Aaron chorused.

Jean-Claude relaxed with his hands behind his head. "This is a pretty cool place. I sometimes study here."

Tyson and Aaron both agreed.

Harlie walked over to the balustrade and beheld the moon amongst the stars. She replaced the air in her lungs with a deep breath and realized how much easier it was to cope thirteen stories over the lively Honolulu.

CHAPTER 17: LOOKING FOR MARA

Ashley's eyes were sorrowfully glazed beyond her rain saturated windshield. The hypnotic drops coated the shiny white Lexus as it cut through the stormy weather. The brightly lit up buildings created a bustling atmosphere, but the excitement was lost on Ashley. There was a nervous feeling deep within her when she thought about how she traded her soul for a flashy car, expensive clothing, diamond jewelry and prestige. A tear trickled down her cheek at the thought the betrayal and lies that she had committed in her ruthless scramble to the top.

Ashley finally pulled up to the rear of the valet line at the Komiama Block, the elegant restaurant where the spirit named Mara demanded she meet him. There was a line of five cars in front of her. Ashley inched up in her car as her place in the procession drew her nearer to the door. As she crept up to the canopied curbside in front of the exclusive restaurant, she was greeted by an impossibly polite valet who opened the door for her. He faultlessly regurgitated the greeting he spoke to every guest at the restaurant hosted that evening.

"A very good evening to you, Madame," he spewed after he opened the door. Ashley put her feet out of the car, exposing her tan, shapely legs and her silver high-heels. She stood up gracefully out of her opulent conveyance and exposed her form-fitting cranberry dress. Ashley garnered the attention of everyone lined up under the canopy.

The men imagined being the lucky man waiting for the elegant lady in the red dress. The women with them were jealous of the stunning blond woman who seemingly glided towards the entrance.

"Sheer perfection, *Madame*," the doorman politely complimented as he held the door open and gave a 'look-at-you' gesture with his hands. Ashley nodded in gratitude as she entered the grand foyer of the restaurant. Black velvet carpets with ornate design lay under her feet. There were impeccably dressed waiters and waitresses who made their rounds with trays of esoteric *hors d'oeuvres*.

As Ashley made her way towards the main ballroom, the foyer became a lounge with various furniture pieces that appeared to have never been occupied. Giant French-doors with a clearance of approximately thirty feet separated the guests in the lounge from those in the main ballroom. Guests were seated at tables surrounding the marble dance floor at the bottom of the double wrap-around stairs within the glorified cafeteria.

Ashley noticed a man standing at balcony just beyond the great doors. She couldn't help but be drawn towards him. She neared the man in the white dinner jacket and black pants who held a glass of champagne. He sipped from it delicately as he observed the satisfied guests below him.

She tapped his shoulder, smelling a masculine scent as he turned around to greet her.

"Can I help, Madame?" He smiled brightly as he admired her—from her stunning made-up face to her pedicured toes. His green eyes lit up and his sharp eyebrows raised when Ashley's beauty finally sank in to him. Ashley peeked up at him. Her long, feminine eye-lashes were gently curled and heralded the sight of her radiant, yet troubled eyes. She daintily extended her hand to introduce herself to the man.

He gently received her greeting and kissed her hand softly. The masculine stubble that his face hosted tickled Ashley's hand. "What may I call you?" He inquired with a barely noticeable Spanish accent.

Ashley tenderly replied, "I'm Ashley," in a quiet, nervous tone.

"Well, Ashley, I'm remarkably glad I've met you. You're a diamond among the coal." He carefully put his champagne glass down on the balcony, "Why do I have the privilege of speaking with you this evening?"

Ashley thought for a second, basking in the atmosphere. If Mara wasn't in her life, what she said next might be a normal response. If Mara wasn't in her life, this night might be an ordinary evening that would turn into something beautiful. The stark reality for Ashley was that this man, who was possibly the most attractive man she'd ever seen, was just a pawn of an evil being that toyed with Ashley's emotions.

Ashley wondered to herself, what emotion would the evil being fool around with next? She also wondered if was she putting this man, who she already felt a real connection with, in unnecessary danger. She didn't know the answer to either question.

Ashley closed her eyes and let out a short breath, saddened by the fact that she might jeopardize this man who she already had become infatuated with. She refocused on him and answered his question as to why he had the pleasure of meeting her. "...Because I'm looking for Mara."

The man's face immediately lost color. His hand started trembling and his fists clenched. Without making a sound, the man's face cringed and his neck contorted as his brow began to sweat. He tried to fight off the essence that was manifesting itself in him. In his sloppy frenzy, he unbuttoned his top collar button, trying to regain control over himself as he ripped off his green bowtie and concentrated on fighting the beast within him. He let out a few exhalations and gazed at Ashley, not knowing that it was her that was responsible for drawing the essence into his being. He tried to apologize for what he thought was an embarrassing display, this, 'seizure' he was having. Ashley covered her mouth and fought back tears as this man she already cared deeply for tried to fight the essence that was almost completely integrated into his soul. A few more moments of ignored, yet conspicuous facial cringing and neck contortions resulted in the return of the creepy voice that had originally came from the old man at the lounge. His eyes turned from a shimmering emerald green to an ethereal ruby color. The red faded to black.

"Hello, Ashley," he hissed.

"Mister?" Ashley replied, hoping it was possible that he fought off the invading force, despite the evidence in his voice and eyes.

"You wish it was him!" Mara said through the man's lips as he grabbed the glass of champagne in front of him and sloppily gulped down the remainder of the libation.

"I do, but a good man I'm afraid is no longer in the cards for a harlot such as myself." She wished she could take back everything she had done wrong and start life all over again.

"You said it. I didn't." Mara boorishly wiped the excess champagne from the handsome man's lips with his sleeve. "Love the dress, especially the exposed hips." Mara winked.

Ashley cringed, "Can you at least try not to act like the unbelievable hell beast you are?"

"Shut up. Don't forget, you're useful to me, not that useful. Grab my arm and let's get seated," Mara demanded as he held out the man's arm and escorted the woman down the circular stairs at an improper pace.

Once at the bottom of the stairs, an elegant waiter dressed in a tailed server's jacket nodded. From behind a host's dais he politely asked where he might seat the exquisite couple.

"In the darkest, most romantic corner," Mara requested— barely able to contain his seditious laughter.

"Yes, sir, right this way." The courteous host grabbed menus from under his podium and brought them to the table that fit the request.

"Shall we?" Mara mocked Ashley's etiquette as he tugged her along impatiently.

"Does this table meet your needs, sir?"

"Yeah," Mara impertinently took a seat and opened a menu.

The host pulled the chair out for Ashley, surprised at the rudeness of the man opposite her.

"Thank you very much." Ashley made herself as comfortable as possible in the chair being pushed under her.

"May I bring you champagne, Madame?"

"No, champagne is for celebrating. *Kina Lillet* please," Ashley stared across the table at her bizarre date. "I'll need something to stimulate my appetite."

"And for you, Eden?"

"You know him?" Ashley interrupted the waiter trying to confirm his name.

"Yes, Madame, Messieurs Eden Flores, the man you're taking dinner with, has always had rapport with the staff. A very generous and thoughtful man he is. May I bring you champagne, Messieurs Flores?"

The man across from Ashley just nodded.

Ashley was glad the spirit didn't say anything. She felt the room grow colder and her circumstances bleaker when he spoke.

"Very, good sir, I will be back right away."

"Let's get to it," Mara demanded. "What have you got for me?"

"What is it exactly that you want?"

"What do you think?" Mara hissed at his insubordinate dinner date. "Do you even care about living? You knowing what I want and getting it for me is how you get to live."

"I'm not counting on living, even if I did get you what you wanted."

"Have we done business before?" Mara laughed.

"I'm not afraid of dying anymore," Ashley snapped. "I'm afraid of disgrace. I wish I had thought before I acted, but I don't care anymore. You could kill me now," a tear trickled down her cheek as she finished her remorseful sentiment "…and I wouldn't care."

"Oh pipe down. I'm not going to kill you. I just enjoy the scrumptious fear in your darling face when you think that I'm going to. Just find me that blood."

The waiter returned with the glass of champagne and Ashley's *aperitif* wine. He took his guests' orders and assured them they wouldn't have to wait long.

"Don't worry. I found your blood." Ashley whispered to Mara..

"Is that so? Do tell."

"I'll deliver the facts about Omicron's discovery of the Neo-Exa formula to the Zoree. It's that simple."

"Elaborate," Mara demanded.

"Omicron didn't discover the formula. Jim Bankhart paid the former Ahi maven, Dawson, a boat-load of money for the secret. The Zoree will not take this well. They'll feel insulted. And their maven is among the missing. The Zoree are ready for war."

Mara thoughtfully paused, "Do you have a backup plan should this scheme of yours fail?"

"Of course," Ashley shamefully reported. "But it won't fail."

"Good." Mara decided. "I'll leave you to dine with this man for tonight. Keep in mind, I'll be watching you—closely."

"Fine."

"Call if you need me," Mara offered with an ashy laugh.

Ashley felt the menacing essence depart and she was relieved. She noticed that Eden's faculties were being restored. Eden began to speak. "Wow! I must confess I'm completely confounded. One minute we were talking at the top of the stairs, now we're down here and I have a headache that just won't quit." Eden placed a pill in his mouth and washed it down with the glass of water on the table. "I also must apologize. I know I'm sitting with an enchanting Australian woman, whose name is Ashley. I don't know much more about her though. I know despite my overall physical discomfort at the present, I couldn't feel better, or luckier. Can you fill me in on where we were or what I missed out on?"

Ashley beheld the man in front of her. She was truly apologetic for inviting Mara's inhabitance. "You were about to ask me to dance."

"Perfect. That sounds about right," Eden sipped from the glass of water in front of him again and stood up, extending his hand to escort his ravishing date in the red dress.

The elegant couple left their table and made their way through the polite society that separated them from the marble dance floor underneath the largest crystal chandelier. Eden insisted that the striking Ashley lead them out onto the dance floor. All of the heads in the room turned in time to see Ashley as she turned around and welcomed Eden to the next dance, a bolero. A business associate of Eden's saw him take the floor with the beautiful Ashley and raised his glass to him, approving of the woman with the stunning figure who so perfectly filled the red dress. Eden graciously nodded back and looked at Ashley who was unknowingly recognized by many people in the room from the media coverage of Omicron.

The couple interlocked their hands and began to competently dance impressive steps. The men and women followed the graceful couple with their inquiring eyes the entire length of their polished dance. Eden spun Ashley at the proper musical cues and Ashley stayed coordinated in her steps despite her hopelessly uncomfortable high-heels. The two were confident in their inspiring dance steps and Ashley's cares slipped away as Eden began their next conversation. "Now, I know I'm dancing with an excellent dancer named Ashley and I'm amazed. Please, tell me more about yourself."

"Gentlemen before ladies," Ashley smiled back. "What are you doing here in this ugly city?"

"I like DC. I'm visiting for a few days before I take care of business in Hawaii"

"Business in *Hawaii*?"

"Architecture is my business. I guess some buildings in Honolulu require an emergency consult. That's it. That's my story. It's your turn."

"I'm Dr. Ashley Ryker and I'm the new CEO of Omicron Laboratory—in Hawaii!"

"You *are* the woman I saw on the news! I'm sorry to hear about Dr. Bankhart. The media painted him as a saint. If you're his replacement, I'm sure he must've been one."

"Dr. Bankhart was my mentor although…"

"Although what?"

Ashley sighed. "It's a long and *very* complicated story. I just hope they get the one who killed him."

"As do I," Eden agreed picking up on her hesitance about the subject.

"…and I hope I get to see you again if you're coming to the island." Ashley wrapped her arms more intimately behind Eden's neck.

"Of course," Eden smiled.

The bolero ended.

Those around the dance floor politely applauded the beautiful couple. They each gracefully bowed to each other and waved to their appreciative onlookers before making their way back to their seats.

"I'm quite sorry if I made you uncomfortable talking about Dr. Bankhart."

"Not at all," Ashley replied, barely able to face Eden. Ever since her first meeting with Mara, she was stricken with a vulnerability that shook her up at the least opportune times. It was a kind of vulnerability felt by people when they step outside of their moral comfort zone and their conscious has a snowball effect on them.

The server brought the food and Eden thanked the man with a hundred dollar hand-shake. He politely complemented the man's service and the picturesque cuisine.

The befuddled waiter was ill-at-ease with the seemingly bipolar behavior of the man he had met before. The waiter simply did the polite thing and exchanged pleasantries with Eden.

After Eden conversed with Ashley about more trivial matters, she again felt comfortable. The couple enjoyed their meal over a more normal conversation and a few glasses of tawny Port before Eden graciously insisted on picking up the bill. Eden had a profound effect on Ashley. She simply felt better when he was around. Because of this, she wanted him around more. She reached into her purse and scribbled down her phone number, e-mail address and access code for her new executive suite, expecting that she would be spending more time there than her actual home.

"I know it's overkill," Ashley remarked, laughing at how pathetic she felt giving Eden the paper. "But I *need* to see you again."

"Don't worry I'll make use of it," Eden promised, smiling and holding up the paper.

They walked out of the restaurant together as the valet pulled Ashley's Lexus around to the front.

"Oh, fancy," Eden joked. Ashley tipped the valet, dismissing him.

"You didn't want them to pull your car around for you?"

"My baby? Wouldn't let them touch it."

"A Ferrari?" Ashley guessed.

"No, a rental." Eden laughed holding up keys to a Hyundai.

Ashley giggled then leaned in and kissed Eden.

214

"Promise you'll use that paper I gave you."

"You have no idea how much use this is gonna get." Eden smiled and closed the door for her after she got in the car.

Ashley drove off and Eden watched the tail lamps disappear in the distance. He fumbled with the keys he swiped from the unattended valet stand. He laughed then threw the keys on the ground where the cars were commandeered by the valets. "Careless workers," Eden laughed to himself as he began walking down the street towards his black Chevy Tahoe.

CHAPTER 18: FLIGHT SCHOOL

It was another early morning on the football field at Occam High. The daybreak was warm but overcast with a strong wind. Aaron and Tyson showed up on time and met Principle Wright on the gusty football field

"How's it goin', boys?" asked Wright.

"Doing good, Mr. Wright," Aaron responded.

"Same," Tyson agreed.

"Good-good. Aaron, I can't thank you enough for your incredible thoughtfulness the other evening at the hospital."

"I just wish your wife came to while I was there."

"No worries, she came to not long after you left and she's been feeling great. That was a wonderful gesture and you have a bright future, son. If you want, the choice is yours. You can consider this the completion of your discipline."

Aaron casually put his hands in his pockets and thought before speaking, "I'll consider it the end of my discipline, but the beginning of the rest of my life if you have more to show me."

"Trust me, kid. I do." Wright smiled in approval then focused on Tyson. "And as for Tyson over here," Wright neared the admirable young man. "You're an incredible role-model for your peers. Thank you for helping me with Aaron's rehabilitation. You've helped more than you know. Don't ever change who you are, for anyone."

Tyson humbly recognized the compliment and Aaron slapped him on the back.

"You boys have a first-period study hall today is that right?"

"Yes, sir," the teenagers chorused.

"Good! Aaron, today begins flight school. Tyson, did you bring your wet suit?"

"Yes, sir."

"You both have Phys. Ed second period right?"

"Yes, sir," they again replied.

216

"Your attendance is already marked 'present' for both of those classes. We'll be back by third period. As far as your teachers are concerned, you two are helping me with a grant for a food drive. I've already written it, put your names on it and I'll send it out later. My boat is docked under the school's pier. We're venturing about two nautical miles into the Pacific and Aaron's going to learn to fly. I didn't forget about you either, Tyson. You'll get practice too."

"Awesome!"

"Practice?" Aaron asked.

"You'll see that Tyson has a gift as impressive as yours, Aaron."

"Sounds cool."

"There's plenty refreshments that are aboard my boat and I think it'll be a good experience. You told me you were a strong swimmer, Tyson. The current may be rough."

"I can handle it."

"Great! This is going to be a lot of fun guys. Get into your swimming gear and meet me at the boat."

The boys did as Principle Wright directed and met him at his subtle performance boat underneath the pier.

"Wow!" Tyson admired as he streamed his hand over the polished finish of the boat.

"C'mon, boys! The more time we have, the more you'll learn."

"Awesome," Aaron said as he and Tyson ecstatically jumped on the speed boat.

Principle Wright pushed the throttle and they raced off into the distance. The current was strong, but manageable. The boat easily skipped through the small waves that opposed it.

Wright spoke up, "We're going to drop anchor here. Tyson will you put this harness over your wet suit? This was developed by the Avia specifically as a war vest. But we need this because this here can serve as a handle on the back of the harness that will help develop Aaron's coordination. It also has weighteous protection in the front, which will develop his flight strength."

"Sure," Tyson grabbed the vest and slipped it on.

"First, we're going to see if he can learn the hard way. It's quicker." Wright laughed.

"Hard way?" Aaron asked.

"Yep." In the blink of an eye and after a loud snapping noise, Wright widely spanned his wings. "Are you ready?"

"Uh....No?"

"Good." The principle seized Aaron by the arm and hoisted him up over his back. He launched high into the air with a beat of his wings and took upward towards the clouds. Tyson watched in awe as heard Aaron laughing and hollering with each loop, nose dive, and vertical climb further into the sky. The principle climbed higher and higher into the air until they were no longer visible to Tyson.

Wright and Aaron broke through the cloud cover and into the bright blue sky-scape before them. The air was thinner, but it was no problem. The air was cold, but it made no difference. Aaron felt his lungs open wider, and his skin tighten. He and Wright blasted further into the sky.

"Are you wondering why we're this high, yet you're not cold and you can still breathe?" Wright asked Aaron.

"Not...really," Aaron answered, unsure of why the principle asked him that. "Something feels different though. I can't put my finger on it."

"Well, I'm not giving you a lesson in biology now so...bye bye." Wright released Aaron.

Aaron was too scared to scream. He tried to gasp as the harsh opposing wind rushed passed his closed eyes. He reached his arms and cowered. Death was the only thing on his mind. His life flashed before his eyes as he felt a stinging sensation overcome his body. Nothing happened. He simply kept falling while his nerves insisted he was in agonizing pain.

Suddenly, Tyson saw a black dot in the sky that was plummeting toward the water. After just a couple seconds the dot took distinct shape. He could see Aaron in free fall. Wright was nowhere in sight. Tyson reached a concerned hand toward the sky, but there was nothing he could do to stop Aaron. He wanted to help, but he was powerless to do so. Just a few more seconds passed and Tyson could hear Aaron screaming for dear life. Aaron didn't have much time before his erratic plummet was going to drive him into the harsh ocean surface. Tyson was speechless as Aaron neared the water. There was still no sign of Principle Wright.

A ferocious wind blew past Tyson, shaking the boat and creating a crescent in the surface of the water. It left a powerful wake that nearly capsized the little boat. Tyson lost his balance then fell over the edge and met the blue water with a loud splash.

Tyson broke the water's surface and wiped his face. He opened his eyes to a beautiful inhuman face in front of him.

"A...a Zoree!" Tyson stuttered.

Her skin was not porous. It was impermeable—pulled tightly over her beautiful streamline face. Her narrow eyes and her small lips were argent, reminding Tyson of an alien—a striking one. Her skin was a modest cerulean tone. Tyson lost himself in her glare. He was dangerously mystified by the female—trapped in the water, paralyzed and unable to move even his finger.

The Zoree female vanished below the surface. Tyson felt a strong grip around his ankles just before he was violently yanked underneath. Tyson was finally able to move again. He kicked and swatted as he was dragged further into

220

the murky depths. He thrashed as he desperately tried to scramble towards the distant air beyond the darkening water. He could no longer see the light breaking through the surface. He reflexively wanted to scream and mistakenly opened his mouth. Tyson was pulled further underneath as the coarse, salty water filled his lungs and he felt the oxygen escape. He was sure he was about to die.

A resonating, melodic voice permeated his ears. "Come further, Ahi."

Tyson felt the same tug on his ankles as he struggled for dear life and tried to hold onto consciousness.

"Listen, Ahi. Tell your order. We want our maven back. You have one week to deliver our leader, otherwise, your order will be exterminated. No one will be spared, not even you. The Ahi will choke under a Zoree tide, just as you are now. Do you understand?"

Tyson tried to speak, but when he opened his mouth, more water infiltrated his lungs.

"Just nod like the good little Ahi you are."

Tyson nodded as he felt his consciousness fail. The black of death came upon him and sealed his eyes.

"Good," the Zoree grabbed Tyson's shoulders. She spun around and whipped Tyson like a bullet towards the surface.

Tyson's entire body violently shot from the surface. "Ahhhhhh!" he hacked as he gasped for air. He landed back in the agitated water and again resurfaced. Dizzy, he treaded in place as the water poured from his mouth. Tyson coughed, expelling the watery infiltrate from his lungs. He swiveled about and noticed that Aaron was already in the boat. Principle Wright was leaning over the edge of the vessel with a hand out ready to help Tyson. "C'mon, kid! Grab my hand!"

"Pl-please, pull me up," Tyson managed to say.

Once in the boat, Tyson fell to all fours as he vomited the contents of his gut and spilled the water from his lungs. "Damn," he gasped as he tilted his head to the side— attempting to get the water out of his ears. Tyson noticed Aaron was wide-eyed, out of breath, unable to speak and he was shaking. Tyson looked off in the distance, wheezed and gagged.

"What happened, Tyson?" Wright asked.

Tyson keeled over and wretched again. His tired body hit the deck and more water spilled from his mouth.

Wright quickly dragged Tyson to his feet. He leaned the distressed teenager over the side and struck him on the back. The last of the salty water drained from Tyson's mouth. Tyson gasped again and finally nodded.

"I'm ok now. I'm ok. It was …a Zoree." Tyson said.

"A Zoree got you?" Wright shouted as he helped Tyson to the seat next to Aaron.

"Yeah, a female, a young female I believe—about my age. I've never seen one before." Tyson looked over at Aaron, "What about him? Is he going to be ok?"

Aaron was practically comatose.

"He's no worse off than you. Give him about ten minutes. He handled that much better than my first day of flight school. Anyway, kid, what did the Zoree want from you?"

"The Zoree sent me a message," Tyson reported. "The Zoree want their maven back from the Ahi."

"What?" asked Wright, "No, the Ahi maven has been kidnapped." Wright corrected. "I'm helping a friend with that."

"No, after she dragged me below the surface, she told me the Zoree want their maven back or the Ahi will die."

"The Zoree maven is missing?"

"Apparently, the Ahi took the Zoree maven."

Wright hastily pried from more information, "You're Ahi, Tyson! Don't you know?"

"No, Mr. Wright, I'm an exiled Ahi."

"Exiled?"

"I can only return in a time of war, or on summons from the Ahi maven." Tyson deeply inhaled knowing that if there was anyone he could trust with a secret it was Principle Wright. Aaron was too indisposed of to hear or care, so Tyson took the opportunity to get it off of his chest. "Have you ever heard of Red Death?"

"Yeah, who hasn't? He was the integrated Ahi who lost his mind and killed his family?"

"He killed his wife while his 5 year-old boy and 4 year-old girl watched," Tyson asserted.

"What does that have to do with it?"

"I was that little boy."

"What!?"

Tyson remembered the conflagration as if it happened the day before.

The fire raged and young Tyson felt the burly arms around him as he watched the burning bedroom ceiling. His little sister struggled next to him, tugging at her father's pants. The house's pine supports cracked as the fire consumed more of his little home. Tyson looked up at his biological father who held him back. The image, burned into the poor children's' minds that day, was the hellish bed in the midst of the inferno, where their mother, Melanie, lay as she suffocated on the fumes of her home. "Daddy! I'm scared!" He yelled as he struggled, "We've gotta help Mommy!"

Tyson's sister, Calysta, fell to her knees, hacking and wheezing, "Daddy, I can't breathe…" she said just before closing her eyes.

"Come on, Anson!" Melanie glared at her husband. "Get the kids out! Calysta is in danger!" She choked on the fumes. "Tyson! You're gonna be ok, honey!" His mother yelled between her wheezing breathes. Her tears flowed as she struggled to free herself from the ties that bound her to the bed. "You're gonna be ok, Tyson!"

"Mommy! I want you to be ok!" He yelled as he kicked, screamed and bit, trying to get free to help her.

Melanie stared at her inhabited husband, "Kill me! It's fine! But don't you dare let your daughter die there on the floor, you bastard! Save her, Anson!"

The wicked man holding Tyson back laughed as his eyes defined the hateful heart within him. "You're gonna be fine, Tyson—and so am I!" He screamed at his wife, "We'll see if Calysta is so unique."

Tyson yelled as he sobbed and struggled more. The fire was melting his shoes, but it didn't hurt him.

"Tyson!" His mom yelled as she choked again on the carbon monoxide bred by the fire. She hacked and wheezed as Tyson struggled against his father, realizing his mom couldn't handle the fumes that were nothing more than an odiferous scent to him and his father. Tyson's scrambling finally proved useful when the back of his head struck his father's nose.

Anson dropped Tyson and didn't bother holding him back anymore, "It's too late, Tyson! Her flesh is melting." Tyson's father uncapped the gas can by his foot. He slowly made his way over to his beautiful wife who pled for mercy between her hacking coughs.

As her life-force abandoned her sweating, melting body, Tyson's father accelerated the flame, which reached seven feet into the air. Tyson, all for naught, kicked and swatted at his father still. Tyson's father raised his hand and slapped Tyson across the face, dropping him to the floor. "You're emotional and weak, Tyson!" Anson hollered just before he escaped through the doorway. The bedroom ceiling over the bed collapsed —burying Tyson's mother.

Tyson saw his sister there, trapped under a piece of the ceiling, maintaining shallow breaths, but still alive. The rest of the ceiling looked like it was going to fall down on her. Tyson threw himself over Calysta as a piece of the ceiling, just heavy enough to render him unconscious, crashed over him.

"Impossible," Wright said.

"When I woke up, I was in an orphanage. They never told me what happened to my sister." Tyson's face was red and in his eyes there was deep resentment. "I don't know what to think. Maybe she's Ahi and survived. Maybe the fire didn't leave a trace of her."

"Red Death was my father. My mother wasn't Ahi. My sister, wherever she may be, and I are directly marked by the Keaka. I've been exiled from the the Ahi-territory. I wish I could've helped. I wish I could've done something, but he was too strong."

"I don't believe it!" Wright sat down next to Tyson.

"I tried! I really did try," Tyson bit his lip, stifling his depression.

"Tyson you were five! You're not to blame!"

"I've been told that….but nothing makes the imagery go away."

"I'm sorry, Tyson."

"Me too, my poor mom! And poor Calysta! Whatever happened to her? I just want to know what happened to my little sister! I want her in my life!" A tear rolled down his cheeks. Tyson trembled in his anger, "I have a blinding anger now that I have to deal with. It's worse than the characteristic Ahi 'Hot-Head' temper."

"Why did your father ever do that?"

"For some reason, my father welcomed the inhabitance of a Keaka before he met my mother. He hid it so well until the day he killed her. In the Ahi territory, it's a sorrowful day called, 'The Day of Red Death.' No Ahi speaks on the Day of Red Death."

Aaron began to stir and shake off the haziness from his adrenaline dump. Wright touched Tyson's shoulder, "We'll talk more about this later. I'm not going to judge you. I know other's have, but this may be too much for Aaron and he's about to come to. Is that ok if we talk later?"

Tyson nodded.

"Ok. One more free fall and he'll be able to do a few loops on his own. Are you a thrower or a breather, Tyson?"

"I was born a breather. When I'm twenty years old, if I can find someone who will teach me, I'll be able to do both."

"Did you still want to do the target practice?"

"Please, if I can. I haven't returned home and certainly haven't manipulated any fire in all of those years."

"You got it." Wright handed Tyson a lighter, a seal of trust.

"Are you comfortable going back in the water? I'll keep a better eye on you and I'll take care of the Zoree if she shows up again."

"That's ok with me," Tyson said wiping the evidence of his past off of his cheeks as he grabbed the lighter.

"No problem, Tyse. We will revisit this." Wright stood up, "When I yell, 'Fire' I want you to try and take Aaron out of the sky with an inferno."

"Isn't that dangerous?"

"Ordinarily yes, but Aaron's even more unique and more powerful than I realized. His skin will be a remarkable exoskeleton when his wings are deployed. So don't worry, a little gentle target practice isn't gonna hurt him." Wright aimed his amused attention at Aaron, "How's that for flight school, young man?"

"Principle Wright, you dropped me from the edge of the atmosphere…leave… me… alone"

"Oh pipe down, kid. You needed that rush in order to learn. What did you feel when you were falling?"

Aaron hesitated, "Fear, I guess."

"Well yeah, did you feel anything physical?"

"I felt a pain, you know, a twinge in my shoulder and in my lower back." Aaron tried to peep at his back over his shoulder.

"Perfect, this time realize that you can stop yourself from falling. You have the ability. Realize the reality that the pain is your wings as they are breaking through your back."

"That sounds remarkably painful."

"It's excruciating at first, but it won't be for long. It hurts less the more you do it. You need the adrenaline to be able to break out your wings the first time. The adrenaline also helps you deal with the pain from it the first time. That's why I needed to drop you from so high and that's why we have to do it again."

"Ugh!" Aaron said. "I don't want to."

"You just gotta trust me."

"I don't want to," Aaron said. "You can't make me do it. I'm not doing it!"

"Yeah you are." Wright grabbed Aaron again the same way he did before and shot up into the sky even faster.

Tyson watched the sky. He could no longer hear Aaron calling Wright a 'whacky old jerk.' Mere seconds later, it was a repeat of the last flight-trial. Early in his accelerating plummet, Aaron fell without any sign of competence. There was only fear. Another few seconds passed and Aaron began to rearrange his position in the air. He was falling head-first towards the water. Tyson scrunched his face and turned away when he suddenly heard a loud snap. Tyson again looked to the skies and noticed Aaron broke two large complimentary sets of wings. The powerful wings were not like Wright's. There were two transparent and vascular wing sets like those of a hornet. Tyson was astonished as he watched Aaron immediately change direction. He began gaining altitude, flying through the air, defying gravity. He was frolicking about in the air like a kid the first time they can swim on their own.

Aaron stayed there in the air, beating his wings gently. He hovered in the sky surveying all the familiar buildings from his new perspective. He could see his school and the citrus groves near the football field. The gentle wind rolled across his face softly. He looked in disbelief under his arms then over his shoulders at his newly found wings.

"What do-ya think?" Wright asked as he flew up behind Aaron.

"I'm not really sure what to think. It's like a dream."

"Good," Wright said with a maniacal grin on his face.

"Mr. Wright?"

"Yeah?"

"Why are my wings not like yours?"

"It's a long story kid, we'll have to discuss that later."

"Fair enough." Aaron studied Wright's face, "you have a crazy look in your eye, Mr. Wright."

"Tyson! Fire!"

A blistering cloud took Aaron right out of the sky and dropped him into the water. "Sorry, Aaron!" Tyson called out after Aaron surfaced. "Mr. Wright made me do it!"

"Oh, you bastard!" Aaron hollered playfully as he popped out of the water. Aaron beat both sets of wings. He whizzed by Tyson, grabbing his harness and lifting him out of the boat.

"Put me down!" Tyson laughed as he swung at Aaron's hands trying to break his grip.

"If you say so!" Aaron let Tyson go. Tyson plummeted about twenty feet and landed with a splash in the ocean.

Tyson resurfaced, laughing and blowing more blazing waves at Aaron. Aaron dodged all of the attacks. Suddenly, an enshrouding cloud to surface from the water and come up behind Aaron. The haze took Aaron by surprise and an emberous sphere blindsided the young Avia. Aaron crashed through the surface with a grand splash.

Aaron resurfaced and both of the boys in the water laughed at the supernatural scuffle they just had. Wright blew a whistle and yelled, "Back into the boat, guys!"

"How'd you do that, Tyson?" Wright exclaimed as Aaron set him down in the boat.

"With my mind."

"A pyrokinetic. You are indeed still marked by the Keaka."

"The Keaka mark was never taken from me. I've manipulated things with my mind more recently than I've blown fire. So it was safer for Aaron. I have more control over my mind than I do fire."

"Wow..." Wright's mouth gaped.

"Sorry," Tyson looked to Aaron and they shook hands.

"No worries—it's all in good fun." Aaron agreed, "Honestly, thanks for not killing me," Aaron nervously chuckled.

Wright interjected. "There is one more thing I'd like to teach both of you today."

The boys turned to each other and shrugged.

"Aaron, balance yourself at the bow of the boat."

"Ok," Aaron replied as he jumped up and landed on the bow with total balance. "Wow!" Aaron surprised himself.

"Great," Wright said, "Now using your wings, wrap them around yourself and cover up your body, protect yourself. This is your nearly impenetrable wing-shield defense. It's you're literal haven from the rest of the world."

Aaron did just as the principle said. Wright picked up a baseball he had on his boat, cocked his arm back and launched the ball as hard as he could at Aaron. The ball made hard, whipping contact, but Aaron didn't budge.

"Did you just do something?" Aaron asked.

"Stay there," Wright said.

"Ok?"

Wright took a match out of his pocket and struck it. He placed the little match in his palm and closed his hand. Wright's fist burst into an angry flame that clearly didn't bother him. He grabbed Tyson's arm and as if the fire were any ordinary object, he placed the fire in Tyson's hand. "It's your turn to throw." Wright smiled at Tyson who couldn't believe his own eyes. "I'm teaching you."

CHAPTER 19: I'D LIKE TO HELP

'Ethan,

I still haven't found former Ahi maven Dawson Wrangle. The acting Ahi maven and Zoree maven are both being held in the heart of Honolulu. We believe Domovoi is responsible. Since your decree to all Avia is to not engage the phantom, I will leave the task up to your capable hands. You will find the maven in a large building in Honolulu where all floors are illuminated except one. The floor where there is no light is where we believe he' s captive. Please don't go alone.

Your loyal friend,

Victor Farrell'

Wright tucked the most recent note from Victor away and surveyed the mourning crowd for Aaron. Grayson McGrath's funeral was suffixed with a breezy, overcast burial ceremony. After the interment, Aaron made his way through the crowd of heart-broken criers and saw Principle Wright.

"Mr. Wright, you wanted to talk to me?"

"I do. Is your father about?" The principle wrapped a friendly arm around Aaron's shoulder.

"Yeah he's right over there." Alan McNamara looked at the opportune time to see his son waving, and gesturing for him to come speak with Wright.

"Ethan, how are you?" Alan asked as he approached and shook the principle's hand.

"I'm well, Alan."

"You've met my lovely wife, Eva." Eva daintily extended her hand and Wright appropriately responded.

"It's a pleasure to see you again, Eva."

"Like-wise, Mr. Wright"

"How are you today, Alan?" Wright shifted his gaze.

He paused, pensively enshrouded by thought. "I suppose I'm as well as one can be on a day where he sees such a young girl lay her father to rest." He cast his eyes upon the ground, stifling his emotions. He faced the principle with a glistening in the corner of his eye. "He was a good friend of mine too, a real great guy, a hard worker."

"I know it's so unbelievably sad." Wright shook his head.

"You know it's such a shame when terrible things happen to good people, young people," Eva concluded.

"I couldn't agree more. Actually, that's why I wanted to talk to you."

"Why's that now?" Alan asked.

"Terrible things are happening to good people and I could really use your son's help."

"Is that right?" Eva warily asked, "How can he help you, Mr. Wright."

"I'd like to take all of you with me on a little boat ride if I may, so I can explain."

Alan and Eva exchanged glances. Eva shrugged, clearly open to the idea and Alan responded with a subdued grin, "Sure, that sounds nice."

"Great, my boat is docked nearby, just ten minutes away. If you want I can drive." Wright offered.

"Great," Eva responded for her vexed husband,

On arrival at the dock, everyone exited the car and found themselves in a small parking lot near a very quiet harbor. "My word! It's beautiful here!" Eva exclaimed as she surveyed the small oasis-like dock that lead to the vast open waters of the blue Pacific. "I never knew about this place."

"It's a fairly well kept secret hidden right under Honolulu's nose."

"Wow!" Alan still had trouble believing the view. "Ethan, this is quite a place! Is that your boat? He asked with obvious astonishment in his face. He pointed to a different boat than the one Aaron had seen the first day of his flight school. It wasn't a small speed boat, but a sixty-foot black yacht.

"Yes it is."

"Wow!"

"You have two boats?" Aaron asked.

"That's right." Wright wrapped his arm around Alan and Aaron's backs. "Please, lead the way, my wife's all ready on board with some food and drinks she prepared."

The McNamaras lead the way. Just as the principle said, when they boarded the elegant yacht, Mary Wright was there, relaxing in a white arm-chair with a magazine. An exquisite mini-buffet was prepared on the kitchenette's granite countertop. There were hard wood floors under a long bubble patterned throw rug and two white sofas in the lounging area.

"Wow!" Alan exclaimed again as he turned to Wright, "very impressive."

"Do you have any kids of your own, Mr. Wright?" Eva asked. She immediately realized the sorrow in the principle's face. "Oh, I'm sorry."

"Don't be sorry." Wright cleared his throat, suppressing his disheartened reaction. "My son died some time ago."

"Oh my God!" Eva immediately went flush, and her eyes became puffy. "I'm so sorry. That's so sad!"

Aaron met eyes with Principle Wright's wife in the midst of the saddening conversation. He immediately marched over to her and in an humbly kneeled while keeping a polite distance. He sat on his heels and threw his hands in the air as if questioning what he was doing. He shrugged before looked into Mary's eyes confidently and apologetically.

All of the adults stopped talking and respectfully listened to Aaron's apology. "May I apologize for my rudeness and extreme stupidity?" Mary put her magazine down on the table next to her and touched Aaron's forearm as Aaron continued, "I had no right to say what I said, for that I'm sorry. I'm truly sorry." Aaron respectfully averted his eyes, waiting for his tongue-lashing from Mrs. Wright.

"You've more than learned your lesson, young man. Consider the whole thing done and over with. It takes a lot more than that to upset me," she smiled heartily and put up her circling dukes. Her hands fell into her lap and she touched Aaron's forearm once more, "Just don't hesitate to forgive others, young man. There's a shortage of forgiveness in this life."

"Yes, ma'am," Aaron nodded.

"Now, stand up, go get yourself some food and have a good time," she smiled.

"Thank you, Mrs. Wright," he said as he got up and did as she told him. She smiled at him, introduced herself to his parents and invited them to sit down with her.

After twenty minutes, Principle Wright took to the captain's chair at the front of the boat and he invited Alan to the other captain's chair. Mrs. Wright slowly got up and invited everyone to sit at the wrap around sofa that surrounded the two captain's seats.

Eva spoke up, "Mr. and Mrs. Wright, this is all so very lovely. It really is, and I don't want to be rude."

"You're not being rude, dear. Speak your mind," Mary encouraged.

"I've something of a glass-half-full personality. I'll just

238

go ahead and say it. I'm a pessimist. That being said, I just can't help but feel like I'm being 'fattened-up for the kill' so to speak."

"Eva!" Alan jumped, completely embarrassed, "Cold and embittered would've been a step up from how that statement came off!"

There was an awkward pause where Eva grinned nervously, "Uh, wow, I, guess you're right." She cleared her throat, breathed in and tried to rephrase, "I didn't mean that the way it came out."

Mary spoke up, "It's no problem, dear. We know exactly what you mean and how strange you feel, being on our boat when you barely know anything about us and then dining with us. I'm sure it must feel very bizarre." The sage woman's deduction mitigated Eva's discomfort. "Ethan, will you put this beautiful young woman's mind at ease?"

"You know, Mary, I think Alan best tell her." Wright focused on Alan as he passed the conversational hot potato.

"Would you please, Mr. McNamara? I can tell your wife is so confounded. Who wouldn't be?" Mary implored.

"Tell me what, Alan?"

Alan smirked, scratched the back of his neck and let out a breath. "Wow, I, I'm not really sure how to say it. Maybe you can demonstrate how Aaron can help you." Alan suggested. "I'm not really sure if I know exactly how he can help you."

"Aaron?" Eva sternly inquired. "Why did you just call him, 'Aaron?'" Alan forgot that she wasn't yet privy to their adopted son's birth-name. "Please!" she shouted, very agitated and nervous as if she couldn't trust anyone in the room. "Just tell me what's going on!" Eva's worried eyes bounced around as she focused one-by-one on all the faces in the room.

"Eva, I think it's actually best if Pat shows you." Alan patted the seat-cushion next to him and asked his wife to sit down next to him. "Are we far enough out, Ethan?"

Wright brought his eyes to his binoculars and inspected the environment. There was no one in sight. "We are. We're ready. Aaron, are you ready to give 'em a show?"

"Aaron?" Eva again asked, "Aaron?" she repeated her eyes puffy and a tremble in her voice. "What is this?"

"Darling," Alan began resting his hand on her knee, "You're about to see the most wonderful yet scariest thing you've ever seen in your life."

Wright stopped the boat and anchored it. They were miles away from the nearest pair of intrusive eyes. The boaters trotted out onto the yacht's deck and wandered to the railing. They gazed into the reflective water's slow current. A slow breeze rolled in and Wright closed his eyes, feeling the gentle gust on his face, contemplating its direction, its beginning and end. He glanced at Aaron. "Show them," he smiled. "It's ok."

All of the eyes on the boat locked on Aaron. Wright, Mary, and Alan were all very enthused, while Eva was dreadfully uneasy. Aaron closed his eyes, thought about the many lessons from his first flight school and braced himself for his maiden take-off. A surge ran through his body, adrenaline, or maybe something else. His back ached. He cracked his neck as his mother shrieked at the weird contortion and the disgusting popping sound. Aaron felt the pain in his back get worse and he screamed as his map-like veins surfaced on his skin.

"Pat!" Eva exclaimed.

The screaming continued and Aaron's young wings exploded to life, finding their freedom over his loose shirt collar. Aaron surprised everyone, including himself. With one flap of his wings and a forceful push off the deck from his invigorated legs, he took to the skies. He hovered over his parents and the Wrights.

"Patrick Eric McNamara!" Eva shouted, not quite sure what to say next. "Come down here! Come down here right now!" She stared at her husband, "Would ya do something?"

Alan put his finger over her lips then kissed her. "Don't talk, just watch," he said as he smiled at his son, who was still aptly hovering in the air with a proud smile. "Son, I'm speechless! Show us what you can do!"

Aaron, still smiling, shot up into the air. He climbed so high they couldn't see him.

"Mr. Wright! Where is my son?" Eva asked as she aggressively neared the principle.

"Hi, Mom!" Aaron shouted as he dropped from the sky and blew by the boat creating a gust. The surface thinly parted underneath him as he skimmed over the top of the water. The mist on his face was refreshing. He saw his reflection in the water and was proud of himself. He dipped his hand in the water as he flew over the surface and focused on the freedom before him. He looked skyward and ascended again, but not as high as his first climb. He flew in a big loop, twisting about in the air before he dropped his altitude and flew towards the boat. He circled his parents and the cheering Wrights twice before he touched his feet back to the deck and proudly ran his hands through his dampened hair.

Aaron looked to his mother and father for approval, realizing he clearly had his father's complete appreciation. He noticed that his mother's expression was an unchanging testament to complete round-eyed disbelief. She tried to speak, "Uh, I, that..." Aaron began walking towards her.

"Mom, it's ok," Aaron said.

"My son just flew...like a bird. I, uh..." She felt her muscles weaken and her legs give out from under her. She blacked-out completely. Aaron moved swiftly enough to catch her before she hit the boat's wet deck. He surprised himself as well as the others with his quickness.

"That's why I need you, son," Wright said as everyone gathered closer around Eva, investigating her well being. "She'll come to in a few minutes. Let's put her in the lounge chair there on the bow's deck."

Eva was still unconscious when they placed her in the chair.

Wright grabbed a cinderblock then placed it next to Aaron and cut to the chase. "Your son is an Avia, Alan."

"Right…"

"I believe his people and the people of this world will need him soon. He was born to be a protector."

"Of?" Alan warily leered at Wright.

"Everything and everyone, his physical potential was realized before his mental potential, very typical of Avian men. Typically, they immediately realize their physical capability. The exact opposite is true of Avian women. Their mental potential is realized long before their physical potential. The women think. They see the big picture and the men make the women's astute visions happen. Avian men aren't usually capable of thinking on that level until they've aged about 150 years. The converse is true of the women's physical potential."

"Interesting."

"Please, allow him to demonstrate a simple ability."

"O-k?" Alan shrugged.

Aaron picked up the cinderblock that the principle had set down and held it up to his father. "Go ahead, Dad, right over my head!"

"Are you mental?" Alan said, protesting the ridiculous request. "I will never! And I forbid you from hurting yourself."

"Fair enough," Aaron brandished the cinderblock with both hands as Eva awakened.

She looked at the cinderblock. Through her maternal instincts she predicted what he was about to do and she shouted, "No!" as loud as she could.

With a grunt, Aaron pulled the cinderblock into his face and demolished it with his forehead. Three pieces loudly fell on the boat's deck as the cinder's dust gently submitted to the breeze. He held up the other two pieces as evidence of his power.

"Dammit, son! I told you not to hurt yourself!" Alan exclaimed, but then noticed his son's strong, painless expression. Aaron didn't hurt himself in the least. There were neither cuts, nor bruises. "How…did you do that, son?"

"I'm a protector, Dad, a strong one."

"I'd like to mentor your son, Alan." Wright said.

"Judging by your little demonstration I have to ask, 'Is it dangerous?'" Alan asserted.

"Very," Wright admitted. "But so was dealing drugs, which he did for how long? It wasn't always to his friends either."

"I can't argue that. But before we agree to anything, we want answers to certain questions we have," Eva demanded as she walked up from behind her husband.

"Very good!" Wright agreed, "No problem."

"We have a *lot* of questions, Mr. Wright." Alan added as he pulled his wife closer.

"I owe you at least that much," Wright said emphatically. "I'm sorry about how uncomfortable I've made you both. I will gladly answer anything you have to ask." Wright gestured towards the bow of the boat, inviting the McNamaras to sit with him and his wife outside in the pleasant air while they thoroughly interrogated him.

Aaron retracted his wings and confidently walked behind everyone else as they filed one-by-one onto the deck. He took a seat in one of the deck chairs and breathed deeply. While his parents asked every logical question they could and demanded thorough explanations, Aaron watched the birds fly through the air, embracing the idea of his newfound heritage.

CHAPTER 20: HERE FOR AN INSPECTION

It was a lazy sunny day at the repair garage where Tyson worked. Tyson closed the hood of the semi-restored red 1955 Chevy Bel-Air he was working on and began ambling toward the open garage door. He wiped the all too familiar grease stains off of his hands and grabbed a basketball on his way outside, dribbling the ball effortlessly. Tyson surveyed the lot. He dropped his sunglasses over his eyes, realizing he had already finished his day's work and it was only noon.

A sporty black Toyota Venza pulled into the cement parking lot and carefully parked. The door opened and Jean-Claude hopped out of the crossover. He put his keys away and made for the garage door where Tyson was standing.

"Basketball?" Tyson asked as he bounced the basketball then spun it on his finger and looked up at Jean-Claude.

"I think we should talk instead."

"We can do both."

Tyson lead the way to the basketball hoop around the side of the building. Tyson dribbled the ball rhythmically while trying to figure out exactly what to tell Jean-Claude. Tyson couldn't tell him much because of certain rules he remembered that were imposed by Dawson, the previous Ahi maven. Tyson however felt he owed Jean-Claude an explanation as to his heritage. He passed the ball over to Jean-Claude who deftly dribbled the ball weaving in and out of his legs before bouncing it back to Tyson. They got to the hoop and took turns shooting before Jean-Claude broke the silence that Tyson was comfortable with.

"What are you going to tell me, bud?" Jean-Claude asked, sinking another basket then retrieving and stiffly throwing the ball to Tyson. Tyson just continued dribbling rhythmically, thoughtfully.

"What do you want to know?" asked Tyson.

"I don't know. I was just hoping I might get to know my best friend."

"Again, I'll tell you. What do you want to know?"

"Fair enough," Jean-Claude said aggressively, wiping his nose with his thumb before he crossed his arms. "Who exactly are you?" He asked agitatedly. "I've known you, how long? Or I haven't known you for how long?"

"There's no need to be hostile, Claude. I'm still your friend."

"You're supposed to be my *best* friend! Man, you should be able to tell me anything."

"I'm offering to tell you now. What's the problem? What's your question?"

"'Who are you?' Is the question!"

"I'm Tyson, God Dammit!" Tyson raised his eyebrows and let out an exasperated sigh.

"I asked the question of who you are all to no avail. So I'm left with the 'What.' So...*what* exactly are you?"

"I'd like to think of myself as a normal high school kid." Tyson responded, clearly evading the question Jean-Claude was asking.

"I would too, but you're not." There was an awkward pause. "Your temperature is twice any normal humans, you have some funky-ass tats that I've never seen and I've known you since we were kids. It's like I've known you without knowing you. I don't have many friends, but I thought the few I had were great ones!" Jean-Claude yelled.

Tyson stopped dribbling the ball and rolled it to the grass before he shot a defensive glance at his friend. Tyson was frustrated so he just paced back and forth thinking. He then began to speak. "What are you saying? I'm opening up to you. I'm giving you a chance just to ask me whatever you want. You're playing games with me, Claude! And this is an edgy subject for me!"

"You're the one playing games! You're telling me that I can ask whatever I want when you won't even answer my simple questions. I've known you more than ten years man and you'll shout out in front of everybody your little secret, but you won't even fill me in on any more detail than you told them. At least explain it to me!" Jean-Claude shouted.

"It's not fair that I have to justify myself to anyone. It's not fair that my best friend won't just let it go! My past isn't something I'd care to relive, Claude!"

After another awkward pause, Jean-Claude got closer to Tyson. "Vinnie told me some things about y'all at our last game."

"Oh yeah?" Tyson was beyond irate at this point.

"Yeah he did!" Jean-Claude said glaring into Tyson's lying eyes.

"You're going to let Vinnie Tarsa tell you about me? Really? Tarsa!" Tyson shouted.

"What he described was exactly the attitude you're taking with me now."

"For such a smart kid, you sound so unbelievably ignorant."

"I'm just calling it as I see it," Jean-Claude rejoined.

"You're seriously going to listen to Tarsa? He's who you're getting your info from? I mean, seriously, consider your source."

"He's the only other kid I know like you. Ordinarily, I…"

"Like me? You just likened me to Tarsa? I'm just going to go ahead and say it. Quit being a tool!"

Jean-Claude ignored the brash comment, "Ordinarily, I wouldn't have listened to him, but everything he said was dead on and he's told me a damn sight more than you have. He's told me a lot and it's all happening exactly as he said it would."

"Tarsa," Tyson shouted in Jean-Claude's face, "…is just a thoughtless jerk-off that does drugs instead of going to class and beats the shit out of anyone half his size in the halls at school! Not to mention he sells his blood for a frigging car!"

"Even if he did sell his blood, who cares? It's his to sell...and get outta my damn face." Jean-Claude pushed Tyson away.

Tyson could tell Jean-Claude wanted to apologize, but the words didn't come out. This time it was Tyson's turn to let the hasty act go. "You really just don't get it. It's not 'ok.' It's a law governing the Lost Orders. We protect and honor our blood."

"You know what, it doesn't even matter. The issue isn't him and his car. The issue is us. Are you my friend or not?"

"What do you think?" Tyson snapped.

"I don't know, man. Since that one incident at the lab we haven't been hanging out like we used to. We haven't even talked except for homeroom and an occasional study hall. So I want to know where the real Tyson is, because whatever you've got going on isn't the real you." After another awkward pause with no eye-contact Jean-Claude continued, "Or maybe it is and my alleged best friend was actually just a liar."

"Unbelievable," Tyson just shook his head and shrugged in exasperation.

"Yeah you are," Jean-Claude said as he pointed at Tyson.

"I'll see you at the game in Kapaa. You're the

unbelievable one." Tyson walked by Jean-Claude ending the conversation.

"I'm the unbelievable one. Ok."

With a wave of good-riddance Tyson rounded the corner and punched back into work. He made his way to the service desk and waited on the customer at the service desk.

"I'm here for an inspection," the friendly customer requested.

'*You too?*' Tyson thought to himself as he slid a few sheets of paper over to the man. Tyson smiled, "I'll take the key when you're done." As the customer filled out the necessary paper work Tyson noticed Jean-Claude carelessly pull out of the space and drive off the same way.

After finishing up the inspection, Tyson's boss, Al Danley, slapped him on the back. "Get outta here, Tyson. You barely took your lunch and I'm sure you have that beautiful girl that you've been blathering on about waiting for you." Danley laughed as his old cheeks flushed and he raised his stylish orange eyewear over his pattern-bald head. "What do young folks such as you two do these days anyway?" Danley asked as he tucked his grease rag in his back pocket.

"Tonight, we're taking the new six hour super-ferry to Kapaa. I'm meeting the team at the hotel tonight. Harlie and I thought it would be nice to see Mount Kilauea tonight instead of after the game this weekend. I'm all packed up and ready to get going."

"A'right then, superstar, don't return without that trophy!" Al smiled as he shook Tyson's hand, dismissing him for the rest of the day.

Tyson smiled as he pushed the car into the next gear. "I'm so excited! This is going to be so much fun!" Harlie exclaimed. He considered the long road ahead of them. There was a large declining hill followed by a large rising hill. After the hill, there was a long straight away and there were no other drivers on the road. Tyson looked at Harlie with a daring smile.

"Do it!" Harlie exclaimed as she braced herself in her seat.

Tyson shifted into a lower gear for a more rapid acceleration. The RPM gauge spiked to 5000RPMs while in third gear. The sound of the engine resounded through the cabin and Tyson pushed the accelerator to the floor burying the needle beyond the red line. He took the car to the 7700RPM range before shifting to fourth gear. The car's engine stirred and they blasted down the straight road at 80MPH. The refreshing wind rushed into the car. The RPM gauge climbed in fourth gear and the car reached the 100MPH mark as Harlie stretched her arms out of the open window and sunroof. She laughed as the adrenaline surged through her body when they reached 114MPH and her head was pressed to the back of the seat. Tyson kept the car at speed for some time before they finally slowed down and carefully drove the rest of the way to the Oahu inter-island super-ferry that was destined for Kapaa.

When they arrived at the ferry they gave the worker their tickets and were directed to their place on the large blue vessel with black windows. It was capable of carrying 350 cars and 1000 passengers. After about an hour, the ferry was filled to capacity and they departed for Kauai Island.

CHAPTER 21: TWO PEOPLE IN ONE

Rockland awoke from the sedative several hours later. Hearing Mursten's voice, he stood up slowly and he adjusted his eyes to the fluorescent light of the cell. This unit was nicer than the average cell. Two of the walls were padded. A mattress was fixed to the floor and there was personal access to a toilet and a sink. He laughed to himself, wondering why he didn't confront his cellmates sooner. He moseyed over to the wall with a Plexiglas window. Mursten's voice was coming from the TV at the unoccupied guard station.

"Good afternoon, ladies and gentleman," he heard Mursten say. Rockland's vision became just clear enough to see the president's face on the TV. "As you have likely heard, there was a murder at the Omicron Laboratory facility not long ago. The murder was excessively violent and came as a tremendous shock to us all. Dr. James Bankhart, the owner and chief executive officer of the laboratory, was found dead in his office at the Omicron facility. There have been honest questions coming from the community-at-large as to the nature of my visit to the laboratory. There have also been more blunt questions regarding whether or not I knew anything about this terrible act. While I am disappointed in the distrust from some of my constituents, it is my duty to formally express my innocence and fill the public in on where we are with regards to the investigation."

Mursten paused and looked at all the faces in attendance at the dramatic press release. "A once very close friend of mind, as well as personal security liaison, Colonel Richard Rockland of the United States Army has been detained on suspicions of the crime. He is being held at an undisclosed location. His trial has begun and he is being held without bail. My cabinet will keep you posted on the status of the trial and any developments that need to be released to the public. Thank you."

About thirty minutes had passed since the telecast and the guard's station was still unoccupied. Rockland was suspicious. In all his time at the prison, there hadn't been a period longer than ten minutes without seeing a guard. Rockland could faintly hear rowdy behavior coming from down the hallway. He tried to peek out from the cell window, but visibility was limited.

Rockland suddenly heard the cell door's lock rustling. The rustling stopped for a second and began again. The rustling started and stopped another three or four times. Finally, he heard the tumbler of the lock click into the unlocked position. The colonel's brain was working better than his body. The handle turned and the colonel threw his massive body in front of the door, knowing there was something sinister on the other side.

Rockland tried to gather his thoughts and come up with a plan. His brain was up to the task, but his body wasn't. His body felt like gelatin.

There was vulgar and unintelligible shouting coming from the other side of the door. It clearly wasn't a guard opening the colonel's cell door. Rockland refocused his mind and tried to come up with a plan, but to no avail. The yelling from the outside grew louder and the force on the door grew more intense with each push. There was a rallying, war-like shout coming from the outside. A strong push forcefully threw the recovering colonel to the ground.

The heavy steel door swung open and a group of steroid-using, tattooed ruffians rushed through the door. They were of mixed origin, but all shared obvious blood lust in their eyes. A few of them were armed with improvised stabbing weapons, shivs, made from items found around a prison cell including combs, toothbrushes and razors.

The colonel's vision was still somewhat hazy. He was fully cognizant of his surroundings but his body was still too heavily influenced by the sedatives from earlier to be an effective defense mechanism. He closed his eyes and tried to think his way out of the problem. Without effective use of his body, his effort was all for naught.

It wasn't long before the aggressors surrounded the drugged colonel. The men taunted and began kicking him. With each merciless second, the kicks grew harder and more frequent. Rockland was forced into a defensive position on the floor, curling up, defending his head and his vital organs from the torturous blows that were still getting worse. As the taunting grew louder, a few of the men lowered themselves towards the colonel, stabbing him with their improvised weapons. The colonel felt the dull points puncturing and the sharp edges cutting away at his skin. A particular series of blows in the center of his torso released a stream of blood from his chest that became a rapidly expanding red pool in front of him. The colonel felt his life slipping away as he watched the weapons cruelly intrude on his body.

At that moment, he remembered his encounter with the shadow in his cell. He felt crazy for putting his life in the hands of a voice he wasn't sure if he actually heard, but it was the only thing he could think to do.

"Are you there?" Rockland called in a weakened tone.

"What did you say?" The largest inmate mocked as he kicked the field of wounds that lay across Rockland's chest.

Rockland thought hard about his communication with the voice he heard coming from the shadows. He remembered what the essence had said, "Call into the shadows for Domovoi." The colonel adjusted his gaze to the darkest shadow in the room.

"Domovoi!" Rockland strained with what life force he had left.

"You called even sooner than I expected, Colonel Rockland." He heard Domovoi say.

"Please, help me!" Rockland abandoned his pride that very moment, leaving it to stain the cell with the liberated blood on the floor.

A compensatory surge of an unknown vigor immediately restored his pride and refurbished his physical potential. The effects of the powerful sedative were immediately gone. His wounds didn't seem lethal as they had moments ago and his mind was sharp. Rockland was more ready for a fight than he ever felt. He was more willing than he had ever been to take the lives of the enemies in front of him.

Rockland scissored his legs, throwing himself into an evasive ground spin. He pushed off the ground with his massive forearms and landed competently on his feet. The surrounding attackers were baffled at his sudden recovery. They didn't spend much time thinking about it. As far as they were concerned, anyone capable of getting themselves up was capable of getting beaten back to the ground.

The men's blows grew slower and more predictable to the colonel who was now standing competently on his feet. His closest attacker plunged a sharpened toothbrush handle straight towards his neck. Rockland effortlessly evaded the attack as he grabbed the attacker's arm and swung to the man's backside. Using the attacker's momentum, he grabbed the back of the weapon-wielding ruffian's head and slammed him into the corner of the breached door. The man screamed in pain as he dropped the weapon to the ground and likewise fell to the floor, exposing his deeply gashed forehead. The man on the ground closed his eyes and breathed his last.

Rockland then ducked a wide-swinging fist aimed at his face. Using all of the force he could gather, the colonel popped up and drove a dominant roundhouse kick into the inmate's head. The lethal blow dropped the man to the floor a mere second after the brutal contact.

It was at this moment, another one of the dormant attackers noticed the colonel's eyes were completely black; another inmate would've disagreed however. From the other inmate's perspective they were a holographic purple. Nevertheless, no matter what perspective, there was clearly no fear, nor hesitation in the colonel's face. There was only joy in the skillful, lethal defense techniques he was exercising.

One of the attackers fled the room screaming. The other men in the room stood there, paralyzed with fear. The colonel approached the nearest inmate and clutched him by the throat. The lethal defense had now become a merciless offense. He thrashed the fearful man into the wall. With a quick twist of his hand he snapped the inmate's neck. The now-dead man just slid down the wall when Rockland let go of his mutilated throat.

An armed guard, Roger according to his name tag, heard the commotion. With his weapon drawn, he approached the murder scene in the cell where Rockland was administering death sentences.

"Line up against the wall! Now! Get up against the wall!"

The once aggressive inmates quickly complied with Roger's demand, hoping that they were quickly going to be separated from the colonel.

"You too, Shrek! Get up against the wall!" The unnerved guard demanded, stabilizing his iron-sights on Rockland's head. Rockland smirked and slowly faced the wall. The guard approached with his shaky arms completely extended. Roger sensed something wasn't right, but he still slowly and cautiously inched toward the men. He readied himself to detain them.

"Please get us out of here, sir! This big dude is crazy!"

"Shut up!"

Rockland knew exactly where Roger was. It wasn't typically in his nature to hurt lawmen, but the essence within him made it so much easier to do. Domovoi forced Rockland to draw his leg up and thrust it into the chest of the approaching officer behind him. The blow landed square on the guard's chest and despite the ceramic vest, the kick laid him out on the bloodied floor. The soiled gun slid into the hallway.

Roger scrambled for the gun, but the inhabited colonel was right behind him and he drove a cruel kick into the lawman's groin. The helpless guard cursed at the intense pain while Rockland stepped over him to retrieve the unclaimed service pistol. Rockland picked up the Beretta

9mm then aimed it at the first of the men he intended to shoot.

"I don't need these guns," Domovoi said through the colonel's mouth. "But I like 'em." The colonel, heart full of blind hate, rapidly fired two quick shots into the cell, dropping both of the intended targets and intentionally killing only one of them. A crimson blood spatter remained on the wall and gravity pulled the thicker traces toward the floor.

He spied the last one of the inmates that he planned on killing. Rockland smirked and took aim. The jumpsuit-wearing target was trying to get though an exit that was locked down by the security team. The colonel cocked the hammer and let the last two bullets he intended to shoot fly out of the barrel with a loud pair of blasts. The intended target fell on his face and lay there motionless.

With a murderous satisfaction, Rockland walked back into the cell. He gazed upon the floored inmate who was closing his eyes tightly, trying to imagine the pain going away, praying help would arrive.

The colonel tilted his head to the side as he inspected the bleeding man on the floor. "Listen, sport, this may be a difficult thing for a blunt instrument to understand, but I'm actually not guilty of what they put me in here for. Do you understand me?" He squatted down beside the inmate who was nodding at him.

"Please, help me! I'm sorry," the inmate managed to say as he lay writhing in pain.

"Shhh, shhh, shhh…"

Domovoi interrupted, "There's no point in crying over spilt blood."

The inmate's eyes met the colonel's. The man contemplated the irregular tone and unnatural comment. "You're two people in one….there's two of you! I hear it in your voice!"

"The shock setting in is making you delirious." Rockland assured the man lying in the viscous puddle. "Now, make this easier on yourself, who wants me dead?"

"It was Minnow in 'F' block. He knows what you need to know, please let me live, I have a family waiting for me to get out of here."

Rockland smirked and began to speak yet again. "Do they call him 'Minnow' ironically?

"What?"

"Do they call him 'Minnow' because he's the size of a whale?"

The inmate nodded hesitantly.

"Perfect," Rockland huffed.

"Please, let me live! Please!"

Rockland *was* going to let him live, but it wasn't his decision. It was Domovoi's choice. Domovoi had comfortably nestled himself in the brooding hate that stirred the colonel to violence in the first place, it was easier for him dwell in a soul where hate occupied the heart.

The compassion in the colonel's face fled.

"Please, no!"

Domovoi forced Rockland to pick up an improvised stabbing weapon. Swiftly, the crude weapon punctured the side of the inmate's neck. The inmates ruby red blood spilled out, contributing to the wealth of gore on the ground. The colonel turned towards the door. The guard was still lying there in intense pain.

"We're not done!" Domovoi said through the colonel's lips.

"Not him!" protested Rockland. "I will *not* hurt him again!"

"Yes, him!"

"He's innocent!"

Roger still wallowed in pain. The colonel was there arguing with a spirit within him, appearing as if he were utterly insane to the guard on the ground.

"You're not in charge anymore!" Domovoi yelled as he forced the colonel to take aim then fire the first unintended bullet that he ever shot. The bullet went through the top of the guard's head, ending his misery. After Roger ceased to move and breath, Rockland felt Domovoi leave him. "The first one was on the house, Rockland."

CHAPTER 22: THE COOLEST DATE EVER

The evening was clear when the Oahu inter-island super-ferry arrived in Kapaa on the island of Kauai. "It's so beautiful!" Harlie remarked as she surveyed the stars over the ocean. She breathed in deeply, appreciative of the thick forestation surrounding them.

"What floor is the dance team on?" Tyson asked.

"11. What about you?"

"14," he said.

"That's not too far."

"Nah, not really."

"Can we go to Kilauea after we check in tonight?" Harlie asked.

"We'll go now before we meet up with everyone at the hotel. It's only a 30 minute drive."

"That sounds even better!"

Tyson put the car in gear and drove off of the boat onto the cement port where cars made the transition from the sea to land. Before long, Tyson and Harlie were cruising along the curvy road and like before they had their windows open, the sunroof back and the music at a surplus volume.

Tyson and Harlie stowed the little car away at a small lot. After a long hike and a veritable bevy of bug-bites, they arrived at the destined plateau-like lookout that reached out over the water. The plateau was connected to Kilauea by a long runway, down which capillaries of the molten rock occasionally flowed. From their perspective, they could see the ashy sky over the brooding Kilauea. There was a thin, glowing orange stream of lava that flowed over the volcano's angry lip. They couldn't see where the largest amount of lava flowed to, but they could hear the molten stream as it ran into the vast ocean and sizzled into a large plume of noxious gases. They maintained a safe distance from the odiferous plume. They walked over a rough and rumbling terrain until they got the best possible view of the volcano and the ocean.

"I didn't know Kilauea still brooded *this* much!" Harlie admitted. "It's reaching the ocean!"

"It's 7 miles from the lip to the nearest part of the ocean."

"And It feels like the ground is moving underneath us!"

"It does when I'm around," Tyson replied.

"Oh my God! Really?"

"Yeah."

"Will you tell me about your heritage? Is this were you were born?" Harlie asked.

Tyson just nodded and Harlie picked up on his hesitance.

"I don't wanna make you upset, Tyson. We don't have to be here."

"There's nowhere else I'd rather be than here with you, but my past isn't something I'd care to relive. I love Kilauea, but when I look at her, I just see things. These things are forever burned into my memory. Any time I return here, I hope it'll be different, but it never is."

"What happened, Tyson?"

Tyson remained silent.

"Tyson, you can confide in me," she said.

"Harlie, I'm sorry, but…I just can't talk about it yet. Not until I reconnect with Calysta."

"Calysta?" Harlie uneasily inquired.

"Calysta is my biologic sister. And I don't know even know if I'll ever reconnect with her," Tyson's face became a discomfited red. "I don't know if she's alive or dead, and not knowing her fate kills me. I think about her every day."

"I didn't mean to upset you, Tyson. I should've thought before I spoke." A hard breeze rolled in off the near water and chilled Harlie to her petite core. She huddled up next to him, immediately comforted. "You're so warm," she commented. "Have I ever told you that?"

"I don't think you did."

"I like it." She kissed his cheek and kept holding onto

his arm. "Are you allowed to do a little showing off for your girlfriend?"

Tyson freed his arm and walked through the noxious air, ambling towards the dangerous, blazing stream.

Harlie watched as Tyson shoveled a small portion of the molten hazardous material into his hands. Tyson returned to Harlie and dropped the smoldering goop on the ground. The lava plopped on a piece of land that hadn't yet been blemished by the material that scarred the rest of the land. He dipped his finger in the substance and drew a heart on the ground. In the heart shape, he wrote their initials in the same way that any normal young lovers would carve them into a tree. Before the smoldering shape began to cool down and the vibrant red dissipated, Harlie asked if she could take a picture with her phone.

"This is the coolest date ever!" Harlie exclaimed as she viewed her digital token of their evening together.

"How about this one?" Tyson bragged as he put his face in the hot pile of smoldering rock. She nervously clinched her pearly-whites. He deeply inhaled with his face still in the magma and ash. He tilted his head back and exhaled a flame that rolled from his mouth into the air and dissipated.

"Tyson! That was unbelievable!" She threw her arms around him and pressed her face to his. She pushed her eager tongue through his warm lips. "Your lips are still warm," she whispered as she indulged in the comfort of their lip lock.

"There he is!" They heard a very familiar, very distinct voice yell.

"That sounded like Vinnie's obnoxious voice," Harlie jumped.

Tyson defensively rose to his feet. "I think it was."

"There he is!" The same voice yelled. "Get him!"

"Yeah, it definitely is," Tyson concluded. They both figured out exactly where the voice was coming from and there was the conceited Vinnie Tarsa, just close enough that they could recognize him. He was wearing a flashy gray suit and a silver tie that whipped in the swift wind. "Since when did Tarsa start wearing suits?" Tyson asked.

A small group of gunmen, six of them, appeared from all around Vinnie. Dressed in heat resistant uniforms, they leaked out from behind the border of trees in the distance, no longer lurking, but brazenly out in the open, wielding assault rifles, pistols, and what looked like portable wet-vacs on their back.

"That's him!" Vinnie yelled again. The group ran by Vinnie who didn't come any nearer. He was in Tyson's domain. If he got any closer, Tyson could've and would've easily dispatched of him after seeing the hooligans Vinnie brought with him.

Tyson helped Harlie to her feet hastily.

"Who are they?" she shouted.

"Collectors!" Tyson exclaimed.

"For what?"

"My blood."

Gunshots rang out in the evening air.

"What are we gonna do? They're coming from over there and there's nothing but water behind us!" Harlie cried out, "We're trapped and they're shooting at us!" Tyson brought his forearms together, and he stared at the 'Ahi' trace as if deciding on something of crucial importance. Tyson considered the Zoree female's message as well as the prospects of his and Harlie's capture or death. It was at this time when Tyson realized Omicron was actively trying to achieve a battlefield engagement between the Ahi and the Zoree.

"No we're not." Tyson exhaled an angry inferno on the emblem that was permanently marked on his forearms. Gun fire still peppered the ground around them.

"What are you doing, Tyson?

"It's the only chance we've got."

"Why are you burning off your trace?"

"I'm not burning it off," Tyson replied as the last of the inferno dissipated from his mouth and the ground started quaking. Tyson, arms ablaze, whipped his body around then spewed out smoldering waves at the gunmen. Tyson threw a violent offensive firestorm of emberous waves that turned the night sky as bright as day.

They gunmen returned fire.

"What can I do to help you?" Harlie shouted.

The shaking of the Earth intensified and Harlie had no idea what to think. She kept herself mentally sharp and got behind her ablaze boyfriend.

"First, let's make our way toward the edge!" Tyson exclaimed.

Tyson continued to defensively light up the night sky like a fireworks display as they neared the edge.

"Ok!" She was unsure why she did it. She tugged at the back of his shirt, guiding him to the edge of the rocky surface

"Look over the edge! Tell me when you see the land coming from under the water's surface! It won't be long before a small tectonic plate comes into view. It's the Ahi tecton!"

"Ok, I see something moving underneath!"

"Tell me when you actually see the land!" Tyson threw more blistering spheres and emitted more brilliant angry waves as he backed up towards Harlie. The shaking of the ground again intensified. The quake threw Harlie fell off the edge into a deep divot full of water with a loud splash.

"Harlie!" Tyson shouted, neglecting his defensive infernos and affording the men with guns another chance to shoot. In their rapid counter-firing, one not-yet- lethal bullet struck Tyson in the abdomen. Tyson felt the penetration of the round and slipped off the edge. He fell ten feet before his back met the hard stony land just surfacing from underneath the water. The fall knocked the wind out of him and just as Tyson gasped for air, a salty ocean wave crashed over them. Harlie recovered first and wiped the hair and salt-water out of her eyes.

"Oh my God! Tyson!" Harlie cried, seeing the bloodstain all over his soaked shirt. The thin orange blood ran through his hands. She had never seen him in such pain. Tyson lay there choking on the water that had just crashed over him.

"They...shot me," Tyson said, finally catching his breath. "I think I can manage to deal with it later."

"How can you just deal? They shot you!"

"I don't want to find out if they wanna shoot me again."

"Ok! Let's go!" Harlie began pulling Tyson to his feet, using every muscle in her petite, yet sturdy body. Tyson wretched and coughed up a large amount of the gritty, salty water when he finally got to his feet.

The ground beneath them was still trembling and Tyson was having a hard time catching his breath. "When this tecton finishes the ascent, there will be a ton of places to hide, for now just keep running. I'll be fine. You go!

"No," Harlie said. "Not without you!"

"Damn it, Harlie! You're going to get yourself killed!" He yelled, wincing in pain from the bullet in his abdomen.

"I just lost my dad and I'm not losing you too! Besides, I don't know what your plan is with all this!" She looked around at the terrain that was unfamiliar to her. "We both need to keep moving! You're coming with me."

Tyson let out a scream and dug deep within himself to mentally block the pain. "Run, you lead the way! I'll be right behind you. Any direction will get us where we need to be! Just run!" The tecton still rose from below the rough gray surface of the water.

Harlie took off like a shot towards the large upward slope in front of them. She capably sprinted beyond the numerous deep crags and huge boulders firmly cemented in the ground. Tyson yelled to Harlie who was quickly putting distance between them with her little speedy legs, "Once at the top there will be a large slope downward. Keep running when you get there!" Harlie kept running and gave a wave. She heard his directions.

Tyson couldn't match the speed and deftness with which Harlie jumped the crags and maneuvered around the boulders, leap-frogging, somersaulting, Kong-hopping and long-jumping. For every obstacle in her way she had a clever way of efficiently moving her body over or around it. The surface was wet and uneven. Her clothes, like Tyson's, were soaked and difficult to run with. The heavy wind kept hitting them from every direction, strewing Harlie's hair about. She was forced to tie it behind her on the fly.

Despite the conditions being so far from ideal, Harlie was still gaining distance from Tyson. The armed intruders were now at the edge where Tyson and Harlie had fallen, but by now, the gunmen had about a two foot climb to make to reach the rising tecton. Two men with the wet-vacs sucked the puddle of the salty water up where Tyson had fallen. They were collecting what they could of Tyson's blood.

Harlie had already made her way over the lip of the tecton just before the descent into the massive, bowl-like crater where there were many more rocks, crags and openings to caves. The water was soaking into the ground so fast she could still see the water level decreasing. Whoever knew about the tecton had instilled a clever drainage system that made it more functional land.

She peeked behind her just as Tyson clumsily dove up and over the rim she had left behind her. He let his body weight carry him down the slope in a painful and wild sideways roll. At the cost of bumps and bruises, Tyson quickly made up the difference in distance between them. He managed to get back to his feet and he began running with Harlie, this time he was almost able to keep up with her. The intense wind broadsided them again, almost knocking them to the ground. The extreme adrenaline surging through Tyson's veins was finally killing the pain.

Realizing they haven't been shot at in a while, Tyson peered behind him now that they were deep in the crater. He looked just in time to see the gunmen reach the top of the bowl-shaped depression. The gun muzzles flashed and again projectiles tore up the ground all around them.

"Are you serious?" Harlie yelled.

"You're doing amazing! Start cutting to your right, it's the third cave beyond the moldy mass over there!"

Harlie nodded as she rapidly changed directions maintaining an impressive rate and agility that Tyson wasn't able to match. The gunfire got closer still to ending their young lives.

The smallest of the thugs at the top of the crater ran around the perimeter. The attacker proficiently aimed down the sites of the rifle while on the run, effectively avoiding the hazards around the rim of the tecton. A very unlucky Harlie was the new intended target, dead-center of the Steyr-Aug's honed crosshairs. With a pull of the trigger, a bullet was sent down range. Tyson heard the crack of the round as an arterial spray left a mist of Harlie's blood in the air behind her, staining Tyson's clothes and sprinkling his face. Tyson watched in horror as Harlie screamed and crashed to the wet, stony ground.

"Nice shootin', Ryker!" One of the men yelled.

"You're too much like your mother, Harlie," Ashley said to herself contemptuously as she turned and walked away, assuming her crew would finish her dirty work.

CHAPTER 23: WHO'S YEREVAN TREAGAN?

Aaron followed Wright into a massive circular room with black tile floors that mirrored the superficial rays from the dimmed ambient lights. A domed ceiling with ornate circular lights cast dim light upon Aaron's and Wright's faces. In the center of the ornate room was an immense and circular table with a flawless marble finish and a large hollow in the middle.

"Whoa!" Aaron exclaimed. "This place is crazy!"

"This place is called, "*The Chamber*." A lot of significant history happened here, Aaron. Stories are told on those ciphers inside the circle of the table. Take a look."

Wright took the messenger bag off his shoulder and opened it while Aaron went over and investigated the ciphers. Wright retrieved a small marble case out of the bag and placed it on the throne that set upon an stage dug into the North wall of the Chamber. He put the bag back over his shoulder and approached Aaron. "Look at the third depiction down at the two-o-clock position."

"What is it?" Aaron asked as he studied the cipher. It

appeared to be a young man with wings, amongst his peers, "Is that...?"

"You," Wright answered. "Yes, it is. Tyson is two away from you, between you two, there's Jean-Claude. And on the other side of Tyson, that's Harlie. All the space after it," he pointed out, "Would suggest to me...you have a lot of work ahead of you. It appears, *all* of you have a lot ahead of you," Wright said.

"Good?" Aaron supposed.

"The one-o-clock position is my story, which you'll notice is growing shorter."

"But you're still relatively young," Aaron replied.

Wright smiled before offering Aaron the story behind the tales, the significance and the history of the Chamber. He called Aaron over to the throne with the marble case on it. Wright ran his hand over the exquisite chair. "This throne belonged to the supra maven, the leader of it all," Wright told Aaron. "He's a good man. He taught me a lot. His name is Addamas. He's gone missing as all the other mavens have."

Aaron wasn't sure what to say.

"He was an Avia before he took the seat of supra maven. He helped me through many difficult times."

"Well, I might as well go ahead and say it while I have the chance. You've helped me through difficult times, Mr. Wright," Aaron admitted. "Don't think it's lost on me."

Wright rested his hand on his protégé's shoulder, "And I'd do it all over again, kid." Wright circled the seat once and shrugged as if disappointed in himself. "I can't bring myself to sit in it," Wright confessed as he stared at Addamas' former throne. "Once I do, I will age an Avia equivalent of some one hundred years per human year. It finally makes sense why my story appears to be cut short."

Aaron already began mourning the idea of losing his mentor. His face flushed, his eyes welled, but he held back. He bit his tongue and cleared his throat.

"You know, I spent a lot of time trying to figure out that cipher." Wright shrugged as he moseyed behind the hallowed seat and rested his elbow on the high back support. "I never thought it would come to this." He locked his gaze on the arched double doors on the far side of the Chamber.

The door to the Chamber cracked open and an older black man emerged from behind the door then gently closed it behind him.

Aaron's eyes popped open, "Mr. Wright, why is Glenn Jackson the news man here? Is this thing televised?"

"No, Aaron. His real name is Victor Farrell. He's exactly the informed man we need here. He's seen it all and he sees all. He has the sharpest eye of anyone I've ever met. He's a very old friend of mine."

"Sharp eye? He wears glasses though," Aaron replied.

"That's just the news studio being a pain in his neck. They say people listen to you more if you're looking at them through the frames of glasses," Wright laughed.

"Oh yeah, he isn't wearing them now."

The man Aaron knew from the news approached them. "It's always a pleasure to serve with you, Ethan."

"Likewise. Vic. The *Blade of Exa* is on the throne."

"Great," Victor said as he grabbed the case and took the messenger bag that Wright gave him. "Who's this?" Victor asked as he looked at Aaron.

"I'd like to introduce you to my mentee, Aaron."

"Is he the same troublemaker you were at his age?" Victor laughed.

"He's gotten over the plight of the teenager," Wright replied.

"Mr. Jackson, you're an Avia?" Aaron asked.

"Please, call me, 'Victor', Aaron," the man from the TV said with a smile and a pat on Aaron's arm. "And yes, I am." Victor's smile quickly subsided, "Bad news though I'm afraid, Ethan."

"Oh what's that?"

"The Zoree are sending Yerevan Treagan as their representative for acting maven."

278

"What! Why?" Wright squeezed his temples, trying to present the onset of a tension headache.

"I don't know, but something isn't right. It doesn't make sense," Victor agreed.

"But, Treagan!" Wright protested, "No!"

"I'm sorry I didn't tell you sooner, but I just found out yesterday."

"Who's Yerevan Treagan?" asked Aaron.

Wright let go of the bridge of his nose, "Yerevan Treagan is the man who is representing the Zoree today as the acting maven. We're in trouble if they're sending him. His disposition is closer to that of a warlord." Wright informed his mentee.

"A warlord?" Concerned Aaron asked.

Victor answered the question, "The Zoree have picked the most ruthless killer they could send. He's only 24, not much older than you Aaron, but he's killed more men in combat than any other Zoree in history, except one."

"Oh...Who?"

"He's the second most lethal Zoree—only to the man who ended Exa, our previous world. It's said the Keaka don't trifle with Yerevan Treagan because they're afraid he'll possess them."

"That bad, huh?" Aaron asked.

"That bad," Victor confirmed then focused on the chair. "You haven't sat down yet, Ethan?" Victor nudged his head toward the chair.

"No, Vic. I can't bring myself to do it." Ethan eyed the throne

"Well, you must, Ethan. It's your duty with Addamas missing. You're the acting supra maven in his absence. There is no council if no one takes the throne. You're the only man who can. That said, I must get ready for the council."

Victor and Ethan, interlocked grips as brothers-in-arms would. "Keep your eyes sharp, Vic." Wright said.

"Keep your mind sharp, Ethan." Victor said before he turned away and disappeared behind the door he entered through. Ethan let out a breath and took his seat at the throne. Wright's cipher-figure on inside of the table illuminated and faded. Wright felt a strange presence come upon him and invigorate him. His eyes vibrantly shimmered and his clothes became white with a golden cipher—just like the inside of the table. Aaron proudly found his place next to Wright. They awaited the beginning of the next *Council of Exa*.

The doors to Wright's left opened and eleven Ahi respectfully processed into the Chamber. Dr. Morehouse emerged from behind the men. The men all wore gray suits, white shirts, and red ties. They stood attentively around the door and kept their hands in front of them. They almost never blinked. They were battle-hardened warriors known as the *Lumos*, the Ahi equivalent to the secret service. Dr. Morehouse took his seat and remained silent as this was the standard practice.

Soon, the doors opposing the Ahi burst open and a group of eleven angry Zoree stormed into the Chamber. The procession ceased and a young, averaged sized man who wore a tieless black suit broke through his guard detail. The young man's deathly stare and lifeless skin tone, told Aaron it was Yerevan Treagan.

"That dude's pretty scary lookin'," Aaron commented to Wright as he stared at the inert face of Yerevan Treagan. The blank anger in Treagan's face was contingent upon years of battle. Treagan's commanders frequently became his minions. The rulers the young mercenary engaged always bowed before him and begged for mercy from the terrible Yerevan Treagan. The mercy had never come.

Treagan took his seat and stared down Dr. Morehouse.

The lights dimmed, but didn't go out. A bright light shot up from the large circle in the middle of the table that separated the Ahi and the Zoree. Ethan watched the ray of light grow broader on the ceiling. On the lift was Victor

Farrell with the Blade of Exa, a diamond dagger crafted by the most skilled of all the Avia.

The ceiling of the Chamber slowly retracted and opened up to the night sky. Ten Avian guardians of the counsel, both male and female, wings not yet deployed, entered through all three doorways of the Chamber and evenly dispersed throughout the room. Ten more Avian guardians appeared from the sky and flew in through the opened roof. They dispersed amongst the other Avia. There were forty of them in total.

"Matt, Yerevan," Wright addressed the men who looked to him with differing expressions. "Be silent as you endure the burden of your people."

Victor approached Morehouse, who honestly offered his clean left palm. Victor placed the felt textile next to his friend and said, "I'm sorry if this hurts, Matt." Victor swiftly, but gently dragged the sharp diamond edge across Matt's palm. Matt extended his hand over the counter-clockwise current of the ring-shaped basin set into the table and let his blood leak into the suspension. Victor picked up the textile and placed it in Morehouse's hand.

"What's he doing?" Aaron asked Wright.

"Rulers must never forget, the blood given up by other men and women for the sake of their people. They too must give blood before a council is in session." Wright replied.

Victor turned and approached Treagan carefully. Treagan defiantly smirked at the man approaching him, indulging in the fear that Victor tried to hide. Treagan's eye was too keen for nervousness. Fear was never lost on him. Victor placed the textile next to Yerevan's open hand. Shaking, he gently grabbed Yerevan's wrist just before bringing the dagger to the man's palm. Treagan jumped to his feet and aggressively seized Victor's shoulder. Yerevan wrapped up Victor's arm, pulled him over the table and wheeled the man over his hip. All watched in shock as Treagan disarmed the grounded Victor. "Interesting, you didn't grab his wrist," Yerevan observed as he nudged his head at Morehouse.

It took no time before two of the Avian guardians ran for the aggressive young man. The closer of the two was ready to lunge in the air. He would try to pounce on Treagan, but the young man reached into his suit-coat and when his hand emerged, he had two knives ready to find the flesh of the approaching guardians.

Ethan almost considered letting the Avian guards try and subdue Treagan, but quickly decided against it when a vision flooded his mind.

The guards would rush Treagan, something the young killer was comfortable with. He would throw one of the knives and it would journey through the nearest guardian's throat. He'd fall out of the air—dead. The further guardian wouldn't delay. He'd run all the faster and try to tackle the mercenary. Treagan would simply leap frog the guard and leave the second knife planted in the man's brainstem. The Avian men wouldn't have a chance against Yerevan Treagan.

Wright's vision faded and reappeared.

Treagan would defiantly stare across the bloody chamber at Ethan—amongst all the Avian corpses— including Aaron's. Wright wouldn't let this happen.

"Halt!" Ethan yelled stopping the men from approaching their certain death. The running man stopped. The Avian guard who readied himself to leap, halted, and kept his feet planted on the ground.

"Good choice, Ethan," Yerevan defiantly smirked.

"Yerevan! I order you to put the weapons down!" Wright declared.

"Yeah? Well, call your men off, Ethan."

Wright remained silent.

"We both know what happens if you don't."

"Fine, just put the knives away." Ethan submitted in the interest of preserving lives.

Wright and Treagan both kept their end of the bargain. The men retreated to their posts and the knives retreated to Treagan's coat.

Victor got to his feet and climbed back over the table. Treagan sat down. The young mercenary raised his hand holding the diamond dagger. He plunged the exquisite blade through the top of his own left hand. The diamond blade tore through his flesh and penetrated the marble table. He didn't flinch. The black blood oozed between his fingers and leaked onto the table. "Is that what you were gonna do?" Treagan coolly mocked as Victor cautiously approached the young psychopath and yanked the blade out of the man's hand.

"Something like that, you maniac," Victor commented as he reclaimed the blade.

"The Zoree demand the safe return of Leor Tarsa!" Yerevan declared.

"Leor Tarsa?" Aaron leaned in to Wright.

"Vinnie's father, the Zoree maven," Wright answered.

"Vinnie's dad is the Zoree maven?" Aaron whispered back, confirming he heard right.

Wright nodded.

Yerevan continued his ultimatum, "No deals, no exceptions. We want Leor safe and unharmed, or we will rollover the Ahi."

"Just a minute!" Morehouse screamed as he stood up, combatively eyeing Yerevan from across the table. "We are not responsible, in any capacity of Leor's abduction."

"Please, Matt, sit down," Wright requested.

"You lie, Morehouse," Treagan kept his maniacal composure.

"If you so much as harm the hair on any Ahi's head, The Ahi will defend themselves—viciously!" Morehouse stated.

"There's no point in defending yourself, Morehouse. Not when you're sharing a battlefield with me."

"You've never shared a battlefield with the Ahi."

Yerevan stood up and glared at the wise Ahi doctor, challenging him. "You're right, but we can change that tonight!"

"Yerevan, cool down," Ethan declared. "Matt, you've never let your Ahi temper fuel your decisions. Don't start now. Sit down and compose yourselves."

"Fine," Morehouse interrupted. "But let me say this to you Yerevan."

"Matt…" Ethan warned.

"I'm all ears, Doctor," Yerevan mocked as he took his seat.

"You're a young, deceptive mercenary. You're a gun for hire. You're a dark void, a merciless abyss devoid of feeling! You're like a spoiled child who treats life as if it were a toy he didn't want anymore!"

"Matt, calm down!" Ethan commanded as Morehouse's voice grew louder.

"You play with human lives to occupy yourself for a

short time just before you mercilessly throw it away. You don't appreciate life, because you've never lived. You don't try to understand because you only care that you're understood, and when you're not understood, you kill, because for some reason you're good at it. Why you're good at it..." Morehouse paused with a shrug before continuing.

Woefully flattered, Yerevan smiled and awaited the answer to Morehouse's rhetoric.

"I don't why you're good at it. Maybe you're Mars, maybe you're Achilles, maybe you're the Angel of Death in the flesh, but you don't understand mercy because you've never needed it and that will be your downfall!" Morehouse boomed. "And I'll tell you this too; You're no maven because you're no human. You have no right to be here! You have no right to represent the Zoree!"

Amidst the chatter in the room that Morehouse stirred, the delighted Yerevan licked the icy blood off his hand, "That was an impressive speech, Dr. Morehouse. You've paid me far too high compliment. But, you have the ultimatum of the Zoree."

Yerevan pointed at the moon, ready to move its position amongst the stars. It was the first step of a Zoree war declaration. A recession of the ocean's water would follow and result in a tidal wave that could wipe out a major city in seconds.

"Don't get any ideas, Yerevan!" Wright folded his arms and stared down the acting Zoree maven. "Let the moon lie in natural balance this evening! Even you're more sensible than this."

Yerevan didn't listen. He displaced the moon in the sky like a magnet on a refrigerator. The ground shook and the loud tide ebbed ferociously. "We're not playing, Ethan. Dawson sold the formula to Omicron and Leor's gone missing. The Ahi are to blame for each of our problems. The life of the Ahi will come to an end if our ultimatum isn't met." Yerevan slammed his fist on the table.

"This will not be the beginning of the next end!" Wright screamed, "It's not happening while I'm the protector of New-Exa!"

"This will be, whatever it needs to be if the Ahi don't deliver Leor. We don't care how you deliver Leor to us, only that you do so quickly and without causing any harm to him." The moon entered an intense waxing phase that caused it to nearly double in apparent size. "If need be, we will fight and the Ahi will die!" Yerevan said crossly. He marched away from the council, ignoring the useless demands to reconsider the brash decision.

CHAPTER 24: MINNOW

The prison that Rockland was trying to escape from wasn't far from being in total ruins. Fires raged through the hallways and into the main floors of the massive blocks. The sprinkler system on the ceilings sprayed a futile mist over the fires that were exacerbated by gasoline and other accelerants. Rockland heard screams of pain and anger as he made his way from his cell towards Minnow's cell block. Rockland could hear explosions from grenades and numerous gun shots fired.

Rockland wasn't sure how he was still living after the phantom left him as the blood still drained from his wounds. The sign on the wall indicated the medical ward was on the way to Minnow's block. Rockland figured he'd see if there was anything that might help him treat his wounds.

After walking the low-ceilinged, narrow corridors, Rockland arrived at the medical ward. He scoured the hallway and the walls that surrounded the ward's doors for signs of imminent danger or booby-traps. Nothing appeared remarkably dangerous, especially given the environment. A heavy duty flashlight lay there on the ground. It was the same kind of flashlight Rockland had noticed a guard carrying earlier. He decided to take it and re-examine the door. Again, he determined nothing was amiss. With a swift kick, the doors crashed open.

Rockland heard anxious hyperventilating. He saw a long blood trail that immediately grabbed his attention. The trail lead him around the corner where he found the appealing doctor that had given him the injection earlier. Half of her clothes were torn off and she was bleeding from her exposed abdomen. In her arms she held one of the nurses, her best friend, who was now nothing more than an unrecognizable pile of flesh. She was burned to death.

"Look what they did to her!" She managed to shout between breaths. "They tortured her! Then they killed her!"

Rockland examined the scene with his flashlight. Given the state of her clothes and the environment that they were in—a prison that seemed more like an asylum for murders, it wasn't hard to imagine what a group of lawless men tried to do to the woman.

Rockland held his hands up and walked towards her carefully. He wasn't sure if she trusted him.

The doctor wasn't scared. She was relieved to see him. She gently let down the body in her arms and approached Rockland as he began to speak.

"I can't stay for long, but can I do anything for you? Will you let me get you out of here?" he asked.

"I called the guard station a minute ago, no one answered. I'm not sure what to do." she replied.

"Then you should come with me. I have no intention of hurting you."

"I didn't think you would."

"I didn't do what they accused me of."

"You don't have to justify yourself to me, Colonel Rockland. When I met you, you just didn't seem like the others."

"How badly are you hurt?" He asked, noticing the blood coming from her abdomen.

"Hurt enough, but I'll live. They stabbed me when I tried to help her." She pointed at the body that lay on the floor. "How about yourself?" she asked noticing the surplus blood that stained his jumpsuit.

"A group of men rushed in my cell. They tried to murder me, hence, the holes in my chest."

"I think those were the men who did this to me. They said your name a few times. What happened to them?"

The colonel was studying the infirmary. "Whatever happened to them...I'm guilty of."

"I wouldn't worry. I heard the cameras were shut down before the attackers began the assault. You only have to prove you're innocent of the one they're accusing you of on TV," the doctor reported. She put her hands around his wound, doing a quick exam. "Oh my God! I don't know how you're alive!"

"I don't either, but I could use some pain killers and something to stop the bleeding. Can I maybe have some kind of bandage to cover it? I've lost a lot of blood."

"I can tell." She pointed at a room toward the back of the medical ward. "The pharmacy over there is open. The narcotic pain relievers are in the cabinet over the sink."

Rockland studied the ravaged pharmacy from a distance and could somewhat see the cabinet. He began walking over towards the cabinet then motioned for the doctor to come with him.

She led the way through the pharmacy—knowing that there were no threats. She went through one particular medicine bay grabbing a few cardboard cartridges as well as a capped syringe and a vial.

She opened the cabinet and knowledgeably removed all of the drugs she needed as she informed Rockland of what she was getting for him. She tossed the drugs in a knapsack and looked at him. "I'd start with this low dose Norco now," she said handing him a tablet. "This dose will kill some of the pain, but a man of your size should be able to keep mentally sharp. Have you used narcotics before?"

The colonel nodded.

"Good. So for some long term relief, you should use take these Fentanyl patches. Change them every three days. You can use the Norco I gave you for break through pain. As for your bleeding, if you'll let me, I'm going to give you a topical aggregation pad. It will help stop the bleeding. I'm including these cartridges and this pamphlet that tells you how to use it if it isn't enough."

She stopped talking for a minute and prepared the aggregation pad.

"May I?" She asked, holding the pad up—waiting for Rockland's approval.

Rockland nodded.

"I'm also putting antibiotics and antiviral agents in this bag as prophylaxis too."

"I wish I knew how to thank you," he said.

"Getting me out of here would be a much appreciated start." The doctor glanced up at him. She was asking him if it were possible to escape.

The colonel thought for a minute. He needed to find Minnow, however he owed it to the doctor to get her to safety.

Minnow would have to wait for his comeuppance.

"Let's get you out then. Get your things."

"I'm ready," she said holding her pocketbook and the medicine bag. She had also changed into sneakers from her work shoes.

Rockland made his way towards the door. He peered around the corner. No one was there, but he did hear approaching footsteps that stopped. He sneaked out the door and crept down the noxious corridor. He gestured for the doctor to stop at a safe distance behind him.

The smell of proximal cigarette smoke drifted into the colonel's honed nostrils. He cautiously peered around the next corner and noticed an inmate standing there having a cigarette. The man was armed with a tactical pistol-grip shotgun that was slung in an upright position over his shoulder.

Rockland deftly positioned himself behind the unsuspecting inmate, grabbed the barrel of the shotgun and yanked it backwards. The butt of the shotgun connected with the unsuspecting inmate's face. A torrent of blood ran out of the inmate's nose. The colonel wrapped his hand over the enemy's mouth before he could make a sound. He stepped on the back of the inmate's leg, dropping him to his knees. With a hard twist of the man's neck, the colonel ended the inmate's life.

Rockland looked at the gun that the dead man no longer needed. "Hmm, Benelli always made a good shotgun." The colonel confiscated the shotgun and looked it over.

The doctor saw the fatal part of the colonel's attack. It caused her to retch, but she didn't vomit.

Rockland knelt down next to her. "I know you've seen a lot, Doctor, but I want you to stay back. I'll get you out, but it won't be pretty. Your job is to save lives. When it's necessary, my job is to take them." He waited for her dry-heaves to stop and asked her, "Are you ok?"

The doctor shook her head 'yes' and wiped the spittle from her lip. "It was a very impressive maneuver, Colonel

Rockland." She raised her gaze to meet his empowered eyes. "Does it get any easier over time?"

"Unfortunately it does. Then after you've done enough of it, for some people, it becomes difficult again. Anyway, let's get to safety."

The doctor just nodded and followed the expert soldier.

She explained to the colonel the shortest direction to get to the door. They rounded a few corners unseen. The colonel heard chatter before he rounded the next corner. He gazed around the wall and saw that there were three inmates gathered around the next set of doors. They were messing around with a two-way radio that they likely took from a guard. There was no good way of sneaking up on this group. He again peeked around the corner, this time with his shotgun. He aimed carefully down the sight of the black Benelli M1. His finger gently squeezed on the trigger until a loud blast echoed throughout the hallway. A scattering projectile reached the intended target. A large arterial spray violently decorated the wall.

The colonel gauged the men's reaction. He expertly shot two of the men with one very well placed round, knowing he killed at least one of them.

Rapid machine gun fire responded and bullets traced the walls around him. One of the rounds grazed Rockland's shoulder. The doctor covered her ears and retreated around the two previous corners.

"Look-it you, gorgeous!" An ugly oafish inmate was waiting for her. Rockland heard the menacing greeting and then heard the doctor scream.

Rockland's temper flared, but he had to judge the situation dispassionately. He just needed five seconds to finish the job he started. His emotions were telling him to save the doctor now, but his instincts were keeping him defensively planted against the wall.

Amidst the doctor's screams, Rockland waited for his attacker who didn't impulsively round the corner as he hoped the he would. It was up to the colonel to make the next move. He could save the doctor and risk getting them both killed by a hooligan who would surely follow him and shoot him in the back. Or he could risk getting shot by the inmate now and they would both end up dead anyway.

Rockland took the emotional path and tactically made his way backwards. He stepped cautiously around the first corner that the doctor had retreated to and slowly walked around to the next corner.

He saw the man raise his hand before bringing a balled fist down across her beautiful face. She grimaced in pain, but didn't give him the satisfaction of hearing her scream again.

The colonel neglected his tactical approach. He stepped out into the hallway and raised his shotgun, "Hey, handsome," the colonel called to the oaf. The oafish man moseyed around to face his fate. The colonel quickly pulled the trigger with his sights on the oaf's face. Another loud bang resounded, the shotgun recoiled. The now headless oaf fell to the floor. Blood violently discharged from the soft mass where the oaf's head previously rested.

'Threat first then the doc,' the colonel instinctively thought.

He turned around to another inmate waving a gun in his face. Rockland maneuvered around the inmate's arm right before a shot rang out. He grabbed the gunman's leg and brutally drove the inmate's head into the low ceiling. The gunman dropped his pistol. The colonel dropped the paralyzed gunman. He snatched the pistol off the floor then aimed it at the dying man. The inmate didn't have much life in him after the colonel introduced him to the ceiling. The ruffian did have enough consciousness to watch Rockland cock the hammer and pull the trigger. The barrel kicked and the inmate was left with a perfect circle between his eyes. Rockland checked the gun and realized there were no munitions left.

"Are you ok?" he tossed the gun away and rushed over to the doctor.

"I'm fine." She rubbed her face and looked disdainfully at her attacker. "He was weaker than he looked." The doctor got herself off the ground and kicked the man who attacked her.

"He's dead." Rockland informed the frazzled doctor.

"It was for my own satisfaction."

"I like you, Doctor." Rockland smiled then grabbed the doctor's hand.

Around the next corner, a man with an injured shoulder and a grudge with Rockland swung a serrated knife at him. Rockland evaded the blow and pushed the doctor out of harm's way. His emotional defense a few moments prior took over his instincts and he needed to regain his wits. The inmate wielding the knife wasn't waiting for the colonel to recoup. He swung the knife every which way at Rockland—getting a little closer every time.

Finally, Rockland's instincts were back on cue as the assailant jumped into the air. He tried with all his might to plunge his knife downward into Rockland's chest. After Rockland's successful evasion, he smashed the attacker's neck with his large fist. The man immediately dropped the knife and clutched his throat. Before the inmate could begin to fight again, the colonel threw all of his body weight into a spin and his heel connected with the side of the attacker's head. The inmate spiraled to the ground—dead from the trauma of the blow.

Rockland hastily grabbed her hand and ran with her towards the door, stopping to see if the men who he shot earlier dropped anything of use. He noticed that most of the guns were damaged beyond use. The shotgun blast destroyed one of the guns. Another gun was chambered with the wrong round leaving it completely jammed. The automatic weapon had no ammo left.

"Perfect," the colonel said in an exasperated tone.

"We can't use any of those can we?"

"Nope," he let out another sigh. "Do you need a minute to recover?"

"No, I'm good. Let's get out of here." The doctor browsed the floor with the colonel and a silver shimmer caught her eye. "What about that one?"

The colonel rolled the body over and picked the gun up that was concealed underneath the corpse. He inspected the gun and determined there was one properly chambered bullet left.

"One's better than none," he said. "Let's go!"

He led the way to the main corridor based off of the doctor's directions. They saw the sun coming through the window over the main exit. The only thing separating them from escaping was a long hallway.

The colonel rushed full-throttle for the door. As he neared the exit, a scraggly man with a long ponytail popped out from a broom closet. He swung a nightstick into

Rockland's face. The popping connection dropped Rockland to the floor. The gun fell behind the colonel and slid towards the doctor. The man with the nightstick kept smacking the colonel relentlessly while the doctor recovered the gun.

"Hey!" The doctor yelled. The inmate with the baton looked up, facing the doctor. She took aim down the sites of the gun as best as she could before reluctantly wrenching the trigger. The bullet traveled out of the barrel with a loud crack and a muzzle flash succeeding the round. The bullet traveled to the target and penetrated his neck immediately dropping him. The man who attacked Rockland choked on his own blood until he died.

The colonel stood up and wiped the bloody mess off of his face exposing a deep gash and a possibly broken nose.

"Nice shot," Rockland nonchalantly commented as he neared the terrified doctor. "Are you ok, doctor?"

She dropped the gun, mortified with what she had just done.

"You saved my life again," he said. "Think about it that way. You didn't kill him, you saved me. Thank you...very much. I mean it," The colonel said softly trying to calm the woman.

"It needed to be done?" The doctor tried validating her actions.

"Yeah, it did. You saved me. Even more importantly, you saved yourself." The colonel didn't know why, but he felt the need to embrace her. He crouched and wrapped his arms around her, "I'll still be useful to you through the end of the hallway. You can trust me."

The doctor cherished the embrace and so did Rockland. They were lost in each other's comfort until the doctor's eyes wandered beyond the colonel's consoling shoulder. She raised her thin arm and pointed behind Rockland, "Look!"

The colonel turned around and noticed a behemoth of a man standing in the narrow hallway. The gargantuan blocked out the light coming in through the window over the door. The man was about seven feet tall. The giant was remarkably muscular as though his entire diet consisted of steroids. Rockland noticed the severe fear in the doctor's face, despite the giant being garbed in a lawman's uniform.

"He isn't a real guard is he?"

The doctor just shook her head 'No.' "There is only one guard who is as big as him."

"The guard that brought me to you earlier?"

"Right, and he doesn't keep a locker here. He took that uniform from him." She exhaled deeply, "He killed him."

"Who is he?" Rockland asked as the distant giant began slowly approaching them.

"His name is Jack Thompson. But around here we call him, 'Minnow'"

"Really? Minnow? This may be easier than I thought," Rockland said sounding somewhat relieved.

The doctor eyed him as if he were a lunatic.

"You're Minnow?" The colonel called to the immense man as he also began walking towards the giant.

"I am," The giant called back. The two men stopped walking for a moment. Rockland thought about the giant's response. It was less aggressive than he expected.

"I'm Colonel Rockland."

Jack smiled a menacing smile. "You're alive? Impressive." Jack seemed relatively intelligent to the colonel, but it could've been intelligence falsely conferred by his British accent.

Rockland kept speaking in an unchallenging tone of voice. "Who wants me dead, Minnow?"

"Me."

"I don't believe that"

"What do you believe?" Minnow began walking faster towards Rockland.

"I believe you know who does."

"And?"

"And…I'd like you to be a sport and tell me who wants me dead." The two men were getting closer to striking distance.

"No can do, bloke." The men were now face to face. "What are you gonna do?"

"I'm going to figure it out." Rockland lifted a finger in front of Minnow's face. "You're going to help me."

Jack condescendingly laughed. "No, I'm not." He drew his arm back and pushed his fist with 550lbs behind it into the colonel's face—dropping him to the floor.

The doctor gasped. She was no longer optimistic about their escape.

CHAPTER 25: YOU'RE SO BEAUTIFUL

Harlie tried to pick herself up off of the ground, but the combination of fear, anger and adrenaline was not enough. She couldn't fight through the pain from the rifle round that entered her deltoid and exited from her chest. She screamed in frustration as she tried to push herself off of the ground, but she fell onto her side where the bullet had shattered her shoulder. The pain was too much. She rolled to her back. Still semi-cognizant, Harlie figured she had no chance of escaping from the people who were shooting at her. She tried to give up her life—not to be tortured by the coward who tried to kill her from a distance.

Tyson rushed to Harlie's side and saw her eyes fluttering. Harlie was on a mortal tightrope that Tyson had to help her navigate. He quickly inspected her wounds. The exit wound was not much larger than the entry wound. It might equate to enough time for Tyson to make a decision that he would be severely punished for.

The only hope was the very near Ahi territory.

Harlie coughed. A spray of blood flew out of her mouth, sprinkling her face and the dirt on the wet ground around her. Harlie's bloody mouth opened wide as she gasped for air that she desperately needed.

It was time for Tyson to act. He grabbed the petite girl and threw over his shoulder. He did his best to block the pain from his own wound and let his powerful Ahi instincts carry them to safety.

His feet pounded off the ground as he neared the cave entrance they were running towards. The bullets were still flying, kicking up the ground around them and destroying the rocks that Tyson was trying to maneuver around. His wound was of no real consequence. In his mind, it never happened. Harlie's wound was far worse and time was against her.

Harlie felt the pain of the injury overwhelming her mind. She felt the injury making her delirious and there wasn't a thing she could do about it. Her eyes tightly closed and all she saw was a white void. It was a soundless empty space—pure nothingness.

She saw herself in this space on her hands and knees, suffering from the wound she had just sustained. The only color in the void was the crimson color she bled on the groundless ground beneath her. She knew she was crying, but there was no sound. There were only tears that fell into the deep red pool of her blood beneath her.

Tyson maneuvered through the rocks, hoping and praying that Harlie would live. He made it to the entrance of the cave and took the quickest route he could, dodging the stalagmites on the ground and the falling stalactites. Rocks fell off of the walls as Tyson's feet pounded beneath him, occasionally landing in a large water filled hole. He hoped he could remember the way to the secret underground volcano, *Aloha Pumehana*— where he could welcome Harlie into the order that had forsaken him.

It was a gamble, but it was the only chance she had at survival.

Harlie was fading fast.

Harlie's vision of the white void was becoming more vivid. A bright light shined on her face and she raised her squinted eyes. She saw two silhouettes nearing her. She tried to move away while she heard her name being called, "Haaarrlieeeeeee…"

A torrent of memories flooded her mind, memories of her father before his accident and otherwise irretrievable memories of her mother holding her as a baby. She heard her name being called again, "Haaarrlieeeeeee..."

Tyson remembered the way. He found the massive, caved volcano. The brooding was loud and Harlie was nearly cogent. Tyson stood at the positive-pressured lip of *Aloha Pumehana*, which successfully combated the water it was previously submerged in for so long. The torrent of wind blew Harlie's hair into her eyes. Tyson pushed her hair out of the way and looked into the volcano. There would be a five-hundred foot fall before they hit the superheated substance beneath them. He set Harlie down, holding her up so that she was standing in front of him, fleetingly conscious. He threw her arms over his shoulder and wrapped her tightly in his arms.

The Omicron collectors popped around the corner, guns raised.

Tyson faced the assailants. He stepped in front of Harlie who watched with one eye slightly opened as she clung to Tyson. Tyson's mouth gaped. One last screaming inferno engulfed the gunmen, immediately killing them.

Tyson wasted no time as he turned to face Harlie. With Harlie in his loving embrace, they dropped off of the ledge. The wind no longer resisted them. Tyson's back was to the molten substance as they plummeted. Harlie's eyes were opened just enough to see the molten material in which they were about to be immersed. She consciously clung to Tyson for dear life, and closed her eyes. With barely any splash, they were completely submerged in the blistering molten rock.

CHAPTER 26: THE PRIDE OF THE AVIA

The McNamaras pulled up to the impressive Wright home in their red Impala. It was a quiet, starry evening with a possible storm front moving in off the water. Principle Wright and his wife, Mary, were sitting in lawn chairs on the driveway drinking Manhattans and enjoying the evening air when the McNamaras popped out of their car.

"Hey, Mr. Wright!" Aaron waved as he closed the door.

"Glad to see you, Aaron." Wright got to his feet, yawned and stretched, "Are you ready?"

"Ready as I'll ever be."

Alan approached Wright. He didn't shake his hand, but rather he folded his arms. "Ethan."

"Alan, Eva, It's a beautiful night." Wright reported.

"Is it?" Eva rejoined.

"Pat is doing an incredible thing today. He's a walking and flying miracle."

"I hope you're right, Ethan," Eva maternally cautioned him as she tensely tugged the straps on her purse.

"Today begins his rise to the pride of the Avia."

Eva looked at her husband.

Alan doubtingly stared at Wright, "Mr. Wright, I'm having a terrible time with my conscience right now. Why should I put Pat in harm's way by letting you put him in harm's way? No father should do that to their son. I stayed up all night thinking of reasons why I agreed to your request. All I could think of were reasons why I should've said, 'No.'" Alan opened his eyes and threw his hands up in the air, "Why should I, as a father, allow this?"

Aaron spoke up, "Dad?"

"Quiet, Patrick!" Alan asserted himself without his usual stumbling hesitation.

"Yes, sir."

"That's why," Wright pointed his head at Aaron. "If I helped you find your way as a confident father in my limited time with you, imagine what I did for Aaron."

Eva began to protest, "Don't flatter yourself, Eth…"

"Honey, please." Alan interrupted Eva, "I was not a strong father," he said softly. Eva's eyes welled up and became puffy. Alan continued, "Ethan *is* right about that."

"You're not asking that question rhetorically either, Alan." Wright's tone was fatherly. "You want the real answer to a question you are having trouble understanding. Who did you come to ask?" Wright cocked his head to the side, trying to draw an answer out of Alan. "The answer is me."

"True...but"

"Granted, I'm the only one who understands it and you can't exactly shout from the rooftops that your son is a 'bird-kid' as you put it. I understand that. I understand the predicament you feel you're in, but tonight, your son will be an unsung hero for the people on Earth. And he will triumph among the Avia. He will be honored in 'The Aviary.'"

"How's that going work, Mr. Wright?" The now half-consenting Alan asked.

"I'm squaring off with the Keaka and your son is going to save the Ahi and Zoree mavens—an incredible feat. It's like saving kings."

A pallid Mary began to cry and Eva didn't know what to do. She took Ethan's seat and tried to console his saddened wife.

Wright continued, "He's the only Avia I trust is capable of going with me. He's truly the rarest of the rare. His ability will grow immensely with each venture. I need his help. With this objective completed, your son will secure his rightful rank in the Avia and a haven for you and your wife if the Lost Orders of Exa should clash. Right now, he's the first chance we've got to prevent the war. We need the Ahi and Zoree to communicate soundly so the Keaka can't continue their treachery. The mavens are our last hope. The mavens can make everything all better again. And they will after we save them."

Alan huffed and grabbed his wife's hand, raising her from her chair. He lead her over to their son. Eva hugged him, "Be safe, Pat. Please be safe…just be safe!"

"No worries, Mom. I love you," Aaron said hugging her snugly.

"I love you too, son." She let go and grabbed her tall son's shoulders fondly. "I'm more proud of you than you could ever know and I don't even understand what you're doing! But you've changed in the most wonderful way!"

"Thanks, Mom."

After Eva's tearful goodbye, Alan led her to the car and closed the door. He turned around to Aaron, who was standing right behind him. He pulled his son into him and hugged him tightly, "I love you, Pat, Aaron, both of you" he laughed frantically.

"I know, Dad. I love you too."

Alan released his son and beheld his countenance proudly. "When in question, whatever you're doing, preserve your life first, above all else. I mean it. You're coming home to your mother and I."

"You got it, Dad. I *am* coming home to both of you."

Alan hugged his son one more time before retreating to his car. He sped off, doubting himself and the choice he made. Aaron watched the car race off before he turned to Wright.

"So it's gonna be dangerous?" Aaron asked.

"Extremely," Wright replied.

Aaron focused on the ground, stoically pausing. He raised his awakened eyes and grinned at the principle, "Cool."

"Ha! Blind bravery, you *are* an Avia! All right, let's get to it!" Wright threw his arm around his young protégé then led his way to the tool shed. Wright opened the doors and there was nothing in the shed, but neatly organized lawn tools.

"We're gonna do battle against the forces of absolute evil with...lawn tools?"

"Very funny, smart ass," Wright shut the door, closed the blinds then turned on the light. The ride-on lawn mower was deliberately parked in the center of the shed. Wright disengaged the parking brake and pushed the lawnmower towards the back of the shed. The principle grasped the seam of a large piece of plywood and slid it away from its place, revealing a secure trap door.

There was a white keypad where Wright completed a long code. The trap door automatically slid open and Wright descended into the secret room. Aaron followed Wright into the fluorescent blue room and wandered the indigo perimeter. The secret room was a home armory.

"These are weapons that I secured from a distributor who supplies militia-men in Bosnia. No one knows who he really is or what he looks like, but he gives me the best prices for these weapons."

"Nice!" Aaron replied as he admired the weaponry on the floor. A variety of pistols, automatic weapons, and explosives neatly decorated the velvety panels where they rested.

Wright picked up a heavy duty flashlight and tucked the flashlight away. Wright walked over to another set of equipment and black uniforms. Wright handed Aaron the uniform and a flashlight. "Should you get scared, don't lose your wits. It's very easy to breakdown when confronted by the evil we're to face. Use this weapon if you're confronted by him."

"Weapon?" Aaron laughed holding up the flashlight.

Wright smirked, "We're dealing with the shadow dwelling Keaka."

"Right..."

"They're soul inhabiting, wicked beings who call literal and figurative darkness home. The flashlight dispels darkness and uncertainty."

"O-k."

"Do you get it?"

"I guess I understand. A flashlight though...I don't get to use one of those?" Aaron pointed at one of the firearms that appealed to him on the shelf.

"Absolutely not! That firearm will be totally useless against the phantom. If you should be cornered by the Keaka, or someone he inhabits, take this light and shine it in his eyes. It'll disorient him long enough for you to escape. Do not attack him."

"Why?"

"As sure as I'm talking to you, he'll kill you. Understand?"

"Completely."

"Just one more thing for me," Wright said as he pressed a button near the guns on the wall.

A clicking noise signified a latch coming undone. The display where the guns were hanging recoiled into the wall. Wright hit another button on the keypad and another arsenal appeared.

A slew of bladed weapons appeared, including swords, knives and elaborately designed daggers. Engraved on all blades were the words,

'This side toward enemy'

with an arrow pointing at the tip. Wright grabbed one of his many combat daggers, sheathed it and attached it to his belt. "Ok, let's go."

Wright held the door for Aaron who was first into the kitchen. Mary was bawling into her hand-towel. "Mrs. Wright? Are you ok?" The uncontrolled crying began to make Aaron nervous.

"Mary?" Wright called as he walked through the door and heard her hyperventilating. "Mary!"

"Ethan! Why do you have to do this?" she sobbed.

"I was dealt this hand."

"No, it's not fair! I don't want to lose you!"

"That's not going to happen!" Wright definitively said. "Not a chance in hell."

"Well there is a chance in hell and here on Earth! Don't forget that thing you're fighting *is* from hell, Ethan!"

"You've seen one?" Aaron asked.

"Oh yes, yes I have. It's a story for another time, young man. They are despicable, evil phantoms."

Wright grabbed his wife's shoulders and sank his posture, staring deeply into her eyes. "Nothing can stop me, not even Domovoi when I have Aaron with me. I've beat the phantom before and I will beat him again." Mary just nodded, she wasn't convinced. "Let's go, Aaron." Wright's voice boomed.

They walked out through the backdoor and down into the middle of the Wright's dark yard. Wright looked around and noticed there was no life stirring outside, no birds, no ground creatures, nothing at all. A gentle breeze rolled in and the two Avia neared the fountain in the yard. Wright closed his eyes and listened to the trickling water as it moved effortlessly from spout to pool—beginning to end.

"Peace means so much more after you've known war. You don't really understand how incredible solace is, the feeling of no weight on your shoulders. It's called, 'freedom.' At the end of all this, the end of the war, we're going to sit near the water and just listen, it'll sound a thousand times sweeter to you."

Aaron felt the butterflies and nerves finally getting to him. "So, my job tonight is to just find the guys that *don't* look like a spirit-hijacking phantom and grab them."

"Precisely."

"Where do I bring them?"

"To safety. If anything happens to me, fly above the clouds and then listen. Only Avia can hear the melody of the Avian Sirens. They'll lead you home."

Aaron was becoming less sure that he wanted to embark on this journey. "So, if he's a shadow dweller, why are we doing this at night then?"

"The maven's are being held in a building in Honolulu. The building will be completely lit up except for the floor they're occupying."

"How do you know that?"

"Victor Farrell told me."

"Oh."

"So, final chance, I'm picking up on your hesitance and I understand. That's the human side in you trying to break through. Are you in or out? I won't be offended if you're not up for it. No problem…"

"I'm in." Aaron broke his wings open and felt a surge of adrenaline rush through his veins.

"Good, because I lied when I said, 'No problem,'" Wright joked.

"I figured as much," Aaron replied.

The sky was hazy and humid.

"We're in for nasty weather soon." Wright broke his wings.

Mary watched from the window as her husband and his young protégé both launched themselves high into the air and took to the skies heading towards the Honolulu lights.

She shuttered in fear as her blood pressure rose and her heart doubled its rhythm. Visions of the Keaka flooded her mind. She felt her heart flutter as she lost her breath and grabbed her chest. Mary lost her balance as her heart pounded and her vision blurred. She rushed for the medicine cabinet—to no avail. Her knees weakened as her weight finished dropping her to the floor. The pain in her chest raged and her heart felt like it was on fire. "Etha…" she gasped, hungry for her next breath. Her eyes closed and her heart stopped. Mary died on her kitchen floor.

CHAPTER 27: LOOKIN' KINDA STRESSED

Tyson awoke with Harlie next to him. She coughed up trace amounts of blood onto the sandy floor of a place he hadn't seen in twelve years. He swiveled his neck nervously. Nothing was different than what he remembered. The sky above was a light red hue. The clouds were differing shades of whitish grays and three suns shone brightly overhead. There was nothing but infinite sand dunes surrounding the flat sandy circle where they lay. It was an endless desert surrounding them. It was a tangible illusion that the Ahi created to keep invaders at bay.

Tyson got to his feet. Harlie was just conscious enough to notice the ugly, heavily-muscled man named Mica, appear from behind him. "Tyson," She weakly called out.

Mica picked Tyson up and slammed him to the ground on his back. Tyson screamed in anguish. Mica thrust his foot into Tyson's ribs and dropped his other heavy foot on Tyson's chest and spit on him.

"God damn, that hurt," Tyson wheezed.

"Tyson!" she called out again a little more strongly as she feebly attempted to raise herself and help Tyson.

"Around here, he's 'The Son of Red Death!'" Mica snapped.

"What?" Harlie mouthed, unable to speak. She wept seeing the pain on Tyson's face. "Tyson," she tried to say, but again she couldn't make a sound. Her chest hurt, the blood loss was evident in the clotted sand beneath her. The blood filled her lungs.

"He's not welcome here and neither are you! You will die from your wounds and he will again be punished then exiled!"

"You," a pained Tyson began speaking, "You! You can't do that!"

"Quiet, you unwelcome devil!"

"I *will* kill you if she dies! Believe that, you son-of-a-bitch!" Tyson protested.

"In fire you came and in fire you return!" Mica yelled as he raised his hand. An inferno from the ground engulfed Tyson.

"No!" Harlie shrieked. The pain was still too much for her to try and intervene. She again felt her life waning. The inferno receded into the ground and there was no sign of

318

Tyson. Harlie cried out, presuming Tyson was murdered by the vicious Mica. Mica turned to Harlie and raised his hand. She felt the burn of the inferno that came from the ground. It surrounded her. It burned her thighs, abdomen and chest the worst.

"Mica!" A powerful voice called. Mica immediately put his hand to his side obeying the mysterious voice. "You shall not hurt the girl! Give her space. She is now one of us."

"She is not! She was not brought here by an Ahi, Dr. Morehouse!"

"As far as I'm concerned, she was!"

"She deserves to die," scoffed Mica.

"She does not, Mica!"

"But..."

"I have spoken, Mica!" The voice boomed with a fury beyond anything Harlie had

ever heard.

"Yes, Dr. Morehouse!" Mica fearfully obeyed as he backed away from Harlie. She realized she was referred to as, 'One of them.'

She saw a thin, middle-aged man with an honest face wearing Khakis and a white shirt step through the horizon into the sandy circle. He had salt-and-pepper hair and was very clean cut. He kneeled down next to her and very gently lifted her head up into his lap.

"Mica, bring her to the crisis center near Serenity. We must try to stabilize her. If fate is on her side, we'll integrate her then complete her total convalescence."

"Yes, sir!" Mica said as he swiftly, yet gently lifted the small beautiful girl into his arms.

"My dear," Morehouse said to Harlie who lay in Mica's arms. She had just enough strength to look at him, but she blacked out again, and reentered the vicinity of delirium.

Harlie saw herself there in the same white void and heard her name called one final time, "Haaarrlieeee…" The blood retreated to her chest and the tears into her eyes. She was able to stand up and she examined her wound. The holes in her arm and chest were gone. She raised her eyes, finding herself face-to-face with a woman she had seen in her nightmares. Her father was next to the woman with his arm wrapped around her. The woman reached out and gently stroked Harlie's cheek.

"You're so incredibly beautiful," the woman said. "And I'm sorry!" The woman started crying, "I'm so sorry!"

"Mom?" Harlie asked as many tears journeyed down her cheeks.

"Yes, dear. You deserved so much more than me!"

"You're with Dad. So, you—are—dead?"

The woman slowly nodded her head. Harlie got as close as she could to the physical apparitions and threw her arms around them. She didn't care if this was the end of her life. She didn't care if she died. She could be with her parents.

"Harlie," her father paternally roared.

"Yeah, Dad?"

"You must fight to stay alive!."

"What?"

"You must try to live!"

"Why?"

Her mother spoke up, "Your place is with the boy who carried you. It's now your turn, *your job*, to carry him. I can tell you things are going to get very bad for him long before they get any better. He *needs* you otherwise he will fail."

"Fail what?"

"It's his destiny to be a significant force in fighting the eve of destruction where the world now waits. I was one of the Keaka's casualties of this doomsday, as was Tyson's father. You're both directly marked by the Keaka. You both need each other's love to prevent the derangement of the phantom within you." The apparitions faded and Harlie heard one last message. "We love you and so does that boy. He can't do it without you. You must live, Harlie! You must...please...try!"

Tyson awoke on the floor of his home just outside of Honolulu. His feet remained in the lit fire place and no one was home. He inspected his abdomen and noticed it hadn't healed.

The process of returning home through fire should've been a cleansing and healing process— it was available to Tyson no longer. He swung his head to the left and right. There was no sign of Harlie. "Oh my God! I killed her! I frigging killed her!" He wept as he slammed his fist on the floor and thought about her, lying on the ground in the Ahi territory, breathing her last, then closing her gentle eyes and being buried in the endless Ahi desert.

Tyson's emotions got the better of him and he looked towards his feet in the fireplace. "Harlie," he said as he reached out towards the hearth, "Please come back." He cried out. "I'm sorry, I'm sorry! Please, come back!"

Tyson tried to refocus his mind and get to his feet. He tried too quickly. The pangs from the bullet wound were too great. "I should've guessed as much," he commented as he slowly reattempted to get to his unsure feet. "Mom?" He loudly called out, but there was no reply. "Dad?" He called out just as loudly and there was still no response. He checked the clock and noticed it was 8:00PM. He walked over to the computer and realized that it was Tuesday evening—after the game in Kapaa.

"What?" Tyson asked himself. "How many days have I been gone." He looked to the left of the computer screen. There was a little note pad with a message.

'Tyson,

If you get home and we're not here call us immediately! We're all looking for you!

Love

Mom & Dad'

He took off his sandy shirt and looked at the bloody wound on his abdomen. "What the hell am I going to do about this?" Tyson thought for a minute.

First, he needed to let his parents know he was alive, but he also needed time to confirm what he expected was Harlie's fate. He needed to be able to answer Harlie's grandparents Dave and Doris when they asked what happened to their sweet grand-daughter Harlie—the only part of their late son they had left.

Tyson picked up the phone and dialed the number to his mom's cell phone. He walked about the kitchen, getting the closest thing to a medical station ready for his self-treatment of the wound while he waited for his mom to pick up the phone.

"Tyson?" He heard his mom after just one ring.

"Yeah, Mom."

"Oh my God, Oh my God! Thank God you're all right! Wait, are you all right?"

"Yeah, Mom. I'm ok."

"Oh, my God! Thank God! We've been worried sick! Your father is in Kapaa with a lot of the guys from the department. They're turning the island upside down trying to find you! Harlie's grandmother and I have been around here with the local search squads looking for you and Harlie! Ok, so she's with you right?"

"No, she isn't," Tyson said again. He shed a tear as he found the clothes iron in the utility cabinet. He plugged the iron into the wall socket and allowed it to heat up.

"Oh my God! Oh my God! What happened? Is she all right?" Doris got on the phone and took over the hysteria for Tyson's mom.

"Tyson, where's my Harlie? Tell me she's ok!"

"Mrs. McGrath, you must do exactly as I say."

"Tyson! Now! Where is she?" Doris demanded.

"Put me on speaker phone," Tyson ordered.

"Ok, Tyson, you're on speaker." His mom took over again and was nervous. "What's going on?"

"Harlie and I were attacked on our trip to Kilauea."

"We've both been shot and I needed to take her to the Ahi territory."

"Oh my God!" Tyson heard both of the ladies shout at the same time. "Shot? Tyson you said you were ok!"

"I am ok, Mom. Right now I've gotta go so I can try to fix this. I'll keep you posted."

"Ahi territory?" He heard Mrs. McGrath ask, hysterically crying, "Where's my Harlie?"

"Tyson, no, no, don't hang up!" His mom yelled. "You have to leave this to the police."

"You know I can't do that."

"Leave it to the police, Tyson!"

"How many Ahi policemen do you know who can come with me to a nether realm?" Tyson retorted.

There was no response.

"I need you to try and explain it to her, Mom." Tyson disconnected the phone—terribly unimpressed with himself on the whole.

He made his way to the medicine cabinet. He looked in the mirror and saw the dried spots of Harlie's blood on his face. He searched the cabinet and found an unused surgical pack from when his mom was still a nurse. He grabbed the forceps, hydrogen peroxide, benzocaine and antibiotic ointment. He also took two tablets of Vicodin they had from when his mom had a root canal. Tyson then prepared gauze patches and rubbing alcohol. He dry-swallowed the Vicodin with then made his way to the kitchen where he already had the hot iron waiting.

He heard the news on the TV in another room that his parents forgot to turn off before their search. Glenn Jackson was filling in for the usual studio anchor.

"Recapping the local news from earlier, in an impressive 21-0 shut-out, Coach Martin's team at Occam High defeated the number one seated Kapaa Knights. It was an impressive victory, especially since their star quarterback, Tyson Lynd, was a no show. As of an hour ago, we still have no report about where the rising star or the last person he was known to be with, Harlie McGrath, also a student at Occam high, have gotten off to. We would like to extend our help to Tyson's and Harlie's families. If you kids can hear us out there, let us know you're ok! The football team will be hosting a vigil at 9:00PM this evening at Occam High's auditorium." Tyson sat down on a kitchen chair. Vinnie has to be there Tyson thought.

Tyson went about his procedure. "Ugh, this is gonna hurt." Tyson prepared a bag of ice for the end of the procedure. He grabbed the benzocaine spray and sprayed his wound until the entire area around the wound felt numb. He grabbed the tweezers and with some hesitation, plunged them into the bloody wound as he screamed in pain. After twenty minutes of excessive swearing, Tyson dug the bullet out from where it was lodged, about two inches into his abdomen. He irrigated the wound with a mixture of the peroxide and rubbing alcohol, again cursing from the intense pain. He grabbed the iron and pressed it to the wound. He heard the sound of his skin singeing, but felt no pain as he pressed the iron all-the-firmer to the wound, cauterizing it.

Tyson wiped his wound dry, dressed it and slipped his shirt back on. Before leaving, he grabbed a zip-tie hand-restraint out of his father's police bag. Tyson bolted out the front door and into the hard rain. It was a torrential down pour and the wind gusted erratically. Tyson was determined to get to school and find Vinnie before the vigil started. He sprinted the two mile trek to school.

Tyson arrived in short time. He eyed the crowd of people hiding under their umbrellas with their candles lit and sheltered from the rain. They were standing around Vinnie's lit up car. They shook hands with him and complimented him on the victory at Kapaa. Some girl who wasn't Vinnie's girlfriend clung to Vinnie's arm in her semi-sheer white top that barely covered her chest and her short white skirt. The rain dripped down her body as she kissed Vinnie under the parking lot's bright lights. Her clothes soaked up the rain, exposing what she wasn't trying to hide.

Tyson furiously walked toward the group and stopped in the middle of a large puddle about twenty feet away from the car as the rain poured off of his clothes.

"Tarsaaaaa!" Tyson screamed in a deep, angry tone that immediately got everyone's attention. Vinnie released the girl from the lip lock and looked up smiling.

Vinnie flipped his hat on backwards and stood up from his laid-back leaning position on the back of his flashy car, "Hey, check it ya'll! It's 'No-win-Lynd.'" Vinnie and everyone around him laughed. Vinnie took his over-sized watch off and threw it to a sophomore friend of his, expecting the same physical escalation that Tyson expected. "Son, I'm glad you didn't show up at Kapaa, we woulda lost!" He arrogantly rubbed his chin and continued his jargon, "The hell happened to you?"

Tyson gritted his teeth and shook the water off his face as the very physical Vinnie neared him. You know exactly what happened to me! You, mother-"

"Easy!" Vinnie interrupted. "I don't know where you been. You just bailed, bro. And now, you want the glory of the winner's circle, yo." Vinnie said in his brash slang talk.

The rain kept blanketing the ground.

"Hey, Vin, come on man, tone it down. You know Lynd isn't like that." Jordan paused seeing that Tyson's enraged expression didn't change at all. "You alright, Lynd?" Still, there was no notable change on Tyson's face. It was like he didn't even hear Jordan. Tyson began walking towards Vinnie who began to speak again.

"See, man, he ain't even interested in what-ya gotta say. Yo, Tyse, me and your boy Jean took this team the whole way. I had to finish what ya'll started man. It was all me...and Jean...mostly me though."

Jordan ignored what Vinnie had said, but the majority of Vinnie's football playing friends weren't happy with his arrogance. Jordan spoke up, "Where's Harlie man? Is she good?"

An uneasy silence was suffixed with a bright flash of lightning, Tyson looked to the sky. The cold rain ran off his face as the wind picked up speed. He broke the silence with a stoic tone, "I don't know, Jordan," Tyson said, eyeing Vinnie, accusing him. "Your *boy* Tarsa led a gang of gunmen right to us and she ended up suffering for it!"

"What?" Jean-Claude replied, not believing a word of it. "You can't be serious, Tyse!"

"That's what I've been tryin' to tell ya'll, man! He don't know nothin'. This dude is impossible. Man, he's crazy." Vinnie replied nonchalantly. "This kid is crazy enough to think I tried to have him killed." Vinnie turned his back to Tyson and spoke to his friends. "Seriously, I've been tied up in some things. I'll be the first to admit that. I know I'm not the teacher's favorite student like No-win-Lynd over here, but seriously, do any of ya'll think that I'm the kinda guy that kills folk?"

The group didn't believe a word of what Tyson said.

"Vinnie brought men to kill you?" A girl in the crowd scoffed. "That's impossible...no....that definitely didn't happen."

"So seriously, where's Harlie?" Tyson heard Vanessa ask. "This is a sick joke, Tyson."

"I watched as she choked on her own blood!" Tyson roared.

"What?" Another one of Tyson's teammates said. "Are you feelin' ok? You're lookin' kinda stressed. You're lookin' off today."

"You don't seem well at all, Tyson," Vanessa agreed.

"Tyson, why don't you and I walk to the pier and get to the bottom of all this? We'll forget all about the garage the other day," Jean-Claude offered. "We may be able to figure it all out. You don't look like your normal self."

Vinnie approached Tyson and leaned in to whisper something in his ear. In plain English, he stated, "You and I exist in a different way than them, Tyson. Consider your audience, man. These are average humans. They haven't seen and they haven't known what we have seen or know. They'll never believe you. To them, things like this don't happen. You know silver-spoon Hawaiian kids."

"You're an asshole," Tyson scoffed.

"Fine, go ahead, swing at me and see what happens, yo," Vinnie let out a small laugh. Vinnie coughed on his own shoulder and sniffed some phlegm back into his throat then continued to speak, "…because you and I both know they're not gonna believe your bitch is dead until they see her pretty face in the obituaries, partner."

Tyson balled his fists, the exact response Vinnie wanted.

CHAPTER 28: A MAN NAMED DRAKE

The Colonel was face down on the floor after the steroid abusing behemoth named 'Minnow' punched him in the face. He shook off the blow and slowly pushed himself away from the ground. The effects of the blood loss were setting in and the colonel was losing strength. He propped himself up on his forearms and knees, still recovering.

Minnow was growing impatient with Rockland's moseying recovery. He drew his beastly leg back and screamed as he kicked the colonel in the ribs, flipping him over to his back.

"You're too light in the ass to be such an arrogant man, Colonel Rockland." Minnow examined the man on the ground in front of him. "That won't get you too far in this place." Minnow positioned himself over the colonel and viciously trounced him with his oversized boots. Blow after blow, Rockland felt more of his life force fleeting from him. He tried the best he could to defend himself competently, but the 550lbs stomping on him repeatedly didn't lend itself to a strong defense.

Rockland thought about calling upon the force that had saved him earlier. He was afraid of what he might do to the doctor under the phantom's influence. For now he sustained the beating, trying to figure out a safer plan for the doctor.

Time wasn't on his side.

"No! Stop!" The doctor cried out as she ran at the goliath, swinging her balled fists as she had done in her cardio-kickboxing classes. Minnow laughed as she landed her inconsequential blows and kicks on his thick skin. He kept stomping and raining his huge fists on the colonel. The doctor realized her blows weren't working so she tried scratching his eyes. It was her only hope.

Minnow became irritated with her attempts to dissuade him from his attack. He wrapped his arm over her shoulder and swiftly swept both of her feet out from under her. Her dainty body met the unforgiving floor and her head followed, crashing against the floor. Her neck cracked as a wave of pain came over her body.

"Ow! Dammit!" she shouted.

Rockland's strange ally from the shadows was his and the doctor's only chance for survival. The colonel was still suffering the blows from the behemoth as he glanced over at the doctor. Her extreme pain was very apparent in her beautiful face.

Rockland owed her nothing less than his life. He remembered he had some degree of control as the spirit manifested itself. If worst case scenario played out and he sensed harming the doctor was the spirit's intention, he would implement whatever means necessary to protect her.

"Domovoi!" the colonel shouted, much to the confusion of the man kicking him. Minnow stomped the colonel again. "Domovoi!" The colonel's plea was strange enough to get the doctor's attention despite all of her physical pain.

Just as before, the essence surged through the colonel's body. The attacks again slowed down in the colonel's perception. He caught the giant's next kick and brought him to the floor with a clumsy thud. Rockland rolled in the opposite direction of where the towering man fell.

Minnow, enraged, slapped the ground and got back to his feet as Rockland put up his tightly balled fists. Minnow rushed the colonel, swinging his fists like a drunken boxer. Rockland capably ducked the flying fists, blocked two widely swung blows and returned a stiff cross to the giant's face. A sanguine river flowed from the man's nose and Rockland followed the punch with an upper-cut into the giant's wide chin then a jumping overhand swing that heavily touched-down on top of Minnow's head. The force of the overhand blow drove Minnow's head towards the floor. Rockland followed up with a downward elbow strike to the back of his enemy's head. The sloppy giant fell to the floor.

The colonel left Minnow there and rushed to the doctor's aid. He supported her as she ambled towards the door. She limped, fighting back the tears from her aching spine.

She peeked over her shoulder, realizing Minnow's pained grunts had stopped. "Look out!" she shouted.

Minnow stealthily rushed the colonel, thrusting the knife at his back. Rockland pushed her out of the way. He quickly and competently evaded the thrust, spinning around to Minnow's backside. Rockland horse-collared Minnow and with all his might slammed him into the nearest wall. He turned the giant and elbowed him in the face, severely stunning him. Still grasping Minnow, Rockland wheeled around then threw his enemy into the opposite wall. Enraged, Rockland left merciless traces of his knuckles all over the giant's face then swept the behemoth's legs out from under him. Minnow again crashed to the floor and Rockland retained Minnow's knife. Without hesitation, the colonel skillfully flipped the knife in his hand and sunk the blade a half inch under Minnow's whiskery mandible. "It keeps going until you tell me who wants me dead."

Defeated, Minnow protested, "Stop! I don't know who he is! Please!" Minnow defensively seized the colonel's arm and Rockland stopped to listen, leaving the cold steel blade against Minnow's neck.

"So it's a 'he'?" Rockland asked.

"I guess, the notes are always signed, 'a Man named Drake'."

"Are you serious?"

"Swear to God!" The giant wheezed. "He's your man, I swear! The bloke is 6s and 7s."

"What?"

"I think he's crazy. I never talked to him, but we've communicated though letters and other routes. You know, no direct contact."

"Thanks!" Domovoi butted in as he forced Rockland to raise the knife and plunge it into the giant's chest repeatedly, puncturing his heart numerous times.

The doctor gasped at the viciousness of the attack. "What the hell!" she exclaimed after hearing the absolute evil that came out of the Colonel's mouth and realizing it wasn't him. The voice was too supernatural to be human.

Rockland was losing control over himself. The doctor noticed a seizure-like struggle within the Colonel. Domovoi grabbed the gun off of Minnow's belt and raised Rockland's tremoring arm, aiming at the doctor. Rockland threw himself on the floor, smothering the gun.

"No!" The doctor yelled.

Domovoi pulled the trigger. Bullet after bullet penetrated the colonel's chest cavity then ripped through the back of his jumpsuit until the hammer of the weapon clicked and no more rounds discharged. The ammunition was spent and the colonel was still alive. Domovoi prevented him from dying, yet the Keaka wasn't totally in control of the colonel anymore. Rockland found a way to control Domovoi, but he wasn't sure what it was.

"This time, I'm permanent!" Domovoi persisted in his attempts to regain control over the colonel's free will. "You can't stop me! I'm not leaving this time!" Domovoi yelled as his influence somewhat dissipated.

Slowly, the colonel got to his knees, rested his hands on his thighs and sunk his head. "I'm so confused right now."

"I'm not," the doctor replied as she knelt down with the colonel in the hallway. The visible sun gleamed through the window at the end of the hallway and it was warm on their faces. "It's simple really. You're dealing with the inhabitance of a Keaka, a phantom that corrupts souls that are prone to corruption. This can't be your first inhabitance. He would have left you. They always leave after the first inhabitance. No one knows why."

"I called on him earlier today when the other inmates tried to kill me." Rockland answered.

The doctor put her hand on his and gazed into his eyes. "It's how you survived the initial trauma from all those wounds in your chest. Sometime after the attack he must've left you. You would've died if you didn't come to the infirmary. The Keaka saved you from the lethality of the blow's penetration. A miracle kept you alive long enough to get to me after he left you. Love will ultimately save you from the Keaka, but you need him right now to survive and he needs you for something, otherwise he would've left you to die already."

"What? How?"

"What you did was a selfless act, trying to end your life to save mine. Right now, the Keaka is keeping you alive and affection is keeping you from total corruption of the Keaka."

"Who are you?" he asked.

"My name is Nicole Risk," she said, kissing the part of his cheek that wasn't bloody. With her lips pressed to his cheek, the influence of the spirit waned again, but Rockland felt his life slipping away as well.

"Let me get you out of here, Dr. Risk." He moseyed himself up to his feet.

"Call me 'Nikki.'"

Rockland walked with Nikki to her car, the stiffness in her back and the pain in her neck from getting tripped by Minnow was getting worse. "I don't know how to thank you enough, Nikki," the colonel said as he finally stopped with her outside of her blue Ford Focus. "I hope…"

"Oh, no you don't! You're not getting away from me that easily. You need me," she said as she looked at the colonel thoughtfully.

"It's too dangerous!"

"You won't be able to keep that spirit in you at bay without me."

"I can't put you in any more danger."

"I can't let *you* put yourself in anymore danger, or any innocent people in danger for that matter. A man as powerful and smart as you colonel is dangerous enough, but with that Keaka in you…you just might be the most dangerous man alive. I took the Hippocratic oath. I owe beneficence and non-malfeasance for the population at large. If you don't need me, then the innocent people you risk hurting need me. I'm the person in your life that can prevent collateral damage." She paused knowing that the thought had occurred to Rockland. "You know I'm right."

The colonel thought for a minute, "I've got a place we can go," he said. "I've got an untraceable car ready to find whoever set me up. I need you to be sure that this is what you want to do. You've gotta consider that you may not be able to see your family or friends for a while."

"Well, most of my family is dead or back in the Ukraine and my only friend is dead too. I could really use a friend." Her eyes began to glisten in her sorrow. "No, I need a friend and I could be useful to you. It's win-win!"

"Ok."

"Thanks." She wiped the tear-buds from her eyes. "Would you mind driving? I have a terrible headache."

CHAPTER 29: IS HE DEAD?

Aaron beat his wings at a hasty rate as he followed Wright to Honolulu, soaring some three thousand feet over head. After they dipped below the clouds, the hard rain beaded on their faces and drenched their clothes. Aaron dipped a little lower and saw the grandeur of Omicron in the evening. The chrome-by-day 'O' emblem was a cool neon blue by evening. The blue color transitioned to a neon red via a sharp purple. The well placed lawn lamps highlighted the edifice with a cool indigo aura.

"We can land in the 'O' then find our destination from there," Wright said. He beat his wings once and drifted effortlessly towards the 'O' on the building's facade.

Aaron followed closely behind Wright, but he wasn't able to drift with the same unhindered acceleration.

Wright noticed the bright lights coming from the top floor. He turned around to Aaron, "I'm going to investigate the top floor, kid. Keep pushing towards that 'O' logo."

Aaron nodded.

With a gusty flap of his wings, the principle shot further in the sky like a determined jet-fighter. He ably circled twice around the building before something inside Omicron caught his eye.

"You're a busy girl, Ashley." Wright laughed as he flew around the building. He noticed a Hispanic man buried between her legs. Wright eyed the room for clues as to the man's identity, but there was nothing—just clothes carelessly strewn about the suite. The lightning cracked and the thunder roared as the man apparently finished his work on the satisfied naked woman in the bed. Her chest heaved as he kissed her lips and walked stark naked to the bar in the suite.

The storm began to settle and Wright came to a realization as he examined the man one last time. "La Tormenta," he said under his breath.

After deciding he'd seen far too much of the lovers' escapade, Wright blasted off to the 'O' emblem where Aaron await him. Wright circled the building one more time before coming in for a swift landing.

Aaron stood in the 'O' shaking his water logged wings and ringing out his clothes and hair. "Did you see anything?" he asked.

"Yeah," Wright answered. With a snap of his wings he effectively drained the water from them.

"What's that?"

Wright warily cleared his throat, "I'll explain later. I saw a little more than I'd care to."

The unworried Aaron just shrugged his shoulders, "Fair enough."

The storm still raged as Wright and Aaron overlooked the city. "Wow," Aaron said, "I feel like I've never been able to see so far in my life, it's crazy!"

"That's called 'eagle eye.' Now that your wings have been deployed for the first time, you can use it at any time." Wright pointed at the skyline as he continued, "You focus on something miles away and you can hone in on it." He pointed at the cars on the ground, "Look down below and even though it's night, I guarantee you can read any of those cars license plates."

"Wow, you're right!"

Wright stared into the distance and pointed across the city. "There's where we need to be, the old finance tower across town!" Wright kicked off the 'O' and launched himself into the air. "Let's go!" he shouted.

Aaron kicked off the 'O,' launching himself over the city in the same manner as Wright did. He eventually caught up to his mentor. "That's it, son! Good work! The more you push yourself, the more you learn—every time you push harder and you learn more. You're not just any Avia, Aaron. You're a truly unique individual. Not all of us are the same. Like humans, we have our 'Olympians' and our 'couchpotatoes' so to speak. More analogous to your situation, we have our pigeons and our eagles." Wright was smiling as he effortlessly cruised along with his mentee.

"Is that right?"

"You bet," Wright said to his protégé. "And you're an eagle through and through. Your vision confirms it. You're just like your father. Trust me, kid, that's a good thing. Your father was the most powerful Avia I'd ever taught."

Aaron closed his eyes. He sadly gazed at the city far below. "Mr. Wright, I'd like to know more, but not right now. Eva and Pat are still my parents."

"You're right, I'm sorry to upset you." Wright wasn't comfortable with how Aaron's adoptive parents just became, 'Eva and Pat.' "Son, they're not 'Eva and Pat.'"

"What?"

"Call them, 'mom and dad'. Your *mom and dad* are still—and always will be your parents."

"Thanks," Aaron said.

Wright spied the building and focused on the floor that had no power. Using his keen sight, he saw a man inside staring at him, trying to focus on him. It was Dawson Wrangle—or at least his inhabited body. The lights on the building started to flicker like a pinball machine.

"We've been spotted kid. I thought the approach would be easier than this."

"What's that mean?"

"New tactic, going in hard, our cover is blown. I'm going to destroy the glass and I need you to go in like a shot, focus on nothing but the mavens. Grab the mavens and draw them into you, shield yourself and them with both sets of your wings. I'll let you know when it's safe to come out."

"You got it."

"Gain altitude. Then on my signal, nose-dive and blow through the glass. You'll get minor cuts on your face, but that's all."

Aaron shot straight up, increasing his altitude as he watched the building with the flickering lights. The rain picked up and the wind was at his back. The adrenaline teemed through his body and he was ready for his part in the rescue. Wright put a 'hold' fist in the air and the vigilant Aaron continued to climb.

Wright's 'hold' fist turned into a 'go' signal with a downward swipe of his arm.

Wright shot like a bullet towards the windows where he suspected Domovoi was. Aaron changed his flight pattern and began his nose-dive. Aaron felt the wind behind him and the friction of the air as it blew over his face, through his hair and contoured to his streamline silhouette as he raced towards the building.

Wright collided with the glass in a resonating and thunderous slam that shattered all of the windows on that floor he hit. Aaron raced by Wright and broke through the cloud of sharp glass, suffering the predicted cuts on his face.

Aaron honed in on the bleeding and defeated man in the middle of the room. The man knelt there next to the dead body he was selflessly trying to preserve as he was abused by a grim specter of a man standing over him. Aaron blew in fiercely. He grabbed the maven and the dead body next to him. He took them away from the abusive man and hit the floor. Aaron heard the wind pick up and he felt a powerful force almost dragging him off the ground. Aaron sheltered himself and the mavens in anticipation of the attack to come.

"Wright!" Aaron heard a wicked voice yell. "Tonight, you and this boy will die!"

"Dawson!" Wright called out. "Can you hear me?"

"No, he can't," the grim man answered. "I killed him before I took his body."

Aaron heard a high-pitched howl as the wind picked up. Aaron looked through his clear wings and saw the grim man standing there boldly, meeting eyes with Wright. Wright hovered outside of the window, lightning cracking behind him. Wright beat his wings strongly, keeping a circling wind current around the building.

The glass, caught in the wind, circled the building as a murderous tornado. Wright let out the same howl that sounded like an angry eagle. He flapped his wings much harder one more time.

Wright sent a barrage of glass shards from every direction—straight for his enemy. Aaron prayed for his life as he felt the piercing glass penetrate his wings. He remained unharmed.

The maven lay there motionless under the cover of Aaron's wings.

"Thank you, young man!" he heard the man say. "I'm Ellis, the new Ahi-maven and I appreciate your help." Aaron was nervous. He wasn't quite sure how the man was so calm.

Aaron could barely hear over the wind torrenting around them.

"You're doing very well, kid. Thank you for also showing the compassion to Leor that he deserved. We must preserve his body. He was the Zoree maven and he was a good man. I know the dead can be unnerving, but he deserves all the dignity we can afford to give him."

"I understand."

"I can tell you're nervous, but just stay focused. Ethan is the greatest Avia in history," Ellis stated.

"Yes, sir."

"Just do as Ethan says we'll be ok,"

Aaron felt the barrage end and heard the evil man curse as he ripped the deeply implanted glass out of his body. "That was a cute little magic trick, but it will take more than that to end me, you irritating son-of-a-bitch!" He removed that last significant piece of glass and tossed it over his shoulder.

After the last shard fell to the floor, Wright darted towards his target. The man dropped to the floor and left a dark vapor in the air that Wright flew into. Wright fell to the ground, cringed, and then got to his feet in a psychotic frenzy. Wright grabbed his own hair and tore it out as he thrashed from left to right, fighting with something within him.

The storm roared and Wright madly flapped his wings. The glass rose up off the ground while Wright tried to gain control of his flashlight. The spirit within him stifled the principle's defense and forced Wright to fly head-first into the hard ceiling. Wright yelled in pain then continued fumbling for the flashlight on his belt.

Aaron knew he had to do something, but if he did, the spirit would surely engage him. 'Mavens first, Wright second,' Aaron thought. He saw the nearest building was easy to get to. He grabbed the mavens by the collar and shot like a bullet towards the nearest rooftop. Aaron reached his destination through the harsh storm and dropped the men off at the rooftop. He circled back and could still see Wright struggling in his defense against the spirit inside of him. Aaron grabbed the flashlight Wright had given him and returned to the skirmish as fast as he left.

Wright continued struggling with the spirit within him. Wright had a large shard of glass in his hand that the spirit was trying to force him to thrust into his own heart.

Aaron immediately acted. On his way to Wright, he gusted past the grim body that the haze left behind. He seized it off of the floor and hurled the corpse out the broken window. He swiftly circled around the building picking up speeds beyond which he'd ever felt. The wind blew past him even harder than his first free fall the day of his flight school. He straightened his flight pattern and honed in on Wright. Still picking up velocity, Aaron darted towards his mentor and crashed into him—sending him to the floor. They skidded across the ground until they reached the paneless window ledge. Wright swatted his fists at Aaron as he writhed under his protégé. Aaron grabbed Wright's left arm with both hands. The inhabited Wright balled his right fist and swung his arm. His knuckles met the unguarded side of Aaron's face. Aaron felt his brain scramble and his vision blur. The blood pooled in his mouth, but Aaron held on tightly.

"You're a strong one!" Domovoi shouted. "You look just like your father! He was pretty young too when I killed him!"

"Shut up!" Aaron demanded.

"How old was he when I killed your son, Ethan?"

"What!" Aaron exclaimed.

347

"Kid, focu—s," Wright managed to say while fighting the phantom inside of him.

Aaron was still holding on to Wright's arm. He let go with one hand, reached back and punched underneath the principle's thumb. The glass shard fell out of Wright's hand, reflexive of the well placed strike.

Aaron brandished the flashlight and shined the aggressive beam into Wright's darkened eyes. Wright's body contorted on the ground as a black vapor left his mouth and nose. The haze manifested itself as a humanoid shape that was about nine feet tall with menacing purple eyes and sharp black teeth.

Aaron rolled away and took off in the opposite direction. The humanoid shape rushed towards Aaron. Aaron again raised the light to the demon's eyes behind him. The phantom was disoriented again.

"Perfect, kid!" Wright yelled as he shot up from behind the spirit. He wrapped his arms around the corporeal body then plunged his vengeful combat dagger into the demon's forehead.

The creature let out an ear shattering roar and fell to the ground with Wright. The phantom bled a sappy black blood. Wright and Aaron exchanged glances as the being dissipated into nothing. They only thing Domovoi left behind was the black blood that leaked from his ethereal face.

"Is he dead?" Aaron asked.

"One of him is—thanks to your instincts." Wright stood up and slapped Aaron's shoulder.

"Huh?"

"Outstanding instincts, kid," Wright's breathing was severely labored. "Awesome work."

"Thanks."

"No, thank you," Wright sat back down on the floor near the blood and took out a series of vials from his pocket. "Domovoi learned a new trick. I underestimated him... and you."

"May I ask a question?" Aaron sat down with him.

"Anything, kid," Wright said as he collected the samples of blood.

"My father—your son?" Aaron asked.

"Yeah," Wright said, putting down the vials. Ashamed of himself, he couldn't look at his grandson. "I wasn't sure when was right to tell you. Even after all these years of experience I've had on this Earth. Things like that are hard. You never really figure it out."

"I called my own grandmother such an awful name! I'm so sorry!" Aaron cried out as he threw his arms around Wright.

"Take it easy, kid. Just like she said, 'It's done and over with. She's stronger than you and I could ever think about being… and she's not exactly your biological grandmother."

"What?"

"Your biological grandmother died long ago. It's a long story that I can fill you in on soon. Right now we must focus. Thanks to your help, one of Domovoi is dead. That's where our concentration must be now."

"What do you mean *one* of him is dead?"

"Every century those spirits are around, they are reborn again. They can control a new being. They're totally in control of themselves in more than one place."

"Damn, how many of him are there?"

"They're always born at the turn of a century. So, I can only guess. I'd estimate there are two of him as of right now. Well, one I suppose, now that this one is dead. I fought him in the American Revolution. At that time, there was two of him as I recall. I dispatched of one, leaving the other alive. There was another turn of the century and I dispatched of another in the Civil War. The 1900s came and I killed one in the second World War. The 2000s rolled around and here we are.."

"Whoa..."

"I'm going to the Aviary for a few days to test the blood, and do some investigating. We should be able to figure out the answers to almost all of our questions. And, I, uh, know we have a lot to talk about. You can join me if you want."

"Yeah, I'll come along," Aaron nodded as he wiped the blood, sweat and rain off his face. "One more thing, Mr. Wright."

"What's that, kid?"

"The mavens are on that roof top over there."

"Good," Ethan smiled. "Good."

"No, not really," Aaron said. "Vinnie's dad was dead when we got here."

Wright sighed as he lost himself in a train of thought. "Then, the war's here. Grab your parents and bring them to the Aviary for their protection. The Avia are in their debt to begin with."

CHAPTER 30: WHAT CHOICE WAS THERE?

Tyson's fists were balled and Vinnie's smirk was wide.

"Go ahead! Do it! Avenge your dead bitch," Vinnie challenged while standing face-to-face with Tyson.

The temper that had rendered Tyson foolish at Omicron was resurfacing. His forehead was sweating, his heart was racing and his teeth were viciously clenched.

"The war's about to start, Lynd—and there's no stopping it," Vinnie sneered.

"Why do you want to do this, Vinnie? You and I together can stop the plight of exa—this imminent fighting for no intrinsic reason."

"No...we can't stop it. Look at the moon. The moon will attack the earth just as it did 6 billion years ago." Vinnie laughed as he pointed to the sky. "I've already been conscribed into the Zoree forces. So, I'm gonna make the best of it. There's a pending bounty on every Ahi's head—including you. I'm going to kill so many of you and get so rich in process, Yerevan Treagan will be taking notes."

"You're insane!" Tyson exclaimed.

"We're going to fight whether it's now or later—now is always good for me, Lynd!" Vinnie seized Tyson's collar and thrust his head into Tyson's nose. The blood streamed down Tyson's face and the teenage spectators all reached for their cell phones to record the fight. "Ten-thousand dollars if I bring you in alive or five-thousand if I decide to kill you!" Vinnie hooted.

Tyson swung at Vinnie's arrogant face. Vinnie ducked the blow and thrust his powerful fist into the wound that was concealed under Tyson's clothes. The force was too much. Tyson shouted in pain as he hunched over after the impact. Vinnie stepped on the back of Tyson's leg—dropping him to his knees. Vinnie chambered his hand for the back-hand blow across Tyson's face that would follow.

Vinnie let his hand fly.

Tyson caught the blow. With staunch determination in his face, he wheeled Vinnie over his shoulders—torquing Vinnie's wrist in the process spraining it. Tyson jumped to his feet and regained his balance. Vinnie snapped himself up to his feet and combatively circled around Tyson, subtly getting closer. Vinnie agilely shuffled his feet before he twisted and launched a swift back kick at Tyson's chest. Tyson narrowly caught the blow and dropped his elbow on the side of Vinnie's knee, fracturing it.

"Oh my God!" Vanessa shuddered as she heard the sounds of Tyson's elbow tearing through Vinnie's sinews. Tyson swept Vinnie's stabilizing foot and let Vinnie crash to the ground.

"Stop! This is so scary!" Vanessa howled again.

"Tyse, this isn't you!" Jean-Claude yelled. "You don't need to fight!"

Vinnie got to his feet. The joint-destroying technique should've disabled Vinnie, but it didn't. Vinnie recovered far too quickly and Tyson drew a necessary conclusion.

"You're inhabited."

"Not yet, but soon, Lynd."

"Alright, so when did you start using the formula for yourself, Vinnie?" Tyson hollered.

"Ever since your sister offered herself to the Zoree!" Vinnie screamed as the rain picked up and seemed to empower him. "She's just as Ahi as you and she's just as Zoree as me!"

"What? Calysta! She's alive?" The rain over took the blackening night sky, and thoughts of Calysta flooded Tyson's mind.

"You should know this! You've seen her more recently than I have, Lynd!" Vinnie threw his balled fist into Tyson's sternum. Tyson doubled over and Vinnie thrust each knee into Tyson's chest.

Tyson collapsed to the ground on all-fours.

"What?" Tyson hacked as he tried to fight the pain.

"Oh, you didn't know?" Vinnie laughed, "She wants the Ahi dead more than I do! She's quite beautiful. I think it's her eyes. They're paralyzing aren't they?" Vinnie kicked Tyson in the ribs.

"Vinnie! What the hell? Stop!" Jordan yelled as the rain intensified and almost knocked the spectators over.

Tyson, amidst the pain, made the connection from Vinnie's gloating. Tyson's sister was the Zoree female. The beautiful Zoree female that pulled Tyson under was Calysta. She wasn't just a Zoree. She was an Azoree, a natural diord. Tyson's mother must've been a Zoree. Tyson felt Vinnie's violent foot find his ribs again. Tyson screamed again as his arms gave out and he fell to the ground.

Tyson was left with just enough time to get back to his feet, albeit quite dazed.

Vinnie, somewhat limping, combatively sprinted at Tyson. The galoot grabbed Tyson's legs and planted him into the ground. Tyson got the worst of the fall and Vinnie scrambled on top of him. Tyson wouldn't have a repeat of the library. He evaded Vinnie's blows as he freed his legs from Vinnie's straddling pin.

"Tyson!" Jean-Claude yelled as he began to approach the fighters, ready to help his friend.

"Jean-Claude!" Jordan grabbed his teammate in a wrestler's bear-hug.

"Let go of me, Jay!" Jean-Claude demanded as he wriggled free of Jordan's grip.

"Look at them, Claude! Tyson wrecked Vinnie's leg, Vinnie probably broke Tyson's ribs and they're still fighting! What are *we* going to possibly do to stop them?" Jordan spoke sensibly for a change. "I can't fight like that! Can you?"

Jean-Claude didn't like it, but Jordan was right.

Still on the ground, but capably defending himself, Tyson pulled his right knee into his chest and kicked Vinnie across the chin. Stunned, Vinnie was momentarily defenseless. Tyson capably seized the opportunity—and Vinnie's arm. Tyson threw his legs over each of Vinnie's shoulders and torqued Vinnie to the ground. With a firm grasp on Vinnie's arm and his feet locking Vinnie in place, Tyson wrenched his adversary's shoulder, elbow and wrist in an arm bar maneuver. A succession of crackles and pops confirmed each of the joints in Vinnie's arm were destroyed—dislocated or broken. Tyson rolled to a dominant position on top of the struggling Vinnie. Tyson drew his fist back and blow-after-blow, Tyson rearranged Vinnie's defined face.

The spectators went silent.

Vinnie's blue blood oozed from each of the deep wounds Tyson left on him. Lastly, Tyson gained control of Vinnie's shoulder and dislocated the ball from the socket with a Kimura hold. Vinnie screamed and Tyson landed two more elbows on Vinnie's face.

Tyson let go of Vinnie's arm and rolled away. Pained, Vinnie also got to his feet with a defiant grin. Vinnie drew his barely functional arm back, but Tyson swung his shin into the side of Vinnie's disabled knee, collapsing it. With all his might, Tyson chambered his other leg then kicked Vinnie square in the *solar plexus*. The formula had worn off for Vinnie. Vinnie screamed in pain just before he crashed to the ground.

"Please stop, guys!" Vanessa howled.

Defeated yet conscious, Vinnie lay there coughing and out of breath after the blow to the chest. Tyson grabbed the zip-tie he obtained from his father's SWAT bag. Tyson stood over his conquered adversary, and dropped the zip-tie on his chest. "Put it on and stand up. I'm not gonna ask twice."

"What's this, asshole?" Vinnie screamed between breaths. "Are you arresting me?" he mocked. "You're not a cop!" Vinnie spit at Tyson. The mix of saliva and blood hit Tyson's face and seeped down his cheek.

Tyson drew his foot back and kicked Vinnie across the face. Vinnie flipped over from the force and tried to recover. He pulled his hand away from his face exposing his gashed cheek. Vinnie spit a tooth out of his mouth as the blood oozed from his fat lip.

Tyson pulled Vinnie's hands behind his back. He forcefully fastened the zip-tie around his enemy's wrists then cinched it. "You're gonna wish I was a cop, you scumbag," Tyson growled as he grabbed Vinnie's hand's and dragged him to his feet.

Vinnie screamed in pain as Tyson exacerbated the injuries with the rough treatment.

Tyson roared in Vinnie's ear, "We're finding Harlie, and then I'm stopping whatever you started with Omicron. For your sake, I hope it's not too late to solve either of my problems."

Tyson pushed Vinnie towards the lawn tractor depot on the far side of the parking lot. Tyson looked over his shoulder. The crowd of burbling students herded behind them at a safe distance. Despite the rain, Vanessa's candle was still burning. Though the distance was significant, Tyson focused on the flame. He reached out toward her and his hand combusted. The students behind them stopped in their shock and awe. Cell phones hit the wet ground and some of the students fled in the opposite direction. Still, others kept recording.

"What are you doing, Lynd?" Vinnie shrieked as he began to writhe in angst, trying to get away. Tyson's firm grip gave him no leverage.

Tyson raised his emberous hand and threw an infernous sphere at the gasoline drums, exploding them. The drums burned high and bright as Vinnie tried to free himself. "In fire I return to The Land of Three Suns."

"What the hell is this?" Vinnie protested as he was only an arm's length away from the blaze. "You can't take me to your territory! They'll kill me!"

"Maybe. It all depends on you, Vin." Tyson further cinched the zip-tie then grabbed Vinnie's collar and dragged him closer to the conflagration. "Let's go."

"What?" A look of fear came over Vinnie's face as if he knew his time had come.

EPILOGUE- TRAGICALLY PERFECT

A preoccupied Dr. Morehouse sat on the oasis-surrounded patio behind the Serenity medical center in the

Ahi territory. Enclosed by a wall of lush green palm plants and colorful desert flowers, he studied the upsetting manila folder on the weathered stone table in front of him. When he looked up from his research, he saw his mentor, Maven Ellis.

Dr. Morehouse stood up as Ellis neared him. "It's good to have you back safely, Maven Ellis," he said with a menacing trouble evident in his face. "I enlisted Victor Farrell, who asked for Emperor Wright's help in finding you."

Ellis embraced his protégé. "Thank you, Matt. You did exactly the right thing."

"Thank you, sir."

"It's wonderful to see you, Matt, but you look troubled. Sit down, let's talk."

"Yes, sir," Dr. Morehouse took his seat. "If you don't mind me saying, sir, beyond the trauma, you look even more troubled as well."

"Well, you tell me what's on your mind first, Matt," Ellis requested as he pulled the chair in underneath him.

Dr. Morehouse pushed the folder across the surface to his mentor.

"What's that?" asked Ellis.

"As much as I don't want to believe it, this is the problem that Dawson left us with. In your absence, the project outlined in the folder has gotten out of hand. It was practically overnight that it happened. I don't know how to stop it. The information is courtesy of Victor Farrell."

"Good old, Victor," Ellis said as he held up a paper in his hand. "They pieced together the reconstruction formula?" Ellis guessed.

"Dawson sold it to them. I'm sorry. Being a mainstreamed Ahi I should've recognized this from the start. They want our blood—badly."

Ellis bedded the report back in the folder and closed it. "It's not your fault, Matt. You're a very good doctor and a very busy one too. Don't blame yourself at all. You weren't the Ahi liaison to world officials. Dawson was."

"Yes, sir."

"And we need to start thinking about our options for a warlord. Keep it contained though."

"I was afraid you'd say that."

"Well, I want to avoid this war as much as anyone else—but we need to be prepared. What else do you know, Matt?"

"The Zoree have employed Yerevan Treagan as acting maven."

"Are you kidding me?" Ellis lost his composure, "Treagan! What?"

"I wish I were kidding. Also, there's presently a mainstreamed Ahi who has found himself the target of Omicron laboratory."

"What? Who?"

"Tyson Lynd."

"The name doesn't ring any bells."

"The Lynds are his adopted family."

"Then the name I'm interested in is Tyson....Tyson. It's coming back to me...Wait, No!"

Dr. Morehouse nodded.

"The Son of Red Death?"

"Yes, sir."

"What do we know about him?"

"Plenty, I've met him myself. He's a strong, smart kid and very moral too." Dr. Morehouse hesitated before he spoke again. "Not to mention he's an Azoree. His mother was a Zoree. I don't know if he knows that or not. Another thing to keep in mind, he's also marked by a Keaka named Taro. Taro was passed onto him from his father. Therefore, Tyson has a terrible anger issue and the rage blinds him."

"We abandoned him at the most vulnerable time in his life. That's understandable. Does he have a vendetta against the Ahi?"

"Surprisingly, no. I've talked to Ethan Wright. Tyson has confided in him. Tyson's anger is with his father, not his people. I implore you to reclaim Tyson as one of us."

"Has this Keaka called, "Taro" manifested itself, yet?" asked Ellis.

"Not yet, sir, but it's bound to happen—the poor young man." Dr. Morehouse sympathized. "Maybe we can help him fight the phantom. And there's more you should know."

"Really?"

"The Neo-Exa project has crossed too far over into his life. When he refused to sell his blood, they tried to take it by force. He has survived the attempts on his life, however in doing so Omicron has set foot on our tecton. They've found Aloha Pumehana! The men were found dead though. Tyson killed them."

"All of them?" Ellis asked optimistically.

"It's hard to tell, sir."

"Well, the war's closer than it seems. There's only one thing to do. For better or worse, we have a warlord on reserve." Ellis reported. "He's tragically perfect."

"Please, no, anything but that! He's too young. He's too innocent." Dr. Morehouse argued. "The mortality, suicidality, and psychiatric morbidity rates are far too high! He'll never be the same. We can't be responsible for creating another Yerevan Treagan!"

"You're right, Matt. We have to create something worse than Yerevan. And we need to have the only kill-switch. I hear you integrated his girlfriend. Does he love her?"

"I think so, sir."

"Tell me about her."

"Her name is Harlie. She was shot by Ashley Ryker at Aloha Pumehana."

"Shot by Ryker? The chaser?"

"Yes, sir."

"Ugh! Did Harlie take well to the integration?"

"Yes, sir."

"What else can you tell me?"

"She too is marked by the Keaka. I found the three characteristic lines on the inferior portion of her eye on my examination."

"Huh...it seems as though this young man and young lady were born to bear our burden."

"That's a weak argument for ruining these kids' lives, sir."

"We're on the brink of war, Matt—with Yerevan Treagan no less!"

"Yes, sir, but you're a maven! You're better than that! Think your way out!" the good doctor interrupted knowing that his rebuttal was for naught.

"We need a warlord on reserve otherwise more lives may be ruined. Tyson is the only blood Ahi with a first degree Keaka influence that we know of. He's also an Azoree. We have a triord. It's my burden to ruin as few lives as possible. I must find Tyson before I do anything else." Ellis decided.

"I disagree, sir. You must talk to Leor first! It's the sensible thing to do. We must first try to stop the war from the outset!"

"Leor is dead. He was murdered at the hands of an inhabited Dawson. The Zoree won't want to see *my* face. They're going to flip when they find out. Where's Tyson, now?"

"I don't know, sir."

"Then I guess I best find him," Ellis supposed.

Mica appeared from behind Morehouse and whispered in his ear. Morehouse rose from his chair. "You won't have to look far, sir. He's here."

This is far from over...

www.ingramcontent.com/pod-product-compliance
Lightning Source LLC
Chambersburg PA
CBHW062007170626
46813CB00001B/65